Countess

Countess:
Abernathy the Archer

BOOK II

a novel by
Taversia

HOLON
PUBLISHING

ISBN: 978-0-9915282-3-3

Published by Holon Publishing
& Collective Press

Credits:
Cover Model – Taversia
Artwork – Chris Barr; Photographer
          – Orina Kafe; Digital Artist

Special thanks to Dr. Paul Patton, once more, for lending his scientific
knowledge & expertise in bringing this story to life.

Special shout-out to our loudest supporters in this book's release:
• Karl Dodd
• Habeeb Al Aswad
• Ryan Just
• Joe Mousseau
• Elizabeth A. Smith
• Joshua Roberson

Finally, Taversia extends her deepest gratitude to more healing sources of inspiration:
• Rathmel Fidelis
• Tyler Sevakis

HOLONPUBLISHING

To the masculine presences in my life
who helped move me past inspiration to actualization.

Table of Contents

viii   Interlude to The Great Escape
  1   To Murder, To Kill
  9   A Whole New World
 14   Rafe, the Scorpion
 20   Guardian of the Key
 27   The Power Within
 35   Battle Mage of the Sage
 40   The Brothers Grim
 50   To Catch A Knight
 55   Butthead
 59   The Duke of Widowsgrove
 65   Hi-Yoon
 70   Baiting the Beast
 76   To Fight a Knight
 82   To Seek a Shaman
 88   Zebadiah
 93   Disgusting
 99   Sage's Reprise
104   Seal of Salvation
110   An Unfortunate Turn of Events
117   Pain, Truth, & Choice
122   Burning the Sails
129   Countess of the Clouds
135   From Sand to Stone
141   Rendezvous
150   Reassurance
159   Attack on Fyndridge
165   The Grey Matter In Between
173   Black & White
180   Purgatory
188   Tall Tale
194   Phoenix Rising
202   Three Wise Men

PRELUDE
Interlude to The Great Escape

I remember the moment well, gazing beyond the steel bars which encased me into the piercing blue eyes with specks of brown I'd never before seen so visceral, so vindictive. His name was Blythe, and I could tell by the way he was looking back at me that he meant to keep me in here, to rot and waste away if he had his way about it. I knew then that I would have to convince him otherwise. It was the reason I was here.

"The lamb wanders far from greener pastures," I said softly, my hands rising to wrap around the rusted metal of the bars.

I watched as Blythe's pupils dilated and began to dance, his mind processing the words I had just spoken to him. The mischievous curl of his lips sank and left his mouth hanging partially open in malcontent.

"Wh-what...?" he breathed.

I knew I didn't have to repeat myself. He heard my words well, even if no one else did. I looked past him at the three other faces looking in at me. I suspected the each of them *shared* my sister, all at different points in time, all human but feral by design; Gwendolyn the Ewe, Ovocula the Lioness, and Rivkah the Doe. This was my first face to face meeting with the each of them, although Blythe I had known for quite some time.

"Mister lady ma'am sir," Gwendolyn said, placing a gentle hand to his slender shoulder. "Perhaps it would be best if you let the Viscountess out of the cage so that she might assist us with our attempting to lay siege on the ship? Be as it may that she so chooses to don the garments of this *Bern girl's* lover, I do not see how that is reason enough to keep her in there while she is a perfectly able-bodied body to help us."

Gwendolyn was a woman with an ethereal quality about her, not conventionally pretty in the face with a perpetually startled gaze and glowing gray eyes set far apart from her small button nose. She faintly reminded me of a toad. Her hair was long and cascading in fine, delicate waves that fell over her raggedly knit, pale blue shawl. It looked more white than blonde, especially by the light shining down on her coming in from the deck at the top of the stairs. There was a strangely *familiar* quality about her.

"We're running out of time," Ovocula chimed in. "Whatever we do, we need to be certain that we do it soon!"

Ovocula contrasted Gwendolyn's strange, porcelain appearance, though she herself took on the semblance of a pristine china doll. She wore a long, draping gown, black and frilled with lace. She stood just farther back from them all with cascading curls at the ends of her wavy black hair. Her features were soft and feminine, and I personally found her to be far more aesthetically pleasing. She wore a black ribbon choker around her neck, an oval brass locket dangling from its loop to the meeting of her lovely pale collarbones.

Rivkah did not speak. I got the sense that she normally had much to say at any vital given moment, but at least for now, she had fallen totally mute. Like Ovocula, she too was quite beautiful. Not soft as she, but baring a more chiseled, and sturdy physique despite having a slight frame. Her caramel-mocha skin was covered in soot and a spilling of darkened, dried blood had stained down the front of her blouse. She wore sooty, tattered green overalls over that. Of the three women, she appeared to be the worst for wear.

"Blythe," came a voice from behind me.

I glanced back and then down, my eyes falling over Doctor Orel Fischer, whom I've known long since before I was old enough to even speak. Never before had I seen him so mangled and broken as he lay on the floor of the holding cell we had been put in. I suddenly became very aware of a repugnant smell as I noticed the pool of human excrement and bodily fluids just a few feet from where he had propped himself up against a wall. His eyes were swollen shut and both his arms were held aloft in makeshift slings of torn cloth.

"Blythe," he repeated, "y-you need to… let her go…"

Blythe stood motionless and aghast. I knew what I said to him had shaken him to his core, especially coming out of my sister's mouth, whose body I inhabited, and not my own. He wasn't listening to anyone else around him. I had his full attention, and I had to be careful with it. The next words that came out of me, my sister, would be the difference of escape and ultimate survival.

Do I tell him who I am? No. I could lose him to disbelief. Extortion?
I could tell him I know *everything*. I could threaten to lay all his darkness
bare. I had to think fast as the seconds passed in gritted silence. I would
tell him *nothing*. I reached through the bars and snatched up a fistful of his
shaggy, dirty-blond hair. I pulled inward with all my might, the metal bars
reverberating off the force of his head smashing into them.

Both Gwendolyn and Ovocula gasped. Rivkah clasped her hands
over her mouth in shock. I did not turn to survey Orel's reaction. As Blythe
slumped to the floorboards on the other side of the bars, I crouched down and
reached around him for the ring of keys he no longer held. Once my hands
had found them, I moved quickly to unlock the cell door.

"Viscountess," Ovocula marveled, her emerald eyes wide under long,
fluttered lashes. "Are… Are you sure that was really necessary? Why didn't you
give us a chance to try and finish reasoning with him?!"

"Because I'm not the Viscountess you've come to know," I replied,
pushing hard on the cell door against the resistance of Blythe's limp form.
"Reasoning was taking too long, and you've said it yourself that we're running
out of time. I did what had to be done."

"Bern…" I heard Orel say. I turned to look him over one last time.
"I-It's you, Bern. Isn't it."

"Later," I replied. "I'll explain it *all* later. You just rest now, while we
take out the bastards who did this to you."

I walked over Blythe, being careful so as not to step on him. He
whimpered and shifted slightly, and it was all I could do to keep from reaching
out to comfort him. I hated what I'd done to him.

"Ovocula, I'm going to need you to fill me in on what's going on here,"
I said, looking her over now. Her fine, thin brows furrowed as she registered
my words. I could see it in her face that she was beginning to catch on.
"Where did Blythe get these?" I flashed her the ring of keys.

"Um, I– err… off Gertie," she stammered.

I knew Gertie well. Demetrius's right-hand man. Demetrius, the
cloaked captain of this sky ship currently sailing through the clouds. Gertie
was a bumbling oaf of a man, short and stout with gleaming gold ingots for
teeth who wore stupid black and white vertically striped pants all of the time.
He had an ugliness about him reminiscent of the Governor of Fyndridge, my
hometown. I knew them both, Gertie and Demetrius alike, but they wouldn't
know it was *me*.

"Step one. We need to arm ourselves," I said. "Where is the cargo hold
on this ship?"

"In the cabin next to this one," Gwendolyn responded, melodiously. I noticed then how sweetly she spoke with her every word. "That is what the one you call Blythe informed Mister Doctor Orel."

"So then what's step two going to be?" Ovocula frowned.

"I'll figure that one out after we deal with step one," I replied, starting up the stairs leading out from the cabin. "Come on, now. We need to hurry."

A novel by Taversia

CHAPTER 1
To Murder, To Kill

"About five feet, eleven inches, with burns all over his face and body," I could hear my uncle say, his voice a muffled echo through the only air vent in this small, square room. "Yes, that is correct. The skin healed over his left eye and his entire scalp. He would be hard to miss." I could not hear anyone else right then.

He must be speaking over the phone with someone, I thought. What an idiot I was that I didn't automatically assume he would have had all the locks changed.

I wriggled within the confines of my straitjacket, stretching the chains around my ankles as far as they would reach. I laid my right ear to the padding of the wall, as close to the vent overhead as I could get. "Thank you, officer. Yes, see you soon," my uncle spoke, audibly slamming the phone back into its cradle. "Now, then… Where were we?"

"I have your niece's medical records here, from Fyndridge," came another familiar voice. My uncle was with some man. "When you asked me to evaluate her physical condition during her admittance to Galvinsglade," he continued, "she responded well to sedation; no abnormalities—physically speaking—although I cannot speak for her mental state as you could. Even so… I'm not sure using her for clinical research is the right answer."

I wondered who this man was. I recognized his inflections, jumpy with the occasional crack in his voice, but could not place the words with a face. My head felt foggy having just awakened from a dreamless sleep. With my one good ear, I barely hung on to each of their voices.

"We've measured out one hundred micrograms of lysergic acid for her to drink," my uncle replied. "We need the government funding to fix this place up, Doctor Fischer. This is no longer about trying to fix *her*. We've run every test short of lobotomizing the poor girl, and it pains me to concede that she is beyond our care. If we run these experiments and demonstrate to the public how our recent findings are *helping* our patients, we can alleviate the risk of being forced to shut down."

"Even if we manage to conduct such tests on all the others here with relative ease, how are you going to get her to unwittingly drink this stuff?" the man identified as longtime friend to my family, Orel, replied. "She's been fighting you and the remaining staff since she's come here. Do we need this data from *every* patient?"

"Only from those not escaped," I could hear my uncle snarl. "This is damage control. The nurses are already making rounds with the residents, but we need *you* to give my niece her dose. It carries no odor and no taste. To her, it would be nothing more than a cup of water and I'm certain she must be quite thirsty."

There was a brief pause. The inner lining of my throat felt dry, like cotton. I was slightly nauseated. I needed to get out of here.

I heard my uncle sigh. "You've been treating my niece since before she was born, Doctor Fischer. I'm confident this will be for her own good in the end. She still trusts you, and won't fight you if you are trying to give her a nice, cool drink of water. You can do that, can't you?"

"…How can we be so sure that this is for her own good?" Orel meekly inquired.

"When we were admitting her into Galvinsglade, do you remember what you told me your observations were, as you were sedating her in the holding cell?"

"Well, uhh, she was t-talking to herself," I could hear the discomfort in Orel's voice as he stammered through his response. "And to me. In different voices."

"And each of her voices have their own names, don't they."

"Yes, sir, they do. She was responsive. She spoke to me in this way."

"Indeed, but still she refuses to speak any other way. She clings to these personas to a debilitating degree, and *that* is how we can be so sure! As per usual, Doctor Fischer, I suspect you can handle the medical aspects of her treatment and leave the psychology to me. Now then; her room is—"

"Room 642. I remember. Doctor LaCroix… I know I'm a medical doctor and not a psychiatrist, but I think I should add that your niece's case is nothing like I have ever seen before in all my years of treating psychiatric patients. Her psychotic delusions, if that's even truly what they are, are of

a depth and complexity and *clarity* that is unlike any other patient I have
seen. As I understand it, the diagnosis of multiple personality disorder is very
controversial among psychologists. Some doubt that the disorder even really
exists. Surely your niece's case must be the clearest and most dramatic instance of
it in *all* of medical history. She is a patient of extraordinary scientific interest!"

I could hear the familiar huff of my uncle's disapproval. "Really,
Doctor Fischer," he interjected, incredulously.

"Uhh, ha-have you considered writing up a synopsis of her case for
the Annals of British Psychiatry, or inviting other specialists to see her?" Orel
continued reluctantly. "In fact, sometimes I'm not even sure that what we're
dealing with is mental illness, as we understand it, at all…" I could hear
his voice trail off as his nervousness and uncertainty grew. "It's… It's like
she could… tap into some other world. Think of all the breakthroughs in
physics back before the w-w-war! Ein… Einstein's theory of relativity, and
Niels Bohr's qua-quantum theory! We… We barely understand the world, or
human consciousness at all. Prof… Professor Einstein's theory says that space
is non-Euclidean. There might be other dimensions of space. Other *universes*.
And th-think of the strange things that quantum th-th-theory says about
consciousness. Do you know about Sch… Sch… Schrödinger's cat, or Wig…
Wigner's friend…?"

"Doctor Fischer, you are quite right," my uncle snarled angrily. "You
are a medical doctor and not a psychiatrist, and most decidedly *not* a physicist.
We psychiatrists deal in *real* science; the measurement and testing of behavior,
not whimsical fantasy. I would like to ask you to confine your opinions to
your own professional specialty. See to it she drinks that. You may go now."

I unconsciously flicked my tongue over my chapped and split lips,
swallowing hard to dull the welling dryness of my throat if only for a second
or two. I really was quite thirsty. I could hear footsteps and the opening and
closing of doors. Orel, or my uncle, or both would be upon me soon. My
uncle must not be aware of how Orel tried to help me escape before, when I
was just the Viscountess… I wondered whether he would still help me as *Bern*.

My mind drifted back to where I'd been before all this had happened; the
other time I remembered ever feeling so thirsty, though perhaps not so weak…

*

I held my bow steady, exhaling very slowly as I pulled back on the
rawhide string to rest on my cheek. I could feel the muscles in my arms tense
and flex, my body steeled with the draw weight of the bowstring, two arrows
simultaneously aimed while I clutched them both between my knuckles. It was
early in the afternoon, the sun at its peak, high and scorching from above. I

was perspiring heavily. My water canteen was nearly empty. The more I exerted myself, the more fluids I would need to stay sharp. I had to finish this quick.

Just before my arms would shake with the strain of the bow, I let the arrows fly. I felt the bowstring whip my cheek, the bolts cutting the still air like daggers as they soared several yards into the distance with whistling speed. They each met their marks, piercing the skulls of the two figures in the distance. I watched them waver a moment, dead before their bodies could physically register it—before they could even hit the ground. My heart leapt in my breast with satisfaction. I could not help but smile.

Deftly, I slipped the bow around my back and over my left shoulder to meet with the quiver. I walked hurriedly, the chains wrapped around my heavy boots rattling with each step. It was difficult to keep from dragging my feet slightly, displacing loose sand over the rolling dunes of desert wasteland which spanned all around for miles. My sleeveless leather duster trailed behind me over the ground, wiping away any tracks my trudging boots would make. Its fringe was weighted down by metal links I had sewn into the skin, so I wasn't worried about leaving my mark to be followed. I had been scouting for days now, my body worn and weary and ready to return home.

As I approached, the willowy form struggling within the confines of the net came more into view. The two figures that once stood over her were collapsed in a twisted heap, my arrows lodged in their brains; one through the ear, the other unseen by the way he fell. I presumed I caught an eye socket. They were both scraggly-looking subterran men in tattered clothes – remnants of the people they once were. Beside each of their bodies were dulled, tarnished daggers. They were going to cut this girl apart; probably eat her.

She struggled, clearly disoriented and frightened, unable to see me through her tumbled red hair all about her head and the net which encased her. "Hold still," I said as soothingly as I could muster so as not to further alarm her. "I'm not going to hurt you."

I knelt down before her, and as I did, I caught the glint of a shining jewel in the corner of my eye. Amid the stillness of the hot air, the sweet scent of lavender accompanied my discovery and my gaze was quickly drawn to the sword-sized key that the gemstone was set into. There it lay in the sand just a few feet away, next to the hole in the ground where the girl must have previously fallen. My eyes grew wide and again my heart leapt. I knew this girl.

Looking at her more closely through the netting, I drew my dagger from its sheath strapped to my hip by tied-together belts, the blade clinking gently against ornate buckles as I removed it and began cutting at the mesh knots. I worked fast, my mind racing. This was the first time I had met her face to face, and with my own body... but she did not know me.

My name is Abernathy LaCroix, and I have the power to trade places with a girl at will. I had never met her and yet I feel her in my blood. She is my sister, of sorts. I don't think she was ever conscious of my presence; of even the vilest of situations I had endured for her so she did not have to. My earliest memory is of my uncle—*our* uncle—putting a cigar out on the back of my neck. It would have been her, had I not willed myself into being – had I not removed her from harm's way by inhabiting her body. Only for that briefest moment.

I think that's why I go by Bern now. I've always hated my name. It ties me to my history; my family, my uncle, serving as a constant reminder of how I was never truly heard or listened to. My father is Amadeus LaCroix, proud captain of the Wild Rose, which was named for my late mother, and noble count of Galvinsglade and Fyndridge. He knew my uncle had burned me and he looked the other way then. Even at the tender age of four years old, I could feel the malice from my uncle and I could sense the denial in my father.

Life went on as though it had never happened, while my mother fed my sister stories—myself sometimes, in her absence—of how the burn was the mark of my noble birthright. For a while, this worked. I truly believed I was some kind of chosen sage, destined to locate and unite the other eleven 'chosen ones,' each of us entitled to the twelve magic gemstones to unlock the legendary Castle in the Sky. The only difference is that now I know my branding had nothing to do with it. I just *am*.

It's why I scour the desert wastelands for vagrants in need as often as my own body will allow. I am looking to form a group; a small army to find this castle—but we need the stones. For the time being I decided not to let her know that I knew her, or that sometimes I would inhabit her body. Would she even believe such a thing? Surely she would be aware of lost time. I kept myself quiet and cut away the rest of the netting, throwing it from her body. What was left fell away with ease, and slowly she sat upright and began brushing her hair away from her face. She turned to look me over.

I'd known she had fallen which is why I was out scouting for her, otherwise I would have returned to Fyndridge the night before. I'm not referring to the trap hole in the ground; that was just dumb luck. I mean, I knew she had fallen from the *sky*. I was taking a big risk, because I only rationed for the couple of days spent away from home. How strange it was to be looking back at her now, and not through the glass of a mirror. How strange the sensations I feel of dread, each time I am compelled to take over her body.

It started innocently enough after that very first time with the cigar

burn. There would be times she slept, and in those precious moments of
unguarded subconscious, curiosity would take me. I focused myself, wherever
I was, and with my focus came the separation of mind from body. Though
I've never stayed too long, no more than a day or so at a time, I feel that
I've gained some valuable insights as to the nature of those deemed superior.
Through her, I am both commoner and noble alike. At the time there was only
one who knew…

Part of the padded wall suddenly swung open, a door with no handle
on either side, and Orel now stood before me. No matter where I was in the
room, I could keep track of where that blasted door was by being mindful of
which corner of the ceiling the vent was on. Or sometimes the dirty marks
along the walls would tell me. The chains around my ankles slacked as I
moved back toward the center of the room where they began. I was like an
inching larva on the floor in my cocoon, glaring up at Orel from under the
mess of hair that fell around my face.

Both his arms bent awkwardly at the elbow, encased in off-white
casts to help mend his broken bones. He looked down at me with bloodshot
raccoon eyes inset by puffy swelling. As best he could anyway, in a neck brace.
A bandage had been wrapped several times around his head, catching wisps of
his salt-and-pepper hair. He looked horrible. In one of his hands, he loosely
gripped a clear plastic cup of water.

"Howd'youdo," he greeted me with an abrupt nod. Or, nod-ish.

"Hi," I rasped, weakly. "What's lysergic acid?"

Orel flinched back, twitching visibly. He was clearly caught off guard.
I couldn't tell what shook him more; that I spoke to him under the guise of
my mute sister, or that I knew something was in the water. I could see it in his
knuckle-punched eyes that he recognized my manner of speaking right away.

"B-Bern," he stammered. "I wasn't expecting… How did you—?"

"I'll explain later. You weren't *actually* going to try and trick me into
drinking that stuff, were you? That would be rude."

Orel hesitated there a moment before slightly turning his body to say
something. He looked robotic, being unable to move his arms or neck. "Can
I have a moment alone with her? We'll be alright," he said to somebody on
the other side of the wall. It couldn't have been my uncle, who doesn't miss a
chance to lecture or, more recently, mock my pitiful state. It must have been a
nurse or a security guard or something. Then again, staff was scarce. Another
recent development.

The door closed behind him as he turned back to look at me again.
"Bern, I don't know what more you know concerning your situation right now,"

he said in hushed tone, "but the media are having a field day right now with Roland's escape from Galvinsglade. This is a *very* big scandal by itself, but if that weren't enough, 'the heiress Viscountess' now being held here somehow got out to the public *too* and the papers are headlining the story!"

"It was Demetrius who escaped; not Roland," I replied, somewhat miffed by his lack of distinction. "They share a body, but you have to keep in mind that they're two separate personalities."

"Okay," Orel exasperatedly exclaimed, "but that's not how *they* view things! To everyone else, he's just one single madman on the run, and you just went crazy too. Meaning ownership of your estate gets passed on to your uncle being that you are now legally unfit to assume charge."

I bristled at his words. "I'm crazy, huh? I wonder what people say when they see you twitching and jolting all the time!"

He paused at that. I immediately regretted what I'd said.

"Bern, I'm not calling you crazy," he continued more calmly, "I'm just trying to get you to understand how *everyone else* views you which is something you need to consider if we're ever going to get you out of here."

"I guess my uncle doesn't know, then," I whispered. "How you helped me before."

"Of course he doesn't know…"

"It barely worked the first time. I made it out of the Fyndridge asylum… but this is Galvinsglade. We're not just insane in here, Orel." I could feel my throat close up as I spoke. The words were bitter. "We are *criminally insane*. That's not something I can ever take back."

"Where is the Viscountess?" he asked flatly.

Even then, I could feel her. "Sleeping," I said. "In me."

"Well wake her up. Before I can help any more… I-I need to know neither of you are truly responsible for starting that fire. For the *murders*."

"It doesn't work that way," I replied, knowing full well he didn't trust me. I knew he had little reason to. "She won't come out; not until we're out of here. *If* we get out of here. And even then, do you expect her to talk? What is it you want to hear, exactly?"

"…I just want to look into her eyes," he said, convulsing abruptly into a nervous tick as he stood. "Her moth—…your mother had a cer-certain *look* about her that she gets sometimes. It… It would be peace of mind enough."

My brain was hazy. With little peace of mind all my own, I decided to make the attempt to appease him. It was the only truth I knew.

"I've never taken over for this long before," I said after brief pause. "Sometimes when I'm dreaming I meet with her. As she did with me, for the first time, after the fire. She receded inside herself. That's how she came to be admitted into Fyndridge in the first place. It's what I wanted for her. My job is to keep her safe, and that's what I'm doing even now, just by being here. I sensed the danger; that it would be too much for her to take. Whenever her stability is compromised, I make due for us both."

His eyes were stony as he looked down at me. "So, you have killed."

"Yes," I said. "But I am no murderer."

"Then drink this."

My heart leapt. I stared up at him, incredulously. He stepped toward me and dropped to a knee, extending the cup of water as far as the cast binding his arm would allow.

"…If I can trust you, then you will trust me," he said. His voice was a whisper. "I think I know how to get you out of here, but you're going to have to drink. You've hardly eaten anything, so the effects should come sooner and last longer; eight, maybe a full twelve hours. You will not be harmed."

I swallowed hard as I looked into the clear water, my tongue dancing behind my lips with anticipation. Reluctantly I took the rim of the cup from him, into my mouth. I didn't know what other choice I had.

I drank.

CHAPTER 2
A Whole New World

I thought back to those moments that I lay in the desert beneath a blanket of dusk amber sky, my knapsack a pillow for my head. In the midst of my light slumber, the fire I built from the dry leaves of an acacia shrub kept me warm. Even still, the dread within me slowly began to build and I realized my sister would need me. The electric charge of adrenaline pumped my heart, and when I reopened my eyes I was crouched low in a dark room, the captain's office aboard the Wild Rose, my father's ship. Once more, I inhabited the body of my sister and it was through her eyes I saw the cloaked man. He stood over me, amid toppled bookcases and broken furniture. Behind him was my father, slumped against a wall with blood pooling around his head and cascading from his mouth. He was dead.

Demetrius. Even with his features obscured by the shrouding of a cloak, I knew it was him; that he had done this. I turned my gaze from him, down the length of the jagged dagger he brandished now dripping with my father's fresh blood. My gaze fell lower still, to the sword-sized key on the ground mere feet in front of me.

"Do you see what you've made me do, you dumb little bitch?" he said, his gruff voice resonating clearly over the screams heard from all around the ship. He spoke deep, and low.

I lunged for the key. As I snatched it up, Demetrius shot forward, his cloak fluttering with the swift movement of his legs unseen and his dagger wound back to strike. My heart beat like a thunderclap in my breast as I clutched the base of the key, my free hand over the gemstone. My movements were shadowed by fragments of a second slowed down. I felt the blade split the air before me.

"λογία þovis!" I bellowed. A beam of pulsating white light rocked from the base of the key in that instant and exploded in a blinding flash from its end. I could feel the energy kick back through my forearms as I gripped it with all my might, the burst knocking into Demetrius like a shotgun shell and sending him careening into the far wall.

I climbed to my feet, clutching the key close to my body and took off in a mad dash through the open doorway from the office. As I left him there, I was immediately assaulted with harsh smoke fumes that stung my eyes and burned the back my throat. The ship was going down in flames. That was the last I remembered before reawakening in the desert, my eyes fluttering open to rest over the orange embers of a dying campfire. I had abruptly returned to my own body and I breathed easy with this realization.

I knew my sister had come to trouble, and this was happening in a sky ship thousands of feet above my head. I sat partially upright, turning my gaze from the weak, crackling fire and up toward the fiery heavens. I felt my leather duster slip from my body with my hasty movement, having used it as a blanket for warmth in the growing night. A vast flickering flame shone through distant clouds, accompanying an emerging collection of stars to the east.

No, not clouds, I thought. *Smoke.*

It would be more than half a day yet before I'd shoot the first of two men dead to ensure her safety. My mind was wrought with worry whether she would make it out in one piece to begin with. I packed up camp and began my search, my gaze fixed on the chaos in the sky. It was like watching watercolors bleed into a canvas, the reds and yellows fading in and out with each pulse.

Static behind my eyelids suddenly as I was wrenched from my musings by a blinding light. I rubbed my clenched eyes with the backs of my shaking hands, shielding myself defensively. My heart was pumping so fast; what was happening to me?

"Her pupils are dilated with no abnormalities in light sensitivity," I could hear Orel say, standing over me. "How's her pulse?"

I pulled my hands away from my face, now aware of an inflated cuff around my right arm as I lay on my back. I could hear it being pumped from that side, but I was still regaining my vision. My eyes reluctantly fluttered open to see Orel flip off the switch to a small cylindrical light.

"Sphygmomanometer reading is one twenty-six over one eighty,

Doctor Fischer," said one of the nurses.

Esophagusa*what?*

"Also, I have the results back from the patient's x-rays," she continued. "There appears to be a *key* trapped in the large intestine. Looks like we have a swallower on our hands."

"Her heart rate is pretty high," Orel calmly responded. "Blood pressure's normal. You; please report to Doctor LaCroix. Tell him we are ready to begin psychiatric evaluation."

The room was beginning to come into focus just as I turned my head to watch the nurse leave. There was only one other, taking notes over a clipboard she cradled in her arm. Behind her my straitjacket had been strewn over a metal chair. Strange multicolored wisps floated all around the four corners of the small space. The departing nurse had turned the corner to disappear behind the wall as she stepped out into the hallway, but still I could see her aura long after she'd left my sight. It was as though the wall had become transparent, but only to these colored auras.

"And you," Orel said, nodding toward the nurse who remained. "Could you please run by my office and give those notes to the file clerk so that she may type up a copy for my records?"

"But Doctor Fischer," she started, "I haven't finished filling out this document. Do you just want me to leave the rest blank?"

"Yes. I'll take care of it later."

I could see the nurse's aura outlining her body in deep blues which changed hue as she hesitated with uncertainty. While she lingered there, her aura turned green, then yellow, until finally she tucked her clipboard under her arm and left. As with the first nurse, I could still see the colors long after she was gone from my sight. Left to ourselves in the room, I turned my gaze to Orel who deflated and unfastened the number-gauging cuff from my arm and set it off to the side.

"Here, sit up," he said, grabbing at my wrists and pulling me upright. "We need to hurry!"

I either exhaled or inhaled. I'm not certain which. All I knew was that heavy winds were rushing through me, icy cold but from the inside out. It made the surface of my skin tingly. The colors intensified as I sat, the solid board I had laid on before vanishing out from under me. The room began to transform before my eyes. I blinked slowly and wide-eyed, trying to take it all in as the walls became entirely translucent. I could now see the shadowy shapes of people from all around me, weaving in and out of other rooms, walking above and below me. Their footsteps left colored trails that matched their auras and faded behind them. I could sense every living person within nearby radius and pinpoint *exactly* where they were.

Orel grabbed my face suddenly, awkwardly through his casts, drawing my attention back to him. His face was close to mine and his eyes looked intense, *focused*, as his spectacles slipped down the bridge of his nose. He was surrounded by an aura of scarlet and both his hands firmly yet gently framing my jawline simmered me, but did not burn. "I know this must all be overwhelming for you right now," he said, "but you were given a serum that is slowly teleporting you back to your world. Do you understand me?" His tone was dire.

I didn't know what to say. I gave a short nod.

"Viscountess?" he said, giving my head a small shake. "Do I have the Viscountess now, or are you still Bern?"

"…I can feel *everything*," I gasped. "*Everyone*."

Orel released me and reached into his very white coat to pull out a lumpy plastic bag. He winced with the movement, his casts keeping his arms rigid. "Here, get dressed. Quickly."

I took the bag, looking down at myself in my ugly nightgown.

"You won't make it past the parking lot, looking the way you do. There's a black car, err, *carriage…* a black carriage with tinted windows waiting for you outside! It's an old buddy of mine; a private investigator studying your case who said he'd be willing to put you up for a while. *In secret.*"

"My case…?" I said, bewildered. I looked into the plastic bag. Inside were poorly folded clothes and a plain pair of shoes that looked to be a size too small for my feet. There was also a familiar brooch, small and sapphire, which bore the emblem of my family's crest.

"How did you—?"

It was Orel's turn now. "I'll explain later," he interrupted. He moved to the wall adjacent to where I was seated and unlatched the lock to the room's only window. He grabbed onto it with both hands and grimaced with pain as he pulled it up. It was a *portal*. A swirling, bright blue, shimmering mass of a portal. "You've got to get moving."

I dug through the plastic bag and pulled out a buttoned blouse, a large, poofy skirt with some kind of hideous embroidered beast set close to its hem, the shoes, stockings, a white ribbon for my hair, and my brooch. As dexterously as I could muster, I began dressing myself over my nightgown.

"It isn't much," he said, "but it should be good enough for now."

I stood up. The portal was like a rush to my brain, fresh air wafting away the staleness of the room. I could *feel* the oncoming footsteps of a nurse's return and knew it was time that I left.

"Orel, do you remember when you helped me—the Viscountess—escape from Fyndridge, and into the mines?" I said, stepping to the window, the translucent wall revealing a faint expanse of deeper shimmering blues beyond the portal.

"K-k-keep your v-voice down!" he convulsed direly, pushing his glasses up the bridge of his nose with two fingers; his usual nervous tick.

"I *found* what I was looking for," I hurriedly spoke. "It is the Libra gemstone. I hid it in *The Rogue Musket* back at Fyndridge. We can use the stones to communicate with each other!"

He looked at me strangely. "Um, o-okay…"

"It carries a scent! When you're down in the cellar, pay attention to your sense of smell, okay?" My heart was pounding so heavily in my chest. It was now or never. I tied up my hair with the ribbon and slipped into the shoes. They were only a little tight around my feet. "The gemstone smells like mint! Find it! Then activate it, when you do! You *know* the incantation."

I clipped the sapphire brooch, mark of my noble birthright and stone of Sagittarius, to my breast pocket. The sweet scent of lavender permeated from it, and I inhaled deeply. I felt a profound sense of calm wash over me.

Without second thought, I leapt through the window and let the portal take me.

CHAPTER 3
Rafe, the Scorpion

I am accustomed to portals as gateways into the recesses of mind
and soul, my body as the vessel. As much as my sister would read our parents'
books, textbook fact and whimsical fantasy alike, there were times I'd caught
pages, myself. I was only ever able to comprehend pictures, but even then I got
a feel for what she had been thinking at the time. Each time I switched places
with her in the midst of her reading, she never seemed to be the wiser, simply
chalking it up to having spaced out, her eyes moving over words not absorbed
by her mind.

I had yet to use a portal as means of travel from one form of *reality*
to the next. I wondered whether accessing the Castle in the Sky to harness its
restorative powers would bring our worlds together. I wondered whether it
would make me *one*, as well. I wondered these things as I slowly and peacefully
drifted downward through the void, the gemstone on my chest glowing bright
and blue. I could feel the key inside me like butterflies in my stomach, as
though it were answering to the naked power of the stone.

That same stone when set into the key's base had led me to the mines
outside the walls of Fyndridge. It was there, standing just outside the entrance
that I sensed my sister's peril, my deep-seated favor for an act of heroism
tugging at my will. I remember standing at that cavernous mouth, wielding
the key set aflame with staggering white light in an otherwise pitch black
desert where even the moon above offered little illumination. It was there that
I answered her call.

When I took over her body I was met with a throbbing sensation in my left temple, sprawled out over the sand as though I'd been struck. By the vastly diminished light of a lantern, I barely made out the features of my sister's attackers made my own. Two men dressed in guards' uniform were quick to restrain me, grabbing at my arms with the weight of their knees painfully digging into my legs.

"What should her punishment be?" one of the guards sneered, baring a mouthful of gnarled, yellowing teeth.

"The *bitch* kicked me," the other replied. He suddenly brandished a short dagger, the sharp metal gleaming by the lantern's light set on the ground beside him. "I say we cut out her tongue since she ain't usin' it."

My eyes darted between both men hovering over me. I took in each of their features shrouded in darkness. It didn't take me long before I realized who they were.

"How is your brother?" I said to the set of sneering yellow teeth looming over me.

I watched as his mouth curled into an ugly scowl. "It speaks," he disdainfully spat.

My blood boiled, adrenaline coursing through my veins though I lay very still. I spoke slowly, that they might feel the weight of my every word, in recollection of my participation in a recent Rogue Musket pit fight. "It must have been very upsetting to you that a timid little girl a quarter his size managed to claim one of your brother's eyes. And with nothing more than a sharp edge like the one your comrade holds, there. To think it had only been a couple months prior that Bern bested him in combat with *even less* than that. Tell me – do you think him weak, or do you think *us* strong?"

His mouth quivered with outrage, his eyes growing wide under narrowed brows. "What… What did you just say to me…?!"

"That's about enough a' that," the other man snarled, raising his dagger to strike in an instant.

I wasted no time. My head snapped forward with my resolve, forehead smashing into nose with an audible crunch. A geyser of blood exploded from the nostrils of the man with the ugly teeth as he fell back with an agonized shriek. In that split moment with an arm now freed, I deflected the other man's dagger with a palm strike to his forearm. The sand sank his blade to the hilt an inch from my shoulder. I reached up and grabbed hold of his face, digging my thumbs into the inner corners of his eyes. I pressed with all my might, his screams of pain serving only to fuel my bloodlust. His dagger slipped from his grasp as I rolled him off me, straddling his torso.

I gouged deeply into his eye sockets, blood pooling around the open cavity I had made. I could feel what I imagined to be his eyeballs letting go like squashed grapes, or perhaps it was the collection of muscles behind them that I was digging into. Either way, I thumbed through what felt to be the consistency of warm berry jam. Lest I kill this man by my sister's hands, I knew it was time to end this.

I snatched up the brass handle of the lantern on the ground, the metal made slippery with the blood I was now covered in. I left those men to writhe, lost and screaming in the dark without a light. The deed was done. My sister would find the rest of her way to me, and I knew she would be coming; following me. I had always gone to such great lengths to protect her, her childlike innocence an invaluable part of what was keeping me *human*…

In the mines, in pursuit of the Libra gemstone, I'd almost let that go.

*

"Viscountess…?" came a man's hushed voice, snatching me through the ether and seizing me into the present. "Are you… the Viscountess?"

I stood in my buttoned blouse and stupid poofy skirt and uncomfortably tight shoes with my unruly hair tied back. If I didn't look crazy enough only an hour before, I certainly felt as much standing in front of a black carriage within the gates of Galvinsglade, dressed this way. I could just make out a set of baby blue eyes staring at me through black curtains draping the window.

"Don't I look like the Viscountess to you?" I grimaced.

The man pulled back the curtains with a gloved hand. "Don't know," he said with a slow, southern drawl. "Never seen her. Sure hear an awful lot about her, though. I suggest you get in quick; before somebody sees you."

His blue eyes were accompanied by faint crowfeet lines and were set under dark bushy brows. He had a full head of salt-and-pepper hair much like Orel's to match his five o'clock shadow. A boyish crescent smile which traced his lips belied these subtle signs of his age. He appeared neither remarkably tall nor short, his aura broader than he was. Even so, he looked like he would be formidable in a fight. There was something calming about his presence that I couldn't quite place; something soft about his nature to suggest he seldom had to. I just bet he *could*.

"You gonna just stand there?" he said, his voice still a hushed tone. "Your family did a pretty good job keepin' you hidden over the years. Somethin' tells me everyone *in there* knows what ya look like, though."

The man nodded back toward the building I came out of. Hesitating no more, I stepped forward and climbed into the carriage taking up the empty seat next to him.

"You ain't wearin' the scrubs they get them patients to wear," he continued, letting the drapes fall back into place. "I guess Orel meant to disguise ya… That'll work for most people once we get you out of here, but until we do, it won't matter what you got on."

"How do you and Orel know each other?" I asked.

He did something with his hands to make the carriage start moving. I wasn't sure what it was. His aura was projecting far outside himself such that my sitting next to him found me wrapped in it as well. I could only focus on its color, a rich purple pulsating with frenetic energy. This man made me anxious.

"Orel and I go way back. We met while we was in the throes of the *Great War*."

"I didn't know Orel fought in the war," I blinked, truly surprised. "You did battle alongside one another, then? Were you part of the same battalion?"

"Nope," he smirked, his half smile spread ever so slightly to deepen his laugh lines. He was no longer whispering as he spoke. "It was just me. I was pretty badly wounded, once. Orel found me sprawled out on the ground and made a pretty convincing field dressing. Later, he was the one who finished patchin' me up. Had to sew my stomach back together so my guts wouldn't spill on out like spaghetti in runny sauce!"

I felt my stomach turn over in disgust. "…Gross."

"Yeah, it sure ain't pretty," he chuckled. "The scar I got now is his own handiwork. It took me a good couple a' months before I was on my feet again, and the first thing I did was took the man out for drinks. Was the least I could do what with him savin' my life and all. Figured I owed him a favor."

I smiled weakly. "What form of alcohol did this favor come in?"

"The drinks weren't the favor. That was years and years ago," he replied. "*You* are, my dear."

"*I'm* the favor…?" I sat, aghast.

"It's a late comeuppance. Conspirin' to commit a crime, kidnappin' of a mental patient, arguable treason… and that's just off the top of my head. Not only would I lose my job, but I'd prob'ly go to prison for bailin' you out of here. Same goes for Orel."

"But aren't you a private investigator? Isn't what you're doing *part* of your job?"

"Still gotta follow the rules, sweet cheeks," he cooed. I hated to be called by pet names. "There are hoops I'm supposed to jump through, and I'm goin' a roundabout way in all this. Orel seems to think you ain't as crazy as they say. I know you got your issues, but if you ain't supposed to be where they

done put ya, well, I'm all about doin' the right thing and I trust his judgment
enough in what he thinks the 'right thing' is."

The carriage pulled up to the tall, black metal gates where a couple of
guards manned their post. He didn't have to say anything to me; I instinctively
ducked down, peering at them through a small gap in the curtains. Slowly the
heavy bars began to part through the center as the guards pulled them ajar,
allowing us passage. I held my breath with anticipation. After a few moments
we were moving again and I ducked down even lower, shutting my eyes and
bracing myself. My beating heart was like a light pin prick in my chest with
each quick, little thump.

"You can open your eyes now," the man said. I could hear the
amusement in his voice. "We made it through."

I sat upright disgruntledly. I couldn't help but feel like he was having
a laugh at my expense, though with his seemingly quiet nature there was no
laughing. On top of feeling anxious, I now felt insecure. Which made me a
little mad.

"So," he smiled, "as the Viscountess, what am I supposed to call you?
Should I be sayin' 'my lady' or should I call you by name, or what's most
appropriate in this situation?"

"You called me 'sweet cheeks,' and *now* you're asking me about what's
appropriate?" I shot.

"You're offended. I'm sorry," he said, his smile somewhat faded. The
aura around him got noticeably smaller. "Y'know, people either love me or
they hate me. Never an in between, it feels like. Heh. Guess I just got one of
them personalities."

His words were gentle. I decided to relax myself a bit. I knew he
meant no harm.

"Please don't be mad. My name's Rafe—Rafe Edgewood! But you can
just call me Rafe. Hope that's not too informal for ya. I know we just met
n' all. I feel a little weird about callin' ya 'Lady LaCroix' or somethin', so is it
alright if I just—"

"Call me *Bern*," I interrupted.

"Huh, that's unique. Like the way a fire burns? Can't say I ever heard *that* as
a nickname before. I guess it suits ya, with your hair bein' all fiery! But then, I gather
that's not the only thing fiery about ya. Just somethin' about you redheads…"

I didn't know what he was on about. I thought it best to just smile
politely and nod for the time being. Suddenly my insides churned audibly
and there was nothing I could do to stop it. I felt my face go hot with
embarrassment.

"You hungry?" he chuckled.

"I am, a little," I lied. I was ravenous.

"I'll fix you up with a nice, big meal when we get to my hideout. Got a little garden goin' that grows the plumpest, juiciest tomatoes you ever saw!"

I allotted him another weak smile. "That sounds really nice," I said. "Are you planning on making a salad?"

"Nope," he replied with a sheepish grin. "I got some sauce simmerin' in a pot, waitin' for us. Been cravin' spaghetti somethin' fierce!"

CHAPTER 4
Guardian of the Key

At some point during the carriage ride between Rafe's light, airy conversation and my minimalist sort-of-listening-but-not-really responses, my consciousness slipped into the realm of dreaming reverie. My mind was filled with dancing color and surreal landscaping, as though I were part of a canvas painting that got caught in the rain, its integrity all but washed away. I saw the faces of those I once held dear.

I was something of a hero to the people of Fyndridge. It was no asylum in *my* world. It was a civilization, rebuilt; a small settlement of people who somehow managed to survive the Great War, escaping the widespread bombings that ravaged the earth. That which left all the soil a toxic wasteland in the wake of destruction still remained to be a threat. What little I knew was remedied by how it had affected me; how perhaps turning the Viscountess over to the city was one of the most naïve things I could have done.

Galvinsglade was where people deemed unsalvageable were put to slowly die, in every way possible. It was only a matter of time before she would be sent there – and then I'd have to find a way out for us both. Now that I'd escaped, my old allies consumed my thoughts; Blythe, Kael, Alasdair… even Roland. With Orel, we were quite the bunch. So much had changed with Demetrius's escape. So much to result in a *slaughter* among us. I knew I had to see them again.

When I wore my chained boots, I felt almost six feet tall. I liked the way they sounded when I walked, the metal gently clinking with each long stride I took. I've always walked a little brusquely, though on this day like many others, I was in no particular hurry. I had always been like an arrow without aim, or so my mother once said. I remember it well, more because of the way she said it; amused, perhaps even proud, but with a hint of worry. I often wondered what she might think if she'd seen me then.

My sleeveless leather duster trailed behind me as I walked while wrapping my hands with gauze tape past my wrists. I paid particular attention to my knuckles. If you don't wrap your knuckles well enough, they can still be split upon impact. I remember my first brawl, swinging wildly and without control as I treated my adversary to a vicious 'ground and pound.' His face looked like meatloaf when I was through with him, but I couldn't hold a mug in my hands properly for days. I couldn't shoot a bow for *weeks*.

The scars on my knuckles were almost completely faded by then, my nerves deadened. That was a long time ago, and I had grown as a fighter since—much to Roland's dismay. He was a handsome, somewhat rugged man with bright blue eyes and tussled brown hair. He could even be charming at times, soft and sweet with the women in town, though never would he be so with me. Not that I ever cared, really. I wouldn't be coddled or talked down to.

"Evenin', Berny," Bill greeted me at the double doors of The Rogue Musket.

"Not yet, it isn't," I replied, not bothering to look up from wrapping my hands. I was intent on tying them off properly so that they did not loosen with a thrown punch. "The sun's still up."

"Sun stays up longer'n usual in the summertime," he said. "Won't be needin' very much candlelight for the first few fights, I reckon. I heard *you* was up first."

"Oh, yeah? The Governor's got the matches posted up already? I wonder how many fighters we've got this time…"

I stood there a while in front of the doors as I finished with my wraps, finally looking up at him, his big, practically toothless grin the first thing I had seen.

"Roland was gonna be signed up, but I heard he done dropped out when he saw you was fightin'."

"…What?" I stood aghast. I remember my heart sinking with his words.

"I'm just tellin' yeh what I heard, Berny; I only mind the door."

I had to go find him. I threw open the doors leading into the pub and began pushing my way through the cesspool of sweaty, dirty men, all bustling and shouting amongst themselves, drinks in hand. *Bunch of drunks, the whole lot of them,* I disdainfully thought to myself.

He couldn't have been in the pit if he wasn't going to fight. Even so, I made my way toward the railing that ran the expanse of the pub's center in a wide circle, glancing over the bars and into the pit to quickly scan for him. There was just the door leading into the cellar. It was about a seven foot drop from the floorboards which surrounded the makeshift arena. I could easily hop down rather than having to push my way back out of the pub to get around the side of the building to the outer cellar door. The cellar was where the fighters were kept before they stepped out onto the dirt floor down below.

Just as I was considering leaping over the railing on the off chance that the other fighters would know where he was, I felt a large, firm hand clasp around my shoulder from behind. I turned to face the much taller man, the badge on his chest the first thing I noticed alongside the identical one on his helmet, which he held under his arm. My eyes met with his, and he smiled at me.

"Hey, Bern. Just got off my shift," he said.

"Alasdair!" I was surprised to see him. His dark complexion ran together with the dark blue of his button down coat, which looked slightly too small for his broad shoulders and muscular frame. "I thought you were scheduled for night duty this evening."

"They got enough guards manning posts right now," he shrugged. "Figured I'd come watch Roland fight, but I just checked the board and he's not on there. *You* are, though…"

"Have you seen him?" I asked, deflecting his marked curiosity.

"Nope. If he isn't here… but you are… I'm betting he's probably gone to see Lyn."

Lyn. If Roland wanted to get back at me for signing up to fight, it would certainly be through her. She was my private treasure; my deepest, most personal connection. She was innocence, poise, and beauty swept into a couplet of sweet symphony and savory nectar. I felt happiest when I could be near her and the thought of another sharing in that happiness terrified me. It made me *crazy.* How could Roland do this to me? She was mine, and he thought he could just infiltrate my property, my home, and take advantage of her while I wasn't around…

"Bern? You okay, girl?" Alasdair spoke after a bit of a pause, snatching me back from my quiet musings. He must have read the expression on my face, how it changed with his words.

"I'm fine," I deflected him, once more. I'm usually much better about hiding my emotions.

I felt the tingle of fingers tracing along my waist from behind suddenly, startling me to action. I whirled around, nearly striking Kael who narrowly dodged my elbow. My eyes, furious with outrage, met with his as he backpedaled just out of my reach. The shorter man smiled apologetically, raising his open palms in acquiesce.

"Hey, hey now; take it easy on me, beautiful maiden!" he chuckled, flipping back his long, jet-black hair with an abrupt turn of his head. "You nearly took my face off! How am I to admire your lovely features with no face?"

"Your *face* is not what you admire my features with, you oversexed leprechaun," I replied, mostly through gritted teeth.

He laughed. "Leprechaun, eh? That's a new one comin' from you! Idn't that s'posed to be Irish? My skin's too dark to pass for Irish!"

"You drink like you're Irish, though," Alasdair smirked. "The sun's not even down yet, Kael. How much have you had?"

"Bah! *Just* enough to give me the liquid courage I needed to sneak up on Bern."

Kael winked at me and I looked away with a slight scowl, relenting. He did have a certain charm about him, that much I could not deny. My annoyance was only on the surface. Deep down, a part of me appreciated the attention he gave me, even in jest. I could never bring myself to admit it if only for the implications of what that could mean, my demeanor compromised by my mixed feelings, were men like him made the slightest bit aware there was any internal struggle. I had earned the respect of those in Fyndridge for my formidable combative prowess, and I was not about to mar that with frivolity.

But, I was still just a woman. I was made aware of that fact by the subtle nuances in the manner I was spoken to, and how this differed from the way men would speak to each other. What few women there were in town I did not spend a whole lot of time with. I felt so awkward around other women, the things they concerned themselves with, from what constituted *beauty* to their hobbies and interests. Maybe I was just insecure in my femininity, especially when faced with these creatures and their smooth, soft skin, their dainty hand gestures and the way they walked, how Roland would be talking to me one moment and a woman in passing would seize his eyes from me the next, not a single word spoken between them.

If I wanted a man's attention, my only option was to take it by force. I took pride in my solid gait; my boots jingling with each step, my steel toe caps a *promise* which preceded me. If I wanted to be respected, I had to fight for it. There were often times where I wished it didn't have to be one or the other, the base level of respect men allotted one another versus the sense of belonging other women had among themselves, and in turn, the men, which earned them proper suitors—which earned them *affection*.

...At least then I had Lyn. When I had to be so rough, she was my soft place to fall. She was the one other woman I felt I knew, from her plump, pink lips to the gentle red strands of hair that caught the morning light as we lay. I couldn't stand knowing Roland was with her now, leaving me to fight alone. Even Alasdair had come to see only him, and Kael always came for the booze if he wasn't to fight, himself.

"Bern!" a squeaky voice chirped, interrupting me from my dwelling. My vision focused on a shorter boy in shabby clothes, his bushy blond hair falling about his eyes as he looked up at me. "I said 'hello' and you ignored me!"

"Oh, uhh, I'm sorry, Blythe," I shouted over the growing volume of the crowd as more patrons were beginning to pile into the bar.

Alasdair smacked my back, bumping me slightly off balance. "Girl, you can't be spacing off like that so close to the fights! You're gonna be up first! You need to get your head in the game."

"Who's the new kid?" Kael asked, before knocking back a tall drink of something or other.

I saved Blythe from the desert wastelands in much the same way I had saved the Viscountess. All he had to his name were the clothes on his back and a ragged cotton-stuffed lamb with buttons for eyes. Since then, he had stuck to me like a burr on my pant leg. Not that I blame him. He had nowhere else to go, and with me being the only remaining link he had to this world, however brief that might have been so far, all I could do was help him get settled into his new life at Fyndridge.

*

"Blythe," I murmured, opening my eyes.

"Ahh, good, you're awake," Rafe greeted me. He was standing beside the carriage now on the passenger side, his gloved hand holding back the curtains with the door opened. "Was worried I'd hafta carry ya or somethin'. I prob'ly could do it too, but I ain't as strong as I was when I was a boy. It would take a lot of energy, and I took a bath before I came and got you, and sweatin' too much is just no good for an older guy who looks as *pretty* as I do."

I smiled more to be polite than anything and stepped out of the carriage. I was immediately struck with a swirling sensation that wasn't quite dizziness, but as though the world around me were spinning about my stillness. I was standing, but could not feel the earth beneath me. Rafe still had his rich purple aura all around him which expanded and tumbled before me with the rest of the universe. I steadied myself in his arms.

"Whoa, easy now," he said with a bit of a chuckle. "Orel told me you'd be out of sorts. They must'a given you somethin' too, huh? Heard about some of the testing that would be goin' on in Galvinsglade. I wonder if they plan on doing the same kind of stuff in Fyndridge."

"Passed through the portal…" I said, my eyes fluttering to focus on his.

He looked confused for a moment. "The portal?"

"I was given a drink of water with something *funny* in it," I continued, trying to go over in my head the events leading up to now. "There's a Castle in the Sky, and it has restorative powers! I know if we harnessed its power, we'd be able to fix this world. I just didn't know there were other worlds… other manifestations of reality… Maybe if we found the castle, it would bring it all together into one!"

He stared back at me, wide-eyed. After a brief pause, his gaze softened beneath his expressive, bushy brows to smooth his features and he smiled. "I reckon so," he said, knowingly.

"That's how I came in through the portal," I continued. "It was the *drink*. The *serum*. Orel had my gemstone; he must have used it for the serum and *I swallowed the key!* Do you see?!"

"C'mon, sweetheart," he replied with a soft cadence. "Don't go gettin' yourself all worked up now." He took me by the shoulders and began leading me away into daylight receding.

My voice now carried a dire urgency. I could feel the erratic excitement rise up within me as colors danced before my eyes. "You're not *listening* to me!"

"I am listenin' to you. Just settle down so we can get you inside. I'll draw ya a nice bath and then I'll finish gettin' supper ready, alright?"

I hated to be called by pet names. I *hated* being coddled or talked down to. If I tried to shrug him off me, would that be a childish thing to do? Could I fight him in this strange state of delirium? Would that even be wise? My eyes danced all about with these thoughts, from the desert sand I kicked up shuffling in my unfitting shoes, to the carriage and the horse which pulled it. A great, black stallion with red eyes aflame. I hadn't noticed how the carriage was being drawn before. Were its eyes truly burning? I looked back to Rafe, who only kept looking forward.

"…I swallowed the key," I repeated. "I drank the serum."

We made our way toward a steep dune with thick, jagged rocks sticking out from the sand above eye level. Suddenly the sand beneath my feet grew firmer. I could feel where I stepped, now. Rafe brushed the sand aside with his dark boot to reveal a strange stone, flat, but for a single protruding pebble which he stepped on. A passageway opened before us, sand cascading from the dune's side beneath the jagged rocks slightly overhead.

I was uncertain whether what I was seeing was even real. But one thing, I knew.

"I *am* the key."

CHAPTER 5
The Power Within

Rafe held my hand as he led me down a dark tunnel and into his abode. The walls were made of sand and stone, dozens of lanterns gently swaying from overhead bouncing soft light all around us. Occasionally grains of sand would fall from the ceiling between the lanterns and I wondered just how stable this secret hideout of his was. Along the walls were photographs in modest frames of people, all of them common in dress but baring expressions which embodied each of their rich personalities, one man broad and proud with shortly cropped hair and a quiet smile. Another man, bald, whose eyes shone a wisdom disproportionate to his striking, young features. Finally, a girl who looked to be adolescent, her large, bright eyes seeming to smile all their own even without her playful grin, head tilted forward so that her chin-length hair touched her shoulders. Their portraits had clearly been captured with great care.

Eventually the tunnel opened into what appeared to be Rafe's living quarters, wax wicks of all different sizes set aflame all about the room, bringing in a soft, dim light to the humble surroundings. My eyes drank in what I could see – a guitar in a far corner rested over a worn mattress with loose, crumpled sheets. An accordion? No, a camera, next to that. At the room's center, a large cast iron pot with pegs simmered over a divot in the ground where dying flames licked the bottom of the metal. A single wooden chair and a shorter stool were the only places to sit at an end table that barely had room for the two bowls and silverware set over it. One of the walls was covered in dozens of hanging trinkets of presumed sentimental value and hundreds of newspaper clippings from a time long past, before the Great War. Rafe was a rarity, being a common man who could read. This shouldn't have surprised me, knowing he'd grown up before the war took place.

"It ain't much," Rafe said, slipping his fingers out from mine and stepping to the pot. "It'll have to do for now, though. At least until we can figure out what we're gonna do with ya."

I nodded, somberly. I knew this couldn't be a permanent arrangement.

He pulled off one of his gloves and reached into the pot, drawing out a long ladle. "Ow, ow!" he winced, loosening his grip to settle higher up on the handle. "It's hot! Guess I shoulda laid it out over the table before I left."

"Um. Weren't you going to draw a bath first?" I asked, wondering where there even *was*, or *could be* one in this place.

"Oh, right. I forgot!" Rafe said, dropping the ladle back into the pot and stumbling around the table as he made his way to a particularly high concentration of newspaper clippings on the wall. He pushed against a small section and the wall opened to reveal a thin passage into another room. "Just right through here. I trust you can prob'ly figure it out for yourself."

I hesitated a moment before making my way toward him and slipping through the passageway. I wondered how many hidden entrances he had in this place and how he made them all work. How could there even be a hot water system built under a sand dune in the middle of the desert? Back in Fyndridge, the homes of the councilmen were the only places with an active water and heat system. I gazed into the dimly lit room where a large tin wash basin had been set up next to a lid on the ground, presumably a waste hole. I didn't have to relieve myself right then and I wasn't curious enough to find out for sure. Above the basin, a mirror was fixed into the ceiling between two lanterns.

"Thanks," I said, turning to look at Rafe who was already shutting the wall behind me.

"Don't mention it," he replied. "Holler if ya need anythin'. A towel? Maybe a *sexy* back rub if you ain't too young for one?"

I could feel my brows furrow with my discomfort at the thought.

"I'm just kiddin' around," he smirked. "See ya in a bit."

The wall closed all the way with a light thump. I looked down at my silly frock, anxious to slip out of it. I started with the shoes, realizing only then how much my feet ached being stuffed into them. Next to go was the skirt, followed by the blouse, all in a heap on the ground around my ankles. I stepped out of the pile of clothes, loosening the white ribbon in my hair while

I did my best to figure out how to start the water running. I peered into the basin, noticing a single nob next to a faucet and turned it clockwise. I was surprised by the steaming cascade of water which promptly fell, a mild scent of sulfur filling the room with it. I wrinkled my nose. It would have to do. I waited a few moments for the murky water to fill the basin a quarter of the way before slinging a leg over the brim and carefully lowering my foot.

I gasped as biting heat met with my bare flesh, submerging my leg to the calf. I found my footing before slinging my other leg over as well. There I stood with my knees brought together, steam rising about my thighs, my body adjusting to the temperature. Steadily, I eased myself down into a sitting position and let the water take me. I laid back and looked up at the dark ceiling, shadows dancing with the gentle sway of the lanterns. I gazed at my naked body through the mirror, no longer my sister's, but my own; my deep auburn hair set aflame with glimpses of fiery red under restless light, loose and draping from the usual tight braids I kept it in. My sun-kissed skin was warm and smooth, a touch darker than that of the Viscountess whose eyes seldom saw the light of day. My eyes were lighter than hers, like two hazel jewels that pierced back into me. They demanded of me.

A pulsating aura surrounded my shapely form, a ripple in a pool of water, an unrelenting constant that took on the coloration of a blazing fire in reds, yellows, and flashing white. As the water level rose to engulf my bosom, my thoughts began to wander from the here and now. My mind plunged headlong into the recesses of distant memory, taking me back to a time before Galvinsglade. The heavy gate along the outer wall of Fyndridge unfolded before my eyes. Through the gate was not the recovering civilization, the *town* that I knew, but a dreary asylum with uniform rooms, not homes, of all its inhabitants; men and women of varied ages alike. My thoughts drifted to my chambers where I'd spent most of my time locked inside my head, safely confined inside my world. As safely as I could be, anyway. I had special privileges to come and go as I pleased under curfew, free to roam the halls as many of the patients often did under minimum security. As the count's daughter, I sometimes had clearance to leave the grounds altogether, but always with the intent on returning.

*

"So, I just woke up from a dream where we were… *intimately* getting to know each other," Kael remarked, popping his head into my room suddenly.

I was lying on my neatly made bed dressed in patient scrubs, my head resting on a pillow propped up by the metal bars of the headboard. I had to lower the book I'd been gazing at rested over my body in order to see his face. I could not repress my look of annoyance as he locked eyes with mine, playfully grinning from ear to ear.

"Okay," I curtly replied.

"Yeah, it was pretty surreal," he said, stepping toward me and seating himself at the foot of my bed. "I was left feelin' kinda befuddled over the whole thing."

I scoffed and raised my book again, blocking him from my view. "And just what is there to be *befuddled* about, exactly?"

"Well, you know how my ancestors were all about dreamcatchers n' everything, right? I got one hanging in my room. Since I've had it, I don't really do much dreaming. *Any* dreaming, actually. My mother told me when I was growing up that it's meant to catch my nightmares. Used to wake up yelling and drenched in sweat… had some real bad terrors. I think I had my first dreamcatcher when I was about nine. She made it for me out of a willow hoop and dyed red yarn and hung all sorts of little trinkets on it she said would protect me. Haven't dreamed since—yet just last night, there you were."

His words were soft and sincere on the deep rasp of his accented tongue. Why now? I just wanted to enjoy my pictures and diagrams in peace, and forget the whole world for a short while. Oh, how jaded I felt right then, my opportunities for escapism few and far between.

"…Just so curious about the dream, and what it *means*," he continued, contemplatively.

Again I lowered my book with an exasperated sigh. "Don't be. I'm generally physically appealing, you're a man with a starved libido, and it was just a dream. It happens. No sense overcomplicating the simple."

"Generally, huh?" Kael smirked, raising a brow. "Your humility is boundless, my dear mademoiselle!"

"Take out the 'generally' part, then. It is what it is."

He had a twinkle in his eyes to once accompany his goofy grin which now faded with my brusque dismissal of his words. I could tell he was trying to connect with me in some way. Even so, I felt affronted by his approach. He was failing to pay attention to what wasn't being said; I wasn't simply praising myself as beautiful. That was beside the point.

"You're definitely attractive, and I'm definitely attracted to you," he said, resignedly. "But you're right. A dream is a dream."

I had snatched the wind from his sails. I felt a twinge of guilt rise up within me knowing full well I was projecting my cynicism upon him, perhaps unfairly, but I just didn't know how to write it off as playful flirting. Not when I was so sure his dream was based solely on the husk my very being inhabited.

His face half disappeared behind his thick, straight, jet-black hair as he hung his head toward the tile floor beneath his feet. The room was so plain and empty, he in his scrubs and me in mine, and the silence between us then was deafening.

For him to dwell over reasons why suggested to me he only wanted there to *be* reasons. There was no love to be shared between us, no fears I felt safe in sharing with him, that he should be strong enough to carry both mine and his. There was no comfort in knowing that even if I spoke of every dark space in my head and in my heart, he would ever understand. And I wasn't willing to risk it. I was satisfied with our fair-weather friendship and in never truly knowing whether he would leave me to my darkness should he see it.

"Welp," he said, using his hands to push off his knees with a slap as he stood, "I guess I'll bugger off, then. I can see you're busy."

"You know you wouldn't be dreaming of me at all if you didn't want to *fuck* me," I bitterly spat. It wasn't often that I spoke profanities. I felt the Viscountess in me cringe. "And what do you really even know about me, Kael?"

For a moment he looked lost. Hurt. Still, he was ever resilient. "I know you're fiery," he said. "I know it's what attracted me to you in the first place. Ahh… I guess I shoulda just kept it to myself."

He sounded genuinely sorry though he didn't outright say it. I had always brushed off his advances as being mostly in jest, but perhaps there was truth under the guise of his mirthful demeanor. Perhaps there was depth behind lots of things he would say to be funny   a roundabout way of reaching out without being wounded.

I suddenly became aware of Blythe's presence in the open doorway. He watched us intently with a strange expression on his face, studying and focused. It was hard to say, but he looked unhappy about something, wisps of his shaggy, dirty-blond hair falling over his eyes as he stared into the room. His scrubs were crinkled and dirty as usual, with only half his shirt haphazardly tucked into his pants. He was holding what appeared to be a collection of cotton balls in the palm of his hand. I sat upright to get a better look.

"Blythe," Kael said, turning to face him. "Hey, man. What's up?"

Blythe averted his gaze from me, his upper lip curling in what looked to be disdain, if only for a fragment of a second. Or perhaps it was a nervous twitch. Either way, something about him didn't sit right with me.

"You weren't in your room," he said in his squeaky little voice. "I came looking for you. Figured you might be here, with um, Bern…"

Kael clumsily ran a hand through his hair and with that, his playful grin returned. "Aha, I see ya got the present I left you!"

Upon closer inspection I noticed the cotton ball cluster was actually one collective cotton form made to look like a little lamb with toothpicks for its legs. A strand of red yarn was tied around it as a bow for its neck. I remembered thinking that it was fairly well made considering the materials used.

"I wanted to thank you for it," Blythe smiled meekly. He shot me a quick, uncomfortable sidelong glance.

"Well, I know how much you love those sheep of yours," Kael said, warmly. "It was the least I could do for your birthday."

That's right. I had forgotten it was Blythe's birthday. I didn't keep a calendar, the days often blurring together with the passing of seasons. I didn't even know what day it was then, the crisp autumn weather my only indication. Another twinge of guilt I felt in such a short span of time. I hated feeling this way. I resented it, even.

"Happy birthday, Blythe," I murmured.

"Thank you," he swiftly replied, smile fading.

I gasped, displacing water from the basin as I sat upright having abruptly returned to the present hour. It was overflowing to meet with the ground on either side in a pouring patter. I scrambled for the faucet, my slippery fingers fumbling to clasp over the nob. As I turned it counterclockwise the steaming water ceased to flow. I felt somewhat lightheaded, inundated up to my neck. Looking overhead to the fogging mirror, I saw that my face had become as red as my hair.

"Hey!" I heard Rafe call out from the other side of the wall. "You doin' okay in there?"

"Yeah," I said. "I need a towel."

"I brought you one. Can I step in and hand it to ya? I'll keep my eyes closed."

I crouched low in the basin, dipping my chin in the murky water with my arms wrapped around my body. "You can come in," I ambivalently replied.

The same section of wall opened up and he slipped inside the room, feeling out in front of himself with one of his gloved hands. The other cradled a towel close to his body. His eyes were scrunched tightly closed, deepening the lines of age in his face. As he moved toward me, I could hear water splash on the ground. His eyes came open in what appeared to be an involuntary response to his surprise, and as he looked down at the puddle, his expression took on the appearance of mild annoyance.

"You, uhh… I think you done used up all the water," he said.

Before I could respond with mounting anxiety, there were several loud crashes from the other room. My body jolted with surprise and I accidentally took hot water into my nostrils. I coughed and sputtered as my sudden movement displaced another brief waterfall to spill out over the edge of the basin. Rafe didn't seem to mind this time, though. He had dropped the towel and slipped back through the passageway by then. I could tell he was even more surprised than I was.

"What the *hell*…?!" I heard him say.

"Looky 'ere, boys!" came a familiar man's voice, deep and scratchy and shaking me to my core. My blood ran cold in that instant, the hot water I bathed in serving only to amplify this feeling in me. "We got us a *lively* one t'night," the voice said.

With my heart drumming the inside of my chest, I quickly stood. Bad idea. My vision split before my eyes. I couldn't catch my breath. The sudden shift in body temperature sent my blood rushing to my head and I stumbled forward. Barely was I able to catch myself, clutching the side of the basin with both hands and shakily climbing out.

"Who are you people, and what're you doin' inside my house?!" Rafe snarled.

I snatched up the towel from the puddle on the ground and hastily began patting myself down with the dry end.

"I understand yeh 'ave somethin' of ours," the voice belonging to none other than Gertie sneered. I could hear it, the sneer in his words. I gritted my teeth as I pictured his ugly sneering mug and the gold ingots where his teeth should be. I wanted to punch them all out of his mouth. "If yeh 'and 'er over nice, we won't smash up any more a' yer stuff. We know you got 'er, so there's no use lyin' about it!"

"You answer my question first," Rafe shot back. "Now, I ain't gonna repeat myself!"

I dressed as quickly as I could, holding my head to one side so that my very long, soaking wet hair would not drench my clothes as it spiraled down my back and shoulders. I heard another loud crash.

"I told yeh why we're here, and that's all yeh need to know," Gertie replied. "We gonna 'ave yer cooperation? Or would yeh rather say 'ello to good ol' *Susan?*"

There was a click, like the drawing back of a hammer on a gun. Susan was the gun.

"Whoa, now, let's not do anything rash," Rafe said. He sounded considerably less self-assured.

My hand rose up to clutch at the brooch fixed to the blouse I now wore, my wet hair which fell around me dampening the fabric anyway. The gemstone started to glow. I focused my energy forth and I could see seven auras through the wall into the next room, and all of them exactly where they stood. I recognized Rafe's as standing closest to me, like he was guarding the passageway still slightly ajar. These were *skylark pirates* he was speaking to. 'Rash' was the only response I could come to reason with. I slipped through into the next room, the auras transforming into people before my eyes, all where they were supposed to be. Lanterns had fallen to the ground, and Rafe's steeping pot had been toppled. My heart raced with my uncertainty fighting against willful resolve and I extended my arm, my hand and fingers, toward the one I knew to be Gertie, first.

    "Λογία þovis," I spoke, calmed and steady. On the inside I was trembling. That trembling became a physical rock backward in reaction to the beam of white light careening out of me in a typhoon of electrical current.

CHAPTER 6
Battle Mage of the Sage

As the powerful blast left my fingertips, I could feel my heart leap up into my throat. My hair whipped around my body in recoil of the sheer force careening out from me and knocking into my target, Gertie, a mere several feet from where I was standing. He fired off a single shot, the bullet narrowly missing Rafe as it whizzed between us and lodged itself, forming a dent, in the side of the toppled pot. Gertie maintained a tight grip around his gun, perhaps only firing in an involuntary clench with his finger on the trigger. He slammed into a far wall by the tunneling entrance which loosed a downpour of sand from the ceiling, shook candles off their perches to fall against the ground, their flames doused, and knocking the portrait of the girl off its hinge. Only then did the gun slip from his hand.

The others hesitated, surprised by what they had seen. They were no more surprised than I was as I took a moment to look down at my hands, turning my palms over and back again in awe. What just happened – that was *me*. I shot Rafe a quick sidelong glance. He looked back at me, wide-eyed and in clear disbelief. I wasted no more time, returning my attention to the five other pirates who closed in on us now, each of them brandishing clubs or daggers, or other foreign objects with which to bash our heads in.

"Ζεῦ þovis!" I bellowed, extending my fingers to the next closest target. The light radiated through me and instantly shot forth, encapsulating the pirate in a glowing bubble that absorbed into his colorful clothes, his plethora of gaudy chains and jewelry, and the very pores of his tanned skin.

"Defend me," I commanded in the language of my common tongue.

I watched his eyes change shades to match the color of his aura, red, and with it came the swinging of his club into the other pirate nearest him. It connected solidly with the pirate's face, letting loose a gusher of blood. The unlucky man cried out in surprise and pain, falling to the floor. The two fought while the three that remained advanced on me, as well as Rafe, who now stood closer beside me. He was suddenly brandishing a weapon of his own—a hunting rifle, now pointed toward them.

"Where did you get—?" I started to ask.

"Really? You're *really* asking *me* questions right now?!" he cut me off.

His eyes darted suddenly and no sooner had he stolen a glance around the room than he was grabbing at my arm, jerking it down as he crouched to the floor. There was a loud bang. I sank alongside him just as a bullet whisked through the air above me where I'd been only a fragment of a second before. He released me then, clutching his rifle with both hands and bracing against the butt with his shoulder as he knelt.

From across the room I saw Gertie lying on the ground with his gun aimed in his hand, having since recovered. His arm was shaking, his face contorted in anger and pain. He fired another shot, the sound from the blast echoing throughout the cavernous hideout. More sand fell from part of the ceiling a couple of feet away, where the bullet had gone.

Finally, Rafe returned fire. With him crouched to my left, I did not think to cover my ears and in the heat of the moment, he did not mention that I probably ought to have. My right ear, the only one I could hear out of when inhabiting the Viscountess's body, rang with the explosive sound of his rifle going off and I shut my eyes in a flinch. Unexpectedly, so did my left ear as well. I was me. Just as I'd seen in the ceiling mirror, I was *me*. If the key was inside me, then perhaps so was she. That is, if I hadn't left her an inanimate husk the moment I stepped through that portal.

My musings spanned the course of just a couple of seconds. In an instant, my eyes snapped back open to the bloodcurdling cries escaped from Gertie's mouth, the arm that once pointed his gun now dangling uselessly, partially severed. I could see the separation of bone from torn ligament in wake of the hole that was left. Meanwhile, two pirates continued to fight one another blow for blow, the one I seized control over maintaining his upper hand as he continued to loom over the other. Rafe cocked back the hammer on his rifle, lining up for another shot.

I was feeling good about our odds, Gertie's handgun, 'Susan,' being the only firearm at their disposal. One of the pirates resheathed his dagger and made a dash for it, attempting to pry it from the fingers of Gertie's disabled arm. "Ζεϋ þovis!" I bellowed once more, extending my reach to that pirate with worthy aim and engulfing him in the same bubble I had with the one before him. But something happened. The light left me, the bubble popping suddenly, and I felt a sinking feeling in the pit of my stomach. My heart stopped and I collapsed.

Again, Rafe fired his rifle. His aim proved tried and true, the bullet exploding from the end of the barrel and through the wrist of that pirate's hand, severing it completely. The other two pirates got in close enough to swing on Rafe with their weapons. He backpedaled, narrowly dodging their blows, flipping his rifle around and knocking the each of them in their faces with the butt. With each man momentarily stunned and the others indisposed or nursing wounds in that moment, he rushed to my side.

"C'mon, we gotta go," he shouted, wrapping his hands around my waist and lifting me partway off the ground. He shrugged one of my arms over and around his shoulders, and my elbow knocked against his rifle now slung over his back on a strap I hadn't noticed before. I dragged my feet, trying my best to make them move again. All the feeling in my body was gone. What had happened? What had I done wrong?

"Don't let them get away!" Gertie shrieked, enraged. His face was red. I could see the veins in his thick neck visibly popping out even in my vegetative state as I glanced over at him from across the room.

Rafe took me back through the passageway behind the wall leading to the basin and ambled us over to the lid on the ground, again, presumed to be his toilet. He splashed over the puddle left from my bath and kicked the lid open, revealing a dark, bottomless hole. One of the pirates he struck with his rifle was coming in fast behind us.

"You're gonna hafta let go of me now and jump down there, sweetie," he urgently spoke, taking my arm off him and easing me down. Surely he was kidding. I shot him a panicked glare, which he made no indication of noticing. Before I knew it, he had suddenly let me go with a small push. Any doubts I had that either one of us would even be able to fit into the hole were immediately vanquished as I suddenly found myself plunging headlong through the pitch black darkness down a slick metal slide. My hands flailed uselessly in front of me, bracing for the inevitable collision I would surely soon be facing. I held my breath in anticipation and fear, not knowing what to expect as the slide curved around rocky corners and dropping slopes. Finally, like a rag doll, I shot out the end as the tunneling hole had come to conclusion.

I hit the dirt like a newly birthed baby giraffe dropped out its mother.

Like a wad of phlegm hocked from the mouth of a Rogue Musket patron and into a spittoon. I probably shouldn't have been even *mildly* amused, having been so alarmed just moments before. Suffice it to say, I was grateful to be out. My collision with the ground left my garments dirtied and my skin scraped. My damp, loose hair clung to my back as I slowly stood and brushed myself off. The feeling in my body had returned.

Rafe came tumbling after me, hitting the ground solidly with a grunt. "Ugh, I'm really gettin' too old to be doin' this kind of stuff," he grimaced.

"Here, get up," I said, reaching down and helping him to his feet. "They'll be coming for us soon, won't they?"

"Were *you* about to jump down a black mystery hole you never seen before if I ain't pushed ya first?" he asked, in retort. He had a point.

"No, not without you pushing me," I admitted, relaxing a bit. "So, what now then?"

"Well, now, we walk."

"…Where?"

I surveyed my surroundings. The hole we came out of appeared to be a fissure in a tall cliffside. I followed it up with my eyes, its height rigidly spanning high above, the distant outline of sand dunes barely visible overhead. We had dropped into a canyon.

"When I built my home, I figured I'd have a couple emergency exits," Rafe said, brushing off his pant legs and starting in on a light trudge. Ambivalently, I followed. "Figured the edge of the desert would be well enough. It offered up a lot of options. That was one of 'em. Just a shame I couldn't take anything with me… Lot a' memories in that place."

"We can go back for it all, can't we?" I asked. "And your horse, too, right? They wanted *me*, my stone, not all that stuff."

"I ain't all that worried about it," he replied. "Not right now, at least. Got other things on my mind. What in the world happened to you back there, anyhow?"

I thought back to the moment just after I fought off the Viscountess's assailants as she followed me into the mines, where I had located and recovered the Libra gemstone. I remember turning corners as I treaded deeper into the mines, knowing full well that she was right behind me. I wanted to make it as easy and painless as possible; I would wait for her at a corner and get the drop on her. Then I would use the incantation that would give me direct control over her will. I would turn her away, and make her go back home. She could have evaded the two guards I had disabled before – they could have rotted for all I cared. She would have been safe, at least until I had retrieved the stone.

I'd forgotten that the power does not work against another whose sun sign matched that of the stone being wielded; whose sun sign is the same as the wielder, himself. The key was my channel of power then, before it became a part of me. When my magic did not work, it fizzled out and then would need to be recharged. I knew what went wrong now. I also knew that making this same mistake again would be far more unforgiving so long as *I* was now that channel of power.

"I am a Sagittarius," I said flatly. "I attacked another Sagittarius, unknowingly. The magic of the stone cannot work against one of the same constellation."

"...Oh," Rafe replied. "Okay, then."

"What it *means* is that I'm going to have to be extra careful about throwing my incants around," I continued. "It was one thing when it was just a malfunction in the key, but this is *my body*, and shutting down like I did back there could mean irreparable damage or something. I don't know. I felt my heart stop for a minute, and that's enough to tell me I need to be more discerning about when and how I use my powers from here on out. I'd have to ask Orel what he thinks."

"Look," Rafe said. "I don't know nothin' about what all you just said, but uhh, the whole deal with Orel wantin' me to watch out for you a while means we gotta lay low. We can't go bumpin' into him just yet. Not 'til I gather up enough evidence against your uncle and Galvinsglade."

"He is the Viscountess's uncle," I clarified. "I'm just Bern."

"Whatever you say, sweetheart," he shrugged.

I abruptly stopped walking. "Can you not call me 'sweetie' or 'sweetheart' or any variation of a sweet *anything*, please?" I barked. "It makes me feel really weird and uncomfortable."

Rafe continued walking, not bothering to look back at me from over his shoulder. "...You're just Bern," he said. "I got'cha."

The Viscountess in me grimaced at that last line. *'I got'cha.'*

CHAPTER 7
The Brothers Grim

The canyon was a land of decay, a forest ravine where the trees stood as skeletal husks, their bony bark fingers reaching toward the heavens as if pleading to be nourished. No amount of rain nor shine could replenish them now, having long since surrendered to their beleaguered environment. Everywhere I stepped there were dead leaves and the hollow remains of once flourishing life.

I paced with my hand over my gemstone brooch fastened to my blouse. I was covering more ground than Rafe suggested I do during the wakeful hours of my shift. I remembered him telling me not to wander off so far that it would take long for him to awaken and come to my aid, should he hear me cry out. Still, I heard something in the thicket and I could not help but follow it. I was not about to let bandits, subterran scavengers, or anyone else get the drop on me, least of all Gertie and what remained of Demetrius's crew. I moved slowly and carefully, trying not to make more than the sound of crunching dead leaves beneath my feet with each step. Whatever it was did nothing to hide their footfalls.

I eventually drew close enough as I made my way through deadened brush to spy on two larger figures, each with a rolling gait all their own. One of them, while the larger of the two, took the time to amble around the deadened remains of briars and underbrush, but the other strode with a purpose. His strong stride tore through bush and vine without pause, not out of disregard, but more that he seemed in thought. The two hardly appeared

alike. One healthily proportioned with a mane of dark brown hair and short
beard to match, he was taller, wider, and more heavily outfitted; the other,
broader of shoulder and chest in a suit of steel armor, his hair shorn short and
matched with a manicured goatee. One jovial, the other stern, they marched
without care for who heard them, as if nothing in these woods could stand
against them. Bravado or well-earned confidence was something remained to
be seen. Both wore sizable shields along their backs.

As far as my eyes could see, there was only death. The trees stood at
great heights as their dead branches continued to reach outward and into the
barren sky above, ashen and gray with only the moon to offer illumination
enough that I could move with intent. I decided to climb for a better look.
Quietly I slipped off my shoes, wrapping myself around the thick trunk of the
tree closest to me and climbing up the branches until I could gaze down upon
them. The bark was very fragile in places and I had to be careful not to snap
pieces off with my footing. I grimaced when my skirt caught a twig or a sharp
edge, bracing for it to cause noise with a snap. Somehow I managed to make it
high enough without being heard.

At last the pair came to a halt in a small clearing just several feet away,
the taller one curling his lip in thought. "Radiation," he said, his tone a weary
kind of amused.

"Naturally. A flower wilts on this plane and there's a subterran or a
degenerate to blame," the more grim of the two said in an almost bored tone.

"Is it bad that we're so used to this?" the first asked, fishing into one of
his many pouches.

"Zebadiah should be told," was the response, disregarding of the
question. It sounded as though it had been asked many a time before.

"Would you do the honors?" the taller man requested with a sheepish
grin. "I forgot I gave mine to you."

The knight was already pulling something from his satchel. Setting
his feet, holding a gemstone in each hand, he held his arms apart and turned
his head to the sky. After a moment's focus, motes of power began to form
about his palms. He paid them no mind as he slowly drew his arms in across

his chest. "*Zé wa Çassel tu wa Ćuaų y zorbeiji wan kroolios kijt rokka und
hajish,*" he commanded, his deep voice shaking with the force of his spell.
Folding his hands over each of the stones, he forced the raw power within
them together and drove the combined energies into the earth. There was a
rush of light, and for a moment the wilting leaves and gray earth blossomed
into life. It began to spread rapidly, like wildfire in shades of green and brown.
Then the momentum halted, at points the struggling magic visibly combating

the taint, before in a rush, the life that flowed was snuffed and the purity of the land drained of life and hope again.

The knight scowled with an expectant sigh.

"Well, worth a shot," the other said, slapping him on the back.

"It's never this simple," he grumbled, returning the stones to their compartment in his satchel and standing straight.

I was stunned. I could not believe what I was seeing. To my knowledge, I had the only key to the legendary Castle in the Sky, and here were two strange men traveling about this deathly soil at the same time as I was on pure happenstance. I saw no other key, no other vessel by which the knight conducted his sorcery. He spoke words of the ancient castlelark tongue I had never learned, an incantation I didn't know even existed. Which of the stones were his? I could not get a good enough look from where I stood along the branches to decipher what they were. I leaned forward above them, stooping anxiously that I might get a closer gander. As I did, a thick piece of bark snapped audibly and fell to the ground below. I could not stop my breath escaping in a gasp, clasping a hand over my mouth all too late.

It seemed their swagger was not just an ignorant façade. The two sprang into action with the practiced precision of a pair that had fought together for years. The larger man immediately drew his shield up and fired a globe of orange liquid my way with a clean snap of the wrist. The other wheeled about his companion in a smooth turn, setting his back to his and bringing his own shield to bear.

"Réii ma!" the knight chanted. His gloved hand ignited in the glow of a spell poised on the tip of his tongue and ready to be cast.

My heart pumped a surge of adrenaline through my veins as the orange globe came hurtling my way. I flipped backward off the branch of the tree as it flew over me, narrowly missing my head. I grabbed another branch on my way down and by the momentum of my body, launched myself forward in the air with a kick at the nearest of the two I could reach. My heartbeat suspended with the instant rush in anticipation. I suspected I would not be able to take the both of them. Even so, I had propelled myself forward, a snap judgment made in the heat of the moment. My bare foot collided with the shield of the larger foe, but the support of his knightly comrade kept them both rooted with his back to the other. I pushed off with the resistance I was met with, flying backward now as the mountainous man braced his weight against the shield.

The knight took this split second to shift his glance, possibly seeking other targets at their backs, before pivoting to his companion's side and locking their shields together to form a defensible surface. The grim-faced man arced his arm over both shields and shouted his command, "Ζεῦ þovis," sending the glow from his fist toward me as I continued to fly backward.

This was a spell I was familiar with. He meant to bend my will to suit his needs, whatever they may be, and I had no intentions of finding out. Quickly, I activated the gemstone fastened to the brooch on my blouse in a counterattack. I had no choice. "Rεῦun þovis!" I shot, midair.

The blast of power bubbled around me as I connected with the ground, more dead leaves crunching beneath my feet with impact. In a white hot flash, I reflected the spell back at the knight who raised his shield to catch it. It exploded against its surface with a brilliant spark before fizzling out into a brief upsurge of smoke. He rolled his armored shoulders, stoically moving himself back into position next to the larger man.

"This is gonna end badly for you, lady," the larger man said, finally pulling a sword free from its sheath strapped to his belt. "I'd surrender if I were you."

The knight didn't seem quite so interested in diplomacy. Closing his eyes, he extended another hand toward me, attempting to pull apart the workings of my mind once more and force me to submit to him. With his hand still glowing, I could feel him inside my head if only for a fleeting moment. Once again, his power sought to abolish my free will only this time he was spouting no incantation to do it. I was awestruck by his sheer level of focus. How was he even able to project such power unto me without a single summons spoken of the ancient tongue? Still, I was able to *feel* him, able to know that this was what he was doing.

"If you were me," I snarled, "You would surrender to *no one*."

I fought against the knight's workings with every ounce of mental fortitude I could assemble. I could feel beads of sweat forming over my brow as my vision began to tumble and split. I refused to let him break into me.

"It's okay," the knight said, turning his head only slightly to regard his friend. He ignored my words of defiance. "I've almost got her."

"λογία þovis!" I bellowed, thrusting both my arms forth in a beam of pulsating white light that rocked out of me, exploding in a blinding flash and causing my muscles to tense up with recoil. Immediately I felt the building pressure in my head fully release, but all too late for him. He did not drop his concentration fast enough to reflect or move out of the way. All he could do was take on the full brunt of the force against his shield which he raised up in front of him at the last possible moment. The shield smashed into him along with the blast and he was sent sprawling backward onto the ground with a metallic thud like an empty tin can.

Before I knew it another globe of orange liquid came careening toward my head. Also before I knew it, it had broken against my hairline, the glass thin and malleable to the impact. I had hardly known that I'd even been struck before shards of glass were plummeting to the ground around me. It was the intense odor that got me, as it splashed down the front of my face. It was sour like vinegar, and I coughed and sputtered. Everything around me seemed to slow down, along with my own movements. Each of my limbs felt so heavy and sluggish.

"Ahh...!" I called out, in a bid that Rafe might hear me. My cry of distress carried only as far as the wind would take it, and the air was very still. I stumbled in place, barely able to raise my hands to wipe the strange substance from my face.

The larger man extended his sword, pointing it toward me a few feet from my face. "Why were you spying on us?" he sternly demanded.

The knight was climbing to his feet behind him with a grumble. "Perhaps we should take *her* to Zebadiah as well. She has a stone."

"I'll not... go anywhere with... you..." I breathed weakly. I could hardly get the words out. If only everything weren't so foggy. "That is why... spying..."

"You mean to tell me you were *spying* on us... because you won't *go* anywhere with us?" the man questioned with a raised brow, keeping the end of his sword pointed at me.

"In the... beginning..." I admitted. "Wanted to... keep camp safe... But I saw... the gemstones... and then... the *magic*... Must get Rafe... He camps... not far from here... Must tell Rafe... there are *others*..."

What was wrong with me? I could not keep myself from blurting it all out. I was giving these men everything they needed to hear and more, and there was no grasp of discernment I could muster to keep me from doing it. I supposed the orange liquid must be some kind of truth serum.

"Rafe?" the knight said, suddenly. "Rafe Edgewood?"

"You trained with his son, didn't you, brother?" the larger man asked, turning his gaze to the knight and slowly beginning to drop his sword.

"What are you doing with *him*...?"

"Saved me..." I said. "He saved me... from Galvinsglade... Broke me... out..."

Both men looked at each other now, eyes wide and registering what I could not keep myself from telling them. Now would be the perfect time to disable the each of them; to run, if my legs could carry me. The haze that cloaked and smothered my every thought was not subsiding. I barely had the presence of mind to ask a simple question of them.

"How long... does fog last...?"

"Fog?" the knight asked. "What in All Mother's name is she talking about?"

There was a pause before the other man spoke. "I uhh, I *think* she means the *trifleberry* I threw at her," he chuckled. "It does kinda feel like being in a fog." He resheathed his sword. "It lasts for about a minute, give or take. You'll be fine again soon."

I'd never heard of a trifleberry before. I decided to sit down amid the scattered dead leaves for a moment and just focus on my breathing. It seemed for the time being that at least one of them was no longer interested in attacking me, and that was well enough for me in the sordid state I was in.

"I'm Seth, and that's my brother Carlyle," the man continued, pointing to the other. "It seems we've made a mistake. I'm sorry we attacked you."

"*Sir* Carlyle Soot, of Widowsgrove," the knight corrected his brother, his stiff tone softening ever slightly. "Why a girl would be wandering alone in a dead wood, that's what I would like to know," he added. "Especially dressed like that."

I looked down at the grungy blouse and skirt I was wearing, my feet bare, with my naked toes crumpling leaves as they sifted into the sooty earth. They fidgeted with my unconscious discomfort, but as the fog steadily lifted from my mind, I began to relax.

"...You're not from around here, are you?" Carlyle continued. "I don't think I've *ever* seen garments that have looked like that, before."

"*These clothes* aren't from around here. I... had to borrow them," I sullenly replied. Finally I was able to think more clearly again. "Doctor Orel Fischer... from Fyndridge. He gave them to me. He put me in contact with Rafe... I don't suppose either of you would know him too?"

Again, they looked at each other, simply shaking their heads.

"Well," I continued. "I've decided I wish to go there again. I have things there that belong to me. My own clothes... my bow and arrow... Two friends of mine are also there. Among other elements of interest." With the trifleberry wearing off now, I omitted telling them about the Libra gemstone I had hidden in The Rogue Musket tavern for Orel to find. If they didn't know him, they didn't need to know about that for now either.

"Rafe never seemed like the sort to let a girl wander tainted deadwoods alone," Carlyle said slowly, almost suspiciously. I didn't like his tone.

No longer brandishing his sword or his shield, Seth offered his hand to me apologetically with a shrug and a smile. "Car, I'm sure she's perfectly capable," he reasoned.

Carlyle had set his shield on his back again as well. He only shrugged disapprovingly, arms crossed over his broad chest.

Reluctantly, I accepted Seth's hand and he pulled me up off the ground. I brushed dry leaves from my backside and regained steady footing on the ground. "So, if the two of you know Rafe, are you close to him then?" I asked, reasoning that he must at least be in good standing for my mentioning of him to have been enough that it would stop them attacking.

"I make a point not to be close with anyone," Carlyle said coolly, his posture relaxed. He appeared to have already filed me as a non-threat. "I held a line with his son on one or two occasions. I appreciated his methods, though I found the company he kept undesirable," he added.

Seth smirked. "*Girls,* oh no!" he exclaimed in mock fright.

"And a courtesan, of all things!" Carlyle snapped. The two looked ready to start arguing.

"Well, you're obviously close to one another, so, it would seem the point you make is not a very good one," I glared. I decided I bored of being referred to as 'girl' with such dismissive tone.

"He doesn't count," Carlyle said bitterly, glaring back.

"Shucks, he *likes* me!" Seth teased.

Carlyle straightened himself, easing down a fold in his surcoat worn underneath his armor and looking out into the thicket. "Seth, escort this girl back to her camp, and make sure she stays," he ordered. "I will head back into town and see to it Zebadiah is made aware of our findings. No doubt there is a planar tear or permanent magical source continuing this corruption."

The larger man smirked, setting his thumbs in his belt. "Yeah, or maybe the guy carrying all the records we've made should actually do that, and his stubborn brother can do his knightly duty and escort the lady back himself, and then meet up with me after. If she even *wants* to be escorted."

Carlyle didn't take his brother's argument well, shooting him daggers with his eyes.

"I suppose I wouldn't mind an escort," I lied. The effects of a trifleberry would have made that lie *especially* difficult for me. The very last thing I wanted was to be anywhere near this man, but I knew I needed to find out everything I could from him. "I'm not that far from camp. Perhaps a few minutes, at most."

Carlyle ground his teeth a moment before he stepped up to me. "Seth, you *will* be careful," he instructed, looking past me.

His brother smiled and gave him a wink. "It was a pleasure meeting you," he said, his words directed at me. "It isn't every day I get to encounter such a lovely young woman during my travels." He allotted me a small, short bow before departing.

I thought Carlyle's eyes might roll right out of his head. Once Seth was well underway he turned back to me, clearly unsure of what to say. He kept glancing down, either distracted by something, or as though resisting the urge to say anything at all. After a moment of awkward silence he cleared his throat and turned away from me. "Right, then. Stay close to me. If anything attacks us, make a run for it. I will hold them off." He seemed to like barking orders.

"Run? Why would I run?" I sardonically inquired. "…I haven't needed to, so far."

"You will run because it will keep you alive. And also because I told you to," he said in a flat tone, not glancing back to look at me. "Which direction is your camp?"

"This way," I replied, leading the way as much as Carlyle would allow me to do so, stepping over fallen branches and other debris obstructing the path. "Have you ever come across another living soul that *didn't* do as they were told, by you?"

"I encounter quite a few such individuals, actually. They normally have much less to say after I've bandaged them up and saved their lives," he said, careful to keep his eyes on the forest around them and not his temporary charge.

"I'd say you assume a bit much," I replied, continuing in stride and doing my best not to bristle at his words. "I see myself needing to be rescued, by you, about as much as I need you to protect me. And why would you even *want* to? What sense of duty do you have that obligates you to me, a perfect stranger?"

"I do not believe I owe you any explanation, girl," he said in an icy tone. "I wouldn't expect you to understand, nor do I want you to." He paused to glance around, presumably making sure our conversation hadn't attracted any attention.

"You actively wish not for me to understand, or you could passively care less?" I antagonized. "Because you've been anything but passive so far, and not wanting to be understood sounds counterproductive to, well, life. That thing you're trying so hard to preserve. That's dumb. And I forgot my shoes."

I abruptly turned on my foot, making my way back to the tree that was just a couple of yards away from where we had been walking. Of course, I had not truly forgotten. I had to come up with other ways to stall this.

"Look," he replied, "I simply do not want to encourage more small talk with you."

He stood there a moment with his arms crossed before finally deciding to follow me back. Despite his begrudged attitude, I had to take into account that he was being very attentive to our safety, an act he had made no effort in when I spied on him traveling with his brother. If anything, he took my protection seriously. Granted, it was either this or he simply did not believe I was capable of backing him up in a fight. Perhaps he was just more paranoid in the absence of his brother. I stewed over these thoughts in silence for a few moments before locating my shoes, still where I'd left them at the foot of the tree.

I bent down slowly to pick them up. As I did, I looked back at the knight curiously. He made the mistake of glancing down as I retrieved them, perhaps letting his gaze linger a little too long, a moment of weakness before he pulled his eyes away again. I smirked. At the very least, he was susceptible to feelings of lust and far be it from me not to utilize every tool at my disposal to gain the upper hand.

"Everything is so… dead, and dry," I lightheartedly exhaled, rising again with the shoes held loosely in my fingers. "The soil feels kind of nice beneath my feet, so, if it's all the same to you I'll just enjoy it. Doesn't look like I'll be stepping on any jagged stones and the like around these parts. I miss lush, green grass though."

I paused briefly to survey his expression. His eyes were considerably less stony as I idly driveled on. "It's been quite a while since I've enjoyed feeling that soft, springy sensation between my toes. Do you ever do that, *Sir* Carlyle?" I smiled up at him, putting deliberate emphasis on my formal addressing of him.

He seemed to be fantasizing at my description, coming to as I addressed him. "No," he said flatly, and a bit too quickly. He cleared his throat and turned back to the path we had taken. "I don't enjoy the wild much. Funny that I spend all my time away from the schoolhouse in it."

"I would imagine so, if such is your duty that you restore this plane, preserve the life, protect damsels in wanting of escorts through dark, and scary woods," I teased. I did my very best not to vomit on my own words falling out of my mouth. "What would you rather be doing, in a schoolhouse?"

"I teach the local children. Education was a luxury my brother and I were permitted in the city, but it is a rarity in more rural areas. Especially in these dark times. I offer my services for free, and live mostly off of the stipend I am paid for my lands in Widowsgrove. I also work with the local common folk and teach them to read so that they can practice alchemy, like my brother," he explained. "It is not just my duty, but my want. To answer your earlier question, I want to protect you because you have value to me. Not in any monetary sense, so please do not let your simple mind get distracted."

I felt a rush of anger spike through me at his last words. Still, I thought it best that I not say anything about it for now.

"As a living creature, one who at least appears to be benevolent, your safety is my strongest concern. I don't much care that you are a stranger. Your life is precious, and as a citizen of this continent, your freedoms and happiness are my obligations to protect."

"Huh," I said, thoughtfully. "That's... awfully selfless and caring of someone with such a general... malcontent."

Carlyle smirked bitterly. "Like I said, I wouldn't expect you to understand. Helping people without the potential for profit is probably a naïve and foolish notion by your standards. Many people confuse my stoicism for hate. Just because I find most people annoying, idiotic, and lacking restraint does not mean I won't lay my life down for them."

"That's not a foolish notion to me at all," I said, genuinely starting to lighten up a bit. "Many people confuse my constant scouring of the deserts for wayward travelers in need to be reckless and foolhardy, too. I've come a long way from my nights as an exotic dancer. Have you ever heard of The Rogue Musket? I hear they also have decent mead, but I just worked there and left the many indulgences to the patrons. Anyway, this was a very long time ago. They do pit fights now."

"I would never be seen in such a place," Carlyle flatly replied. "Or seek the company of one who held that profession. Though I am sure it suited you."

It would be the first and last time I'd open up to someone about part of my past like this. I decided to change tactics, allowing him to walk ahead of me. He passed, unassumingly. "Kleitijd gelahkkt," I chanted, touching my hand to his back.

He swayed a moment, before falling heavily at my feet.

CHAPTER 8
To Catch a Knight

I watched Carlyle's eyes open blearily a few times before regaining
their focus. Unable to move, unable to even speak, he tried to direct his gaze
toward the weight over his legs, where I had made my perch. I smiled down
at him while batting my lashes, kicking my legs up over torso, crossed at the
thighs so that both my feet would sling over a single one of his shoulders. I
gently glided the back of one of my feet across his cheek, playfully. I could feel
his rough stubble against my foot. As I did this, his expression changed several
times from a groggy coherency to a look of murderous contempt until finally,
as I caressed him with my supple form, complete shock. I was pleased to see a
deep flush beginning to color his cheeks. His lips parted in a nervous gasp for
air, unable to squirm or fight, eyes regarding the sky in desperation.

"What did I tell you?" I said softly. "You assume too much. You
assumed I'm a helpless damsel in distress, and then you *assumed* if I don't listen
to you, I'll surely end up needing you to rescue me. You *assume* I have no
concept of helping others without want for myself. Now you're assuming such
provocative dance suited me, with disdain?"

As he took in what I was saying to him, I studied his features more
closely than I had before. He had shortly cropped hair and eyes of deep blue,
or green, or gray; it was hard to tell by moonlight. I vaguely recognized him
from his portrait hanging along the tunnel wall that led into Rafe's desert
hideout. I only now pieced him with his captured likeness in which he was
quietly smiling. There were no smiles now to cross the angular structure of his

face from his strong, Roman nose that looked as though it might have been broken once or twice, to his masculine jawline that looked like it could have broken the bones in a fist were anyone fool enough to punch him. Despite an intimidatingly rugged presentation, he had a gentle way about him in this vulnerable state I had put him in that I didn't quite know how to take. His nature now belied the layers of steel armor he wore which only suggested he had seen his share of grueling combat.

"Tsk, tsk," I continued, not to be deterred from making my point by his aesthetic qualities. "My, this *is* a predicament you've found yourself in. I hope you're listening carefully, *Sir* Carlyle. You're used to giving lessons, but it would seem as though you could use a lesson all your own. Allow me to oblige."

Carefully, I went digging into his pockets to see what I could find. Trapped within this magical prison I had encased him in, he was quite at my mercy. The creator of the prison had full tactile range within it, able to reach through the otherwise impermeable surface as easily as reaching through smoke. So of course he felt my body upon him, felt me drape my legs over his chest. He would feel everything I would do to him, and at his expense. I dug through his satchel and pulled out the two gemstones first. I was hit with the scent they gave off before anything, the intermingling aromas of basil and sandalwood. As I studied each stone in my hand, they looked remarkably the same, both sort of aquamarine in color. I could not decipher on my own what constellation each stone was a part of, and was wary not to try doing so with my power that it might drop my current spell from Carlyle prematurely.

"Aha," I grinned impishly. "This is just what I had been looking for. Now, before I partially release you from the prison I have built, thus giving you ample opportunity to *apologize*, you need to be made aware that common sense should dictate that if I am out here, camping in the cold of night, willing to subject myself to the many afflictions of the world *least* of which involve enduring the likes of you, then it should stand to reason it beats the conditions I left behind. So, no. You are wrong in your further assumptions that such a lifestyle suited me. And now you may speak."

I watched his brows narrow indignantly, his nostrils flaring with his outrage. I knew he would not comply, but I suspected he would be too proud to cry out for help.

I hovered my hand over his face with a faint glow along my fingertips. "Segahkkt," I chanted, dropping the magic barrier from only his head.

With his head free he looked up, trying to manage a glare, but somehow found it difficult, once more looking distracted. "You have insulted, and now *assaulted* a noble. If you do not release me now, I will execute you here on this spot, you fool," he warned gravely.

I moved up closer along his torso, seating myself directly over his chest, uncrossing my legs at the thighs, knees out, as I recrossed at the ankles. The backs of my feet now rested on either side of his face from his jawline up to his temples. Leaning in close, I breathed hot air into his ear and spoke in a husky, hushed tone from my previously light cadence. "Who's the fool, Sir Carlyle? You are trapped. I can do anything I please with you. I *know* what I do. Now where's that heartfelt apology? Do you not claim to be a man of honor?"

His breath caught, head easing back as I drew closer. I felt him squirm within the ethereal casing that held him, but even his considerable strength could not sunder its magic. His flush grew, and his breathing became more erratic and tense. He moved his head away as I whispered into his ear, inadvertently nuzzling against the foot beside his face. "I do not lower myself to villains," he responded, trying to keep his voice firm.

I knew his disposition well, having known the Viscountess in me to have held it once herself, the sense of superiority he felt over commoners to accompany his sense of duty. "You throw your nobility around and expect it to carry more weight than your good deeds? And are we all supposed to simply look away when you do wrong? ...No. I will be the one who does not excuse you from this. I will hold you to the same standard you appear to hold everyone else to. Learn from me, Sir Carlyle. I am no more the villain than you, for we both walk the same path. The supposed crown you wear atop your head is just another pretty, shiny thing and there are plenty more to play with that it doesn't make you special." I wriggled my toes against his cheeks close to the corners of his mouth. "I like playing with pretty, shiny things. I have no trouble finding them."

This time he didn't seem capable of coming up with a response as I rolled the gemstones in one of my hands raised just over my head. His lips parted with a nervous, perhaps humiliated quiver and he swallowed hard, clearly doing his best to keep quiet the hungry groan that rumbled through his chest. Could my teasing somehow be a source of *eroticism* for him? I raised a brow thoughtfully, but decided to push it out of my mind for the time being.

"I'll tell you what," I said with a smirk. "You can have these back when you're ready to say you're sorry and admit you were wrong to make any lewd insinuations against me, especially where my virtues are concerned." I flashed him the gemstones one last time before pocketing them. "Come find me. When you feel that you're ready to talk *to* me and not *down* to me as I've demonstrated in doing with you, then I'm certain we can come to an arrangement." I stood up, looking down at him with my hands on my hips, one foot over his chest and the other by his head. I was careful so as not to allow him a look up my skirt. "Sound good?"

I felt powerful turning the tables on him like this, even if part of me also felt conflicted in relishing the moment. My plan would be simple. If I could coax him into meeting with me again, perhaps on more even footing with Rafe at my side, maybe then we would be able to employ their help in recovering the other gemstones. If not, I would simply keep the stones and find other, more agreeable sorts, with the astrological alignment to wield them instead. Still, I *had* to find out how he was able to wield them in the first place without the use of the key—*my* key—and two stones, together, at that. As far as I knew, there was one stone to every one sign. How could he have used the other, I wondered? He wouldn't tell me now, at least not without a globe of that orange stuff, and as I went through his pockets I did not find any on him. His brother was apparently the only one who—…

…*Of course!* I beamed, the thought suddenly crossing my mind. *His brother had thrown the first one and it missed me! I didn't hear the globe break. Perhaps it's still intact somewhere!*

"When I come find you, it will be to drag you away in chains," Carlyle said darkly, wrenching me back from my thoughts. It was just as I thought it would be.

"I wonder how the town you hail from handles these sort of disputes," I replied sweetly, "between two nobles? Sounds like an awful lot of 'he said, she said' to me. And do you really want word of this to be getting around?" With the Viscountess in me, the brooch baring my family crest upon it, I revealed myself to him in the heat of the moment. I pondered all too late whether it was an unwise revelation to have made.

I watched his eyes widen with my words before he angrily dropped his brows once more. "So it's *you*, then. *You're* the escaped Viscountess people are looking for. I had my suspicions when you mentioned Rafe had broken you out of Galvinsglade. It is beyond me why he would have done such a thing with the reputation you've made for yourself. They don't call it the 'town of thieves' for nothing."

Word of my travels was getting around much faster than I thought it would, and I had only barely begun my search. I knew then that once I returned to camp, I would need to tell Rafe that it was time we moved on from here.

"You are no noble," Carlyle continued with a growl. "You are a foolish girl who needs to learn her place. Enjoy this brief moment of triumph. You will find it comes at a high price."

I lifted my foot from his chest and placed it directly over his face, pressing it into him in exasperation. I bent at the waist to bring myself closer to him so that I would be heard, my long, loose hair falling over my shoulder to barely brush over his skin. "And *you* are an angry little man trapped by a foolish girl who knows her place well. I'm showing you right now."

I felt all his resistance melt away as I pressed my sole down on him. His body tensed briefly before easing into limp acceptance. My actions were rewarded with a soft, lustful moan. It seemed he had no way of helping it. Just as he had no way of helping the warm, damp pass of his tongue against the flesh over his mouth. It was a gesture made in desperation, my eyes growing wide in shock with his surrender. I let loose a small gasp, but did not let up my foot. Now it was I who needed to save face, unsure of how to react as this was not a factor I had accounted for. I could feel my face get hot. How was I to handle such a display? My mind began racing, flustered.

His erratic breathing became more rapid, his body shaking beneath the links of his armor. After the first timid lick, he had closed his eyes and his lips parted, delivering a second, slower, more loving lick, doing his best, pinned as he was. I ran. I simply couldn't take it. I ran long and far, leaving him there to his prison for it to wear off on its own in my absence. I knew it would drop the moment I was out of sight. I think my greatest discomfort with the whole situation… was that part of me liked it.

CHAPTER 9
Butthead

"Snxx, nngh wharghh—?!" Rafe mumbled, turning over in his sleep as my hand firmly met with his shoulder.

"Yeah. Pretty sure those aren't words," I smiled down at him, kneeling at his side.

"My turn to scout the perimeter already, huh? What time is it?" he asked, groggily.

"Late. Early. Won't be long before the sun is up again, so I figured we may as well get a move on… to Fyndridge."

"Fyndridge?" he asked, incredulously. "Girl, you either gone crazy fer real or them drugs ain't worn off yet! Orel told me I should put ya up while investigatin' to make sure you was safe, and that's what I'm gonna do."

"Yeah? And where do you propose to keep me?" I shot back. "Certainly not in your hideout; at least not anymore."

"Well we gotta go back eventually so's I can gather up some more of my things. And if them pirates haven't taken my horse and carriage, it'd make gettin' from one point to the next one helluva lot easier! Do ya really expect to *walk* all that way with no supplies? I ate some while you was in the bath, but *you're* prob'ly just runnin' on fumes right now." He sounded irate. "Look where we are, darlin'. We gotta go all the way around to get up to the desert planes again. Our best bet would be to go into the nearest town and get some help. That'd be Widowsgrove. I know some people I ain't seen in a while."

I winced at his words. *Widowsgrove.* Should I tell him? I would have to, before too long. "I've never been there before," I said. "I've heard… very little about the place. What's it like?"

"It's got about the only patch of thrivin' forest I seen in all these parts," he replied, considerably less gruff. "Flowers, too, in full bloom. They got a market; whole mess a' people livin' there. Oddly enough, no docking station for visiting skylark aristocrats and their ships, though. You'd think they'd have established a sort of trade system with the outside world, but then again, maybe that's why they been doin' so well. They deal only with their own. Less risk of lettin' in the wrong people, I reckon."

"Well then how are *we* supposed to get in?!" I asked.

"I told ya already," he said. "I know some people."

I decided to keep the events that unfolded within the hour past to myself for the time being. I knew I would see Sir Carlyle again, but I was not certain as to whether he would tell his brother, or anyone else for that matter. I had devised a plan if I should face him alone, but if he brought allies to take back the gemstones I'd stolen from him, I knew I would not prevail. I wasn't sure whether Rafe would understand enough to help me, nor did I think he would help, even if he did. His only allegiance with me was that I was his case to solve. He would not have a portrait of a man hanging in his abode if he did not care for him in some way. I did not have his care, I was merely his burden for now. No matter how kind he was to me, I had to be mindful of that.

I rolled the stones in my fingers concealed in a pocket of my skirt. Whatever was to happen, there was still the matter of Carlyle's power. He was clearly knowledgeable of the Castle in the Sky, as per his ability to harness its restorative properties channeled through the stones. Through *him*. Could there truly be more than one key? I had to find out. It seemed like too much of a coincidence that he too carried such a vessel inside of him. I would never have been able to, had I not traveled between worlds, between modes of reality. If nothing else, I had to find out the signs corresponding with these two stones he carried – that he was somehow able to wield, together, as though they were one in the same.

After packing up camp and walking for a short while in silence, I suddenly became aware of the lack of food in my belly. "How long of a walk is it to Widowsgrove?" I asked, hopefully.

"From here? It'll be 'bout an hour," Rafe replied.

Walking alongside him, I nodded in acknowledgment. We stepped through the dead thicket, maneuvering over fallen branches and treading lightly over uneven terrain. We had long passed the site of battle, Carlyle and his brother Seth at the forefront of my mind; the trifleberries that had been thrown, the orange globe that missed its mark. My plan.

"Rafe," I started again. "…Who are those people in the framed portraits on your wall?"

He was silent a moment before answering me. "Well, uhh, one of 'em is one of the people I know in town. He's a knight there, but not the one who will vouch for us gettin' in. I got other people in mind to go through for that."

I drew a sigh of relief.

"Other one's my son," he continued. "And the girl, well, she's just… someone very dear to my heart, is all. They all are, in one way or another."

"Why wouldn't C—um, your uhh… Why wouldn't your knight friend vouch for us gaining entry into Widowsgrove? The two of you on bad terms with one another, or something?" I asked. Clumsily.

"No, it ain't that. It's just we have some complicated history is all, and he don't like to see me if he don't have to. He's a nice guy and everything and I hold nothin' against him. I know he don't hold nothin' against me neither, but them's just the breaks sometimes, I reckon."

"Oh," I said.

"Since we're on the subject of people we know," he started, a strange lilt in his voice as he spoke, "I'd appreciate if you'd tell me who all those people were in my house last night. They weren't just random pillagin' pirates passin' through; they sounded awf'ly familiar about you, and I think I got a right to know why if I'm gonna be lookin' after you for a while."

It was my turn now to pause. I wondered how much I should tell him. It took me a moment to find my words. "…I'm not sure what of me you already know," I reluctantly said. "But, those were Demetrius's men. I don't suppose you've heard of him? If not from Orel, then by way of what research you've already done…?"

"Well let's see," he said. "I know you got a Viscountess somewhere inside a' you, so you ain't no ordinary common woman. I know that's the reason you was news 'round these parts. There ain't that many people know what you look like for sure though, so we can use that to our advantage; maybe dress you up different or somethin' when we get into town. That can be one a' the first things we do."

"Won't we need some type of currency for that, though? What have we to offer?" I asked, clutching the stones in my pocket, raising a hand to my brooch. I certainly was not about to trade.

Rafe breathed air from his nostrils in a scoff, smirking slightly in response. "Now, you just leave all that to me and don't worry your pretty little head none," he replied.

I scowled darkly at him.

"I'm teasin' you, butthead!" he chuckled, suddenly.

"Butthead?!" I was shocked. The emotions that ran through me were a great many in the span of mere seconds, from outrage, to confusion, until finally all I could do was respond in likeness, a slow smile tugging at the corners of my mouth. "...I can't *believe* you just said that to me."

He laughed. The air between us felt lighter now. I started to relax. "I know you're kinda the daughter of Amadeus LaCroix, the Count of Fyndridge and Galvinsglade," he continued. "I know that his airship burned down, what was it, the Wild Rose? ...Anyway, now he ain't around, his brother done took over both the towns. His brother, your *uncle*, Acanthus LaCroix."

"Well, you've certainly done your research," I replied feeling considerably less defensive.

"And yes," he said. "I *do* know of Demetrius. I just didn't account for word of your escape travelin' as fast as it had, so soon... and I didn't think it would be traced back to me. If them skylark pirates know, what's to say the folk over at Galvinsglade don't?"

I shrugged. "Demetrius is... calculating. He's good at what he does. If he wants me, he won't want the competition, so I can't imagine he would have told anyone else of my whereabouts outside of those in his crew who were successful in tracking us down. His crew are loyal to him. At this point, it's a safe bet that we only have them to worry about. At least for the time being."

"You know the guy better than I do. I'll take your word for it," he said. "There's nothin' *else* I should know about now, is there?"

"...No," I said, quietly. "Nothing."

We walked the rest of the way mostly in silence. I continued to roll the stones in my fingers.

CHAPTER 10
The Duke of Widowsgrove

The secluded town of Widowsgrove stood tall and proud, the buildings reaching as many as four stories up from ground level, each made of sturdy stone and brick. There was a bed of flowers at almost every window of all different kinds, the colorful arrays in each sill sending waves of excitement throughout me, invigorating my hungry, weary body. We arrived at the elegant golden gates just before sunrise, and I looked in through them with bated breath. If this was how the closed in grounds looked from the outside of these metal bars, I could not help but struggle with keeping my eagerness at bay as I awaited Rafe on the other side. He spoke with three others outside my range of hearing. With my hands leaned on two of the bars, my face resting between them, I took in their features.

One of them appeared as tall and robust as my father, his kempt handlebar mustache lining his full beard, curled stylishly at the ends. His facial hair was brown with golden highlights, his sideburns connecting neatly with the hair on his head. He looked to be of noble background, perhaps the head of the town as a whole. He stood with his chest out and his shoulders back, a posture which indicated to me that at the very least, he was a man in charge of his station. He presented jovially, but it was clear he meant doing business. He wore rich robes of deep purple with red lining that caught the dancing light of the torches burning on the other side of the wall. Gemmed rings adorned every one of his fingers.

The other two men were significantly less decorated, dressed in much the same manner as Carlyle had been upon our first meeting, a full suit of chain linked armor over surcoats and pouches of gear, swords sheathed at their sides and shields on their backs. I wondered how many noble knights stood guard in this town. They were certainly more heavily equipped than the guards of Fyndridge, the town of Widowsgrove by far more lavish in comparison.

"You there! Girl!" a similarly dressed man shouted, looking down at me from some kind of perch on the other side of the wall. "Back away from the gate."

I complied with the guard's order, begrudgingly releasing my hold on the bars and taking a couple of steps back. I folded my arms over my chest somewhat spitefully, hoping Rafe would be done in there soon. I knew he was trying to get them to let me in, and that's why it was taking so long. With each passing moment, I grew increasingly anxious. They couldn't possibly turn us away. We would waste away before we made it back to his hideout on foot, with no food and no supplies. The severity of our situation far from eluded me. Up until now, Rafe had done a good job at setting my mind at ease. He would glance at me every so often through the bars, meeting my eyes with a nod or a reassuring wink. I found it comforting if nothing else.

Finally the decorated man looked over at me and made a sweeping arm gesture to accompany his shout. "Let her enter!"

Immediately the bars lifted from the ground for the second time I had seen, the first time only as Rafe had been permitted through. The gates here opened differently from Fyndridge or Galvinsglade and I was just as taken by it this time as the first. They raised up along the much taller walls, and the sound of gears turning from the other side indicated to me some kind of pulley and wheel system was in operation here. Once the metal structure had risen high enough that I was able to duck through, I made my move. I wasn't about to give the guard on the wall a chance to tell me I had to wait until the gate had completed its long journey upward.

As I approached, I could hear my stomach growling angrily in protest at my sudden movement. I flushed with embarrassment. I was certain they could all hear it from a few feet away. "Um, so, what's our first order of business…?" I asked, straightening my posture as I tried to save face.

Rafe smirked. "To get some food in you, girl!" There was laughter in his voice and I found myself torn between relief and indignation.

"I must say," the decorated man said with marvel as he looked me over, his eyes trailing up and down my body. I was instantly uncomfortable. "That's quite an unusual outfit you're wearing. You aren't from around here, are you?"

"The clothes aren't—*Sir*." I replied, trying to mind my manners as best I could. I was tiring of that question, and eager to change into something more conducive to travel, my feet especially aching from the shoes that did not fit right.

"Bern, I'd like ya to meet the Duke of Widowsgrove, his Royal Highness, Sir Archibald Weonette," Rafe said with a grandiose hand gesture in regard of the man standing beside him.

"…Your Grace," I corrected myself, trying to remember how the Viscountess would curtsy with a formal introduction. I awkwardly tucked one foot behind the ankle of my other, dipping at the knees. I hoped my etiquette would be serviceable. Nobody seemed to take issue.

"Why don't you show the girl around," the Duke said. "Shops open at sunrise. All booths and stalls, a little after. It should not be long now. Just be certain that your firearm stays on your back and that the safety is on at all times."

"Will do. Thank ya kindly, for receivin' us," Rafe replied. "Your hospitality is always appreciated. C'mon, Bern. Let's go find ya somethin' to fill up that belly."

Upon closer inspection, I noticed that Duke Archibald was strikingly pale, his light eyes sunken under peculiar dark rings. He looked as though he seldom slept and had not seen the light of day in ages. I tried not to stare, Rafe curling his arm around my shoulders ensuring that I didn't. He led me away, probably having noticed the prolonged gaze I was giving him, before I had noticed that I was staring, myself.

"Do you know him? Personally, I mean?" I quietly asked as we walked away from the group of men and into town.

"We go back a ways," Rafe said, his hand familiarly cupping around my shoulder. "I fought with him in the Great War, too. He wasn't a duke then. He was in my battalion. Had a part in savin' his life, and he's been grateful to me ever since. Said I always had a place in this town, but I prefer to be away from the stress of people. I like livin' out on my own. I don't come 'round here too often; just every once in a while when somethin' of concern catches my eye from the outside and I feel they oughta know about it. Or, when I need help. Granted, I haven't *needed* help 'til now. It's good to have that reassurance."

I blinked at him, bewildered. "You mean, you didn't know for sure whether they would help us?!"

"Aww, don't sound so worried; I figured we'd be fine! Gotta have a little faith in people, y'know?" Rafe flashed two slips of paper at me with his other hand as he spoke, each baring identical emblems on them sealed in red wax and each with thick, black lettering I could not read. "With these, we can go into *any* store and take whatever we might want or need. Within reason, of course. We can take only what we can carry, ourselves. Had to get one for you, too. That's why it was takin' so long."

I was truly impressed. "Fyndridge has limited rations for its residents there, and only the members of the town council have access to running water and heat. Once a week, the Rogue Musket tavern holds its pit fights where the winner is issued a pass to raid the mines of whatever they can carry, or a months' supply of food and sometimes access to a hot water source."

He loosed a low whistle at my disclosure. "Sounds rough, darlin'. 'Round these parts, *all* residents get their share of heat n' water. And everybody works for themselves. There's a strong sense of community here though, so people ain't completely without help if they been needin' it, like if there's a sickness preventin' somebody to work or a death in a family or somethin'. They take care of their own. With vegetation thrivin' here, there ain't no shortage of crops, neither."

As Rafe went on in praise of this town, I started to wonder why he chose to live outside the safety of the walls. There had to be a reason beyond that he simply preferred his own company to that of the townsfolk, especially if they were truly as he claimed.

"I think I'd definitely prefer living here to living at Fyndridge," I said, frowning.

"Or Galvinsglade?" Rafe teased.

I didn't find him funny. "*Or* Galvinsglade. But that was never my home. It was my prison. The 'town of thieves,' where earth dwellers, subterrans, and even degenerates alike all go to rot in one place," I explained, unable to spare him my bitter tone. "None are exempt from the biochemical testing that goes on in there, or the shock therapy among other things. No matter the adverse effects this testing has on the residents there; on the *prisoners.*"

His arm gently slipped away from me and we walked in silence for a short while, passing by buildings as the sky gradually started to get lighter with the break of day. That's when it occurred to me. "Duke Archibald is a noble, *and* an earth dweller. That's different. Most nobles I've met are skylarks with their own ships. Is he not concerned about the dangers of a pirate ship laying siege on Widowsgrove from above? Or the possibility of toxic shifts in the atmosphere? This place is surrounded by dead forest. What's to say such plague won't run rampant on the inside, and kill all the foliage in here too?"

"We're also smack dab at the lowest point in the middle of a canyon, dear," he said in rebuttal. "Ain't no ship's gonna fit through some of the cliffs on the way down. Not unless it were one a' them smaller models with less crew to man it. And if it was, the duke's got *dozens* of knights here to protect the town, and plenty more guards and watchmen after that. Plus, the people here are smart. Plenty of 'em can even read, and that's a luxury afforded only to rich skylark noblemen and aristocrats, most parts. *All* parts, is what most people believe. There're even a few alchemists here, o'course I wouldn't know nothin' about that; just that it can help keep them *atmospheric shifts* at bay, as ya put it. They can defend themselves just fine. The duke's made diggin' his roots in one place work for him thus far. I reckon they'll continue to be just fine."

I felt a little bittersweet about the community he regarded in such high esteem. On the one hand, I was awestruck by their ability to have made their way of life work so well for them. It was a far cry from the adventurous world of the nomadic aristocrat, but just as far removed from those barely scraping by in poverty, under corrupt rulers also stationary. The peculiar duke had it made here. What trial and error he must have endured to get to where he is now, I could not fathom. Rafe saved his life once. I could only imagine what that entailed. Since he did not say, I decided not to press the issue for now.

"What's wrong?" Rafe asked me, suddenly. "You keep gettin' kinda quiet on me."

"I'm hungry," I replied. "And tired. That's all."

"Well don't you worry none. I know the baker here, and he makes some a' the best garlic bread you ever had in your life! Gonna fix you up with somethin' real big and greasy. Like the sailors do. You know sailors eat real greasy all the time, right? Know why that is?"

"Not a clue," I said.

"It's 'cause then all that grease coats the inner lining of their bellies and they don't get motion sickness from the water of the ocean rockin' the boat! Wouldn't be surprised if them skylarks eat real greasy too, air turbulence n' whatnot." He paused a moment. "I can't eat greasy foods like I used to. I get all gassy and then I'm up fartin' all night."

I shot him an uncomfortable sidelong glance, but then I smiled. He was so crass that he reminded me of my old allies; the things the six of us together would talk about. It was mostly Blythe or Kael, but often times Alasdair and even Orel would get involved. *Roland*, on the other hand, was more like me in that he only appreciated such humor in small doses and All Mother forbid if I cracked a joke in his presence, myself. I decided not to dwell. I knew Rafe was trying to cheer me up. The truth of the matter was that I felt somewhat bitter. Why couldn't I have had the luxury of living in a place like this? Why must I have fought so hard, all of the time, simply to maintain what meager things I *did* have?

They were petty thoughts and meaningless emotions. It did not change the way things were, and making any sort of comparison was an exercise in futility. I had what I had, and I should feel grateful to still be alive. I should feel grateful to still be able to pursue my quest for the twelve magic gemstones. I had three of them already; four, if I counted the one I left for Orel. I was in pretty good shape. If only I could find a moment alone to identify the two I picked up off Carlyle...

Zebadiah! I thought, remembering the brothers having spoken of a man in town who may know. He could prove to be a vital source for finding out other things pertaining to the stones and the powers vested in them as well.

"So, umm, who takes care of all the vegetation here?" I casually asked all casual-like. "I'm assuming that there's some semblance of a forest left within Widowsgrove that isn't dead like in the rest of the canyon..."

"Don't know for sure," Rafe replied. "I know this place has its very own shaman, or somethin'. I don't really pay attention to that kinda stuff. All I know is that ever since he come around, the duke ain't never been the same. Avoids the sun so much you'd think he was a vampire."

CHAPTER 11
Hi-Yoon

Before we knew it, the streets were already bustling with activity, townsfolk busying themselves with their morning routine. I had eaten cooked scrambled eggs to go with my garlic bread made fresh out of the oven, accompanied by several cups of maple tea, my *favorite*. We found a clothier and a blacksmith to equip us each with new garments to wear on our travels, Rafe in knightly chainmaille and high collared surcoat, though he kept his same leather gloves, and myself in a simple bustier held up by arm straps to go with formfitting dark leather pants. They were secured by two belts crossed at the center and fastened with a large, elegant metal buckle. We each got new boots as well, which did not go unappreciated. I traded in my own misfitting shoes, knowing full well the value of footwear; how altogether difficult it was to come by in just Fyndridge alone. I tucked my brooch away into a pant pocket for safekeeping.

To my relief, we found a barber shop. My hair was a dreading, tangled, knotted mess all about my head. The Viscountess may have worn her hair loose, or perhaps even in a simple bun, but neither would satisfy a scalp like mine. I looked to Rafe and flashed him my best toothy grin.

"You wanna go and get your hair done too, don'tcha," he smirked back at me.

"Yup," I replied.

"Okay. Here, take yer slip then," he said, handing me one of the papers with the duke's seal on it. "We'll split up for now, and I'll handle gettin' us anything else we'll prob'ly need for makin' our way back to my hideout. I'm guessin' your hair is gonna take a while, so I'll meet back here in a few hours. Don't go gettin' yourself into any trouble now, ya hear?"

"Yes, daddy," I grinned cheekily, pocketing the slip with my brooch. "I promise I'll be good."

"Go on now," he muttered with a crescent smile, briefly rolling his big blue eyes. "Go on n' git. *Butthead.*"

He made a kicking motion with his boot at my rear as I stepped away from him, smiling back before entering through the door of the small building. Inside were a few empty chairs lined up on either side of the room in front of long mirrors on adjacent walls. A woman stood behind a counter, a black veil over only her eyes. She was tall and slender, almost waiflike, her shiny black hair done up in two perfectly symmetrical, tidy buns on either side of her head, and each about as large.

"Greetings," she said in a soft voice. She spoke in almost a whisper, with a pleasant smile on her tiny rosy lips. Her sheer, black bell sleeves, long and slight, caught the air as she elegantly rolled her wrist in gesticulation. "Please, have a seat anywhere you like." Her tranquil words filled the quiet of the room.

I did so with uncertainty, arbitrarily placing myself in the seat nearest me. I watched her as she crossed around the counter, her long gown hugging her willowy form and noticeably just as sheer as her sleeves. Once again I found myself trying not to stare, but then I wondered whether she was even able to see me with her eyes veiled as they were, the fabric not visibly sheer as the rest.

"You've never stepped foot in my boutique, have you," she inquired, making her way over to the chair I had set upon. I looked up at her through the mirror in front of me as she circled behind me, taking up thick strands of my hair in her hands, her fingers long and thin like talons.

"…I'm not from this town," I replied. She spoke so softly, my own voice had come out softer than I would normally speak. I had not even thought about it until after having opened my mouth.

"Ahh, how strange," she said, suddenly brandishing a brush and now combing down the ends of my hair. I could feel her take firm hold of each strand she brushed through so as not to pull my hair at the root. She was markedly careful as she was deft. "We do not allow *any* outsiders in through the gates. Trespassers are led away by the town guard, never to be seen or heard from again. I know of no instances where the gates had been opened beyond excavations on the outside. Only then do appointed members of the town gather gen from the earth that surrounds us."

I wasn't sure what I should say in response to that. "I'm with Rafe," I replied, hoping that would be sufficient enough.

"Rafe? Rafe Edgewood is in town?" she asked. "My goodness. For how long?"

I was somewhat taken aback by how receptive she was to my dropping his name. "We're only here for the one day," I said.

She began combing higher along my neckline and up through the back of my scalp. "I see. I would imagine he may be too busy to stop in for a wash and a trim. My name is Hi-Yoon. Once I have finished with your hair, do tell him I say hello."

"I will do that," I replied.

"Speaking of your hair, what is it you would like me to do to it? You have so very much to work with. Am I right to assume you wish to keep your impressive length?"

I paused for a moment, skeptical of what she could be capable of without being able to see her own hands in front of her face. I wondered if she was even aware how immodest the dress she wore was. "Are you able to braid it?" I asked. "Tightly, so that it's confined and manageable?"

"I can do whatever you so desire," Hi-Yoon cooed. For a short while she worked quietly, brushing out tangles until she had parted off a smooth section. She soon began weaving strands of my hair in and out from one another with surprising dexterity. "Have you ever sailed on a ship?" she asked, suddenly. "Not an *airship*, I mean. A *real* ship, meant just for the open sea."

I thought back for a moment to those rare seldom instances where I had taken over the Viscountess's body on our father's ship, the Wild Rose, during times we had flown low over vast bodies of ocean water. Even now as I recollected such a time, I could smell the salt in the air. What little taste I got, I savored, reveling in the peace of warm wind through my hair and the sound of soft waves crashing in the distance. Though I could not read the texts of our father's books, I remembered looking at drawings of whales and diagrams depicting their size relative to adult human beings. The blue whale incited the greatest sense of awe in me as quite probably the largest living creature to have ever shared the earth, among any other. I had always wanted to see one outside of textbooks, or my dreams.

"No," I replied. "I've never sailed on a ship."

"…You were thinking of something just then," she said, her fingers never stopping as she spoke. "May I ask what it is that you were thinking about?"

I hesitated before answering. "Blue whales."

"Blue whales," Hi-Yoon repeated, thoughtfully. "Have you ever seen one before? Perhaps that is a foolish question to ask of someone who has never had the pleasure of voyage by ocean..."

"I've, um, ...*read* about them," I said. "I've had dreams."

"*I* have seen a blue whale before," Hi-Yoon said proudly, her deft fingers continuing to move along the back of my scalp, coiling braid after braid over a span of what felt like mere seconds. She even seemed to work faster with the zeal of conversation, though her voice never carried above what for me would be a whisper. "They are such graceful swimmers," she continued, briefly lowering her head to mine, "and unparalleled hunters. At least as far as the deepest waters are swum!"

She straightened, turning her head back toward the counter and made a strange repetitive clicking noise with her little mouth. A gray cat with large emerald eyes briefly peeked around the corner before ducking back behind it. "Penelope, on the other hand, is the greatest hunter on land. Always bringing me mice!"

The Viscountess in me cringed. Oh, how she hated mice.

"Tell me, friendly stranger," Hi-Yoon smiled. "...Have you thought about what these dreams you have might *mean*...?"

Again, I hesitated. "They're just dreams," I said.

Hi-Yoon seemed unphased by my answer. "In most beliefs, whales are a symbol of strength and protection. But some believe them to be a sign of our darkness and the possibility of experiencing a great loss in our lives. I prefer not to dwell on such things, so I focus on the interpretation of tranquility they bring, as though they are a sign that whatever turmoil you are facing, in the end it will all be fine."

The conversation was beginning to make me feel uneasy, but I decided to press the issue anyway. "Tell me about the darkness," I said, my morbid curiosity ruling out over feelings of discomfort that lurked within me.

"Other interpretations perceive blue whales as a part of our own personal underworld and are viewed as the things we do not want others to know; a hidden dark side within us," she smiled.

I thought on that for a while.

For the next couple of hours, she worked without another word spoken. There were several times I felt the urge to say something, anything, if just to fill the silence with airy conversation. It seemed that I was the only one between us who felt any sort of discomfort. She worked fast, her sightless fingers gliding over my scalp with ease and precision. Then she stopped suddenly, brushing over the raised patch of skin at the nape of my neck. I could feel her flinch back, and as she did my heart leapt in anticipation for what she may have to say. It was the only time she paused in the midst of her fervent efforts, and yet she said nothing at all. She must have been curious, the pattern of the scarring, how it formed an unmistakable four-pointed star within a diamond, a curved line running through and out its center. Still, she remained silent, perhaps opting for politeness in much the same way I had chosen not to bring up her dress.

She continued along as she had before, keeping the silence. I was grateful to her for not bringing it up. It was because of this that I soon started to relax, finding no more discomfort in sharing the quiet with a stranger. Her touch was so gentle, so easy on my scalp that I somehow even slipped into a brief slumber. I awoke from my nap at the distant sound of a bell, raising my head from the back of the chair with a start. When I opened my eyes, we were done.

"That means it is noon now," she said with a smile. "The sound of the bell toll is certainly jarring at first, but after a while I've gotten used to it. We've finished just in time. I hope you like what I've done."

As I gazed at my own reflection in the mirror, my eyes trailed up the smaller auburn rows of braids along the sides of my head, up to the much thicker ones toward the center. My hair had been raised off my scalp as the braids got larger, coiling around the back of my head in a tight braided ponytail to fall past my shoulders and down the whole of my backside. I looked like a rooster.

"Well, my hair won't be getting in the way now," I said through my teeth, smiling in spite of my furrowing brows. I was glad she would not be able to see my expression. If nothing else, my hair was patterned neatly and obviously tight as I became aware of the dull ache spread all throughout my skull. "…Thank you."

"You are quite welcome, my lady. I wish you the best of luck on your travels."

'My lady.' She knows, I thought. Saying nothing else, I stood and made my way out of the shop as I raised my hand to the back of my neck, running my fingers over my branding; my noble birthright. Amply distracted, it wasn't until I had already left the building that I realized I'd forgotten to show her the paper slip with the duke's seal on it.

CHAPTER 12
Baiting the Beast

I saw him. Walking out of the barber shop, my eyes fell over his unmistakable form. There he was, 'Sir Carlyle Soot of Widowsgrove,' sitting on a curb and watching passersby like some kind of damned petty theft detective. Was this how he fulfilled his knightly duties, I wondered? Policing potential pickpockets and the like? Regardless, I was reluctant to tangle with him a second time. He would see me any moment now, or perhaps he already had. I wasn't going anywhere, and I certainly wasn't about to let on that he made me nervous, especially going so far as to spark a flavor of intrigue in me I never would have known even existed had I not met him; had he not reacted in such a manner to my restraining him. I stood there in plain view, pondering what my next move would be.

Then he locked eyes with mine. In the midst of all these people bustling about, the streets now considerably more crowded, he followed the empathetic echo of my gaze. Standing from his perch, his expression was neutral as he approached me from across the dirt path. Once more that strong stride, that purposeful movement; he was given room as he cleared the distance between us. My eyes were wide with the wild, bewildered sort of intensity I felt in the few passing moments that lasted an eternity before he finally came within speaking range. My heart skipped around inside of me like a trapped butterfly desperate to escape, though I remained very still. He watched me for a long moment, within sword's reach, as if trying to decide.

"We have business," he said at last, his tone brusque and formal.

My eyes narrowed in mock confidence, my head raised, more to convey willful resolve than to look up at him for our difference in height. "Yes, we do," I said, my voice as steady and still as I maintained to be on the outside. "Where?"

I had expected a fight out of him. His hard features softened a little as he turned his gaze up the road, then down it. "I play everything above the table. I am not intending to trap you. You may pick the spot," his lip curled, half-closing one eye for a moment. "Just somewhere quieter," he strained, his request a dichotomy of the relative quiet to the street.

I looked up at him in silence for a beat or two, registering his words. Was he calling me out to duel?

"Please," he added. The nicety seemed foreign to him.

I glanced around reluctantly, mentally preparing myself for whatever he might have in mind for the each of us. "...I don't know this place," I said finally. "I heard something about a '*Zebadiah*', some sort of shaman who oversees the unplagued nature source of this town. I assume if there is a place here more accommodating in the way of quiet, someplace not lost to the deathly hollows would be ideal. Take me there, and we will do business as you see fit."

"It would be a great trespass to take you to Zebadiah's grove," he replied. "But I will take you somewhere safe, nearby. Once again, I will be intending to protect you. I would appreciate it if you did not strike me from behind." He spoke with forced politeness, clearly still raw over the tactics I had used against him from before.

"Agreed," I said, in turn.

This man was a puzzle to me, a well of complexities and contradictions I simply could not work out. He intrigued me just as much as he intimidated me. I kept it all in as I followed closely behind, knowing Rafe would eventually come looking for me in the spot where he'd left me. I decided not to bring him up or to attempt making small talk this time. He squared his shoulders and set the path toward the outskirts of town, the tails of his surcoat flapping, dancing to the heavy clink of the manacles on his belt and the clear jingling of his chain armor.

He would take us far away from the confusion of the town market, to somewhere healthy and green. The place seemed untouched, even the natural trails of wild game seeming sparse in this place, albeit excited that I was to see any such wildlife at all. Easing the weight of his shield from his arm, he set himself down on the coiled roots of an old tree to save his back the burden of his armor. "Before we continue, I would like your view on last evening's events," he said finally, after having walked all this way in silence. "I would like them unfiltered. A half-spoken truth is a lie."

I bit my lower lip, flinching ever slightly with his words. My mind raced. How could I answer that? I hardly had the time to reflect on my thoughts enough to form any sort of view, but before I knew it, I was blurting one out to him. "…I *enjoyed* you," I said simply, doing my best not to sound as awkward as I felt. I wasn't sure whether I had succeeded in that.

He looked as if he hadn't expected that response. He watched me another long, uncomfortable, unblinking moment more. "You *enjoyed* me?" he finally asked slowly. "It had seemed the evening's events revealed the opposite," he added evenly, his tone still neutral. "When I pursued you, I spent some time considering excuses. I admit for a long part of my journey I had dwelled over setting you on the long walk."

I flared up at the last of his words, my defenses rising. "I meant, I enjoyed watching a rude, pompous, condescending man such as yourself *squirm* beneath my feet," I muttered, crossing my arms over my chest as I stood before him. I shot him a stony gaze, stubborn and unrelenting. I couldn't help myself.

He gazed at me evenly, doing a decent job of masking whatever emotions he may have been feeling. Still, I detected a curious rush of anxiety wash over his face. I thought for a fragment of a second that he glanced down at my boots, but I could not tell as he shifted his seating slightly and chewed his lip. Setting one hand in the other, he rested his forearms on his knees. "I *had* dwelled over it," he repeated. "But I find there is no excuse for my behavior, both before and after the event. And to take your life, as satisfying as it would have been to my ego, would be an act of low, self-serving wickedness." He turned his gaze back up to me. "I am not a pleasant man, my lady. I am not sought out for my company. My compassion and intent are always genuine, but I do not allow myself to become lax. In truth, I do not know how to talk to people. I don't really wish to learn, as it is not my place to live among them. There needs to be distance between others and myself."

My guarded rigidness slowly softened with his words as he spoke in earnest clarification. I realized how quick I had been to jump the bow and quiver. I recalled being told these things once before; how I fell for the man's words—*Roland*—how the Viscountess fell. How the inevitable would happen that he'd no sooner push us away. Despite how hurt she had been, she could not help but fall for these similar words now, and neither could I.

"Why is it you feel that it's not your place to live among people…?" I asked, after a moment's pause. My voice was softer now as I spoke.

"The shepherd does not lay with his flock," he said simply. "If I was to devote myself to others, I would have to make that sacrifice. I will hold no life in my charge more valuable than another. This distance protects them, and strengthens me." He sighed, bowing his head. "When you... expressed your *disappointment* in my refusal to comply, I admit there were stirrings. Powerful stirrings. I need you to forgive me. I have made vows to abstain from pleasurable company or act. I devote my life to others. There is no room for myself in this quest."

The living, breathing conundrum continued to unfold before me. I took a moment to absorb the heavy cadence in his voice before speaking further. "Not all are mere sheep among you," I bid. "Do you not hold your brother dearer, and thus his life above those around you to whom your only binding is in self-imposed duty, and not in a deep familiarity, a bond, that you share?"

"You confuse my symbolism for disregard; I do not feel everyone needs my protection, I feel they deserve it," he said firmly. He sighed again, shaking his head. "I am not interested in mapping out my psyche, nor do I care to discuss my brother. Seth does not need me to protect him. I came here to offer an apology for my debased behavior, and my less than tactful words. I hope that will be quite sufficient enough to have the stones returned to me without further issue."

I smiled at him, deciding to leave it at that. "Well, then, I accept your apology. The stones are yours."

He nodded, seeming glad to be resolved of the matter. "You are more than welcome." He stood, dusting off the front of his coat. "Would you like an escort back to the market?"

"I would," I said with another smile. I extended the gemstones to him, which he abruptly snatched from my hands before I had anything else to say about it. I did my best in that moment to conceal my anxiousness. I simply reminded myself of the plan I devised, turning it over in my mind as backup should I need it. It was risky and I hoped that I wouldn't.

"Rafe has probably discovered that I've gone missing and he's likely concerned," I continued. "That being said, once I've returned to him, I would like to discuss the prospect of our joining hands in pursuit of the other gemstones. They're still scattered about, all over this world. I'm sure you know this. We can search for them together; me and Rafe, you and Seth!"

He looked uncomfortable with the suggestion. "I'm not sure how safe, or *appropriate* it would be to have the two of you traveling alongside me and my brother. And even then, you would need to take it up with our mentor, Zebadiah, as well as Duke Archibald who gave Zebadiah clearance to perform his shamanistic practices in the first place. As it is, we are only permitted relatively short missions in keeping within a days' travel of Widowsgrove on foot. What you speak of would be much greater than that." There was a short pause as he started to walk away back toward the town market. "Also, I simply *won't* justify leaving the children and the schoolhouse unattended for so long," he added.

"You are the only one who tends to them?" I asked, raising a brow.

"Well, no, but I still would not be there should they need me. And as I've said before, I don't enjoy the wild much."

"Surely you must know of the Castle's legend and what it would mean for your people, for the *whole world* once we've gathered all the stones together," I urged, following in step a few paces behind him. "What if I had you along as my knight to advise me and keep me safe, then? Granted, I'm sure you're well aware by now that I have little trouble handling myself," I added with an impish grin.

"Yes, provided your opponent has their back to you, and believes themselves to be on your side," he muttered, not without a little sting.

I hesitated for a beat or two, taking in the full force of his words before deciding to laugh it off. "Oh, stop sulking. I take whatever opportunity would present itself to gain the upper hand. As a knight, you should know well enough to always be on guard. Especially when you find that you're as susceptible as you are to pretty lost girls in the woods!"

"You're right. I should not have trusted you," he continued, not bothering to turn and look at me. "Thank you for the lesson. To be truly distanced from my charges, I should consider them just as potentially wicked as any threat." He spoke through his teeth with a slight growl, not at all happy that I had discovered that particular weakness of his. "Just keep your boots on. And perhaps a bit of quiet for our walk."

Now it was my turn to narrow a brow angrily. "You *just* admitted you deserved it, and I don't act without good reason! Obviously trust is not the issue here, but wounded ego. For which I have little use or patience in nursing. I'll leave that to you, if you *really* do insist."

"If violence is how you react to anything that doesn't please you, that is your prerogative," he replied condescendingly. "I admitted I was wrong. I hardly think your reaction was justified. If I must be honest, I would say your behavior was akin to a child throwing a tantrum."

I glowered. "If I had truly been violent as you say, believe me, you would have known it. A tantrum suggests I was anything but in control… and I think you would agree that I was well within my power. And *you* were well within my power, too."

"The power of a little girl who got lucky," he said simply. "I hope for your sake all of your encounters are against trusting allies."

I brandished three loose arrowheads I picked up earlier in the day from the town market, tossing them at him without second thought. They each whizzed passed his ear, jaw, and neck to connect with a tree just a few feet in front of him where he was walking. Each lined up one over the other, their pointed ends embedding into the bark with a soft 'thunk.'

"…Try me," I dared.

CHAPTER 13
To Fight a Knight

Carlyle finally turned, meeting my stare with an exasperated expression. "Réii maij!" His fist ignited in energy, and with a snap of his wrist, a mote of light struck the arrowheads and blew them to splinters of wood and iron, leaving the tree itself unharmed. "I am not interested in this exchange," he said angrily. "Nor do I care to play father to another one of your fits. Do not test me, girl. I will not apologize a second time."

"You won't need to—Réii ma!" I said, flaring up a fist of energy all my own. "Your defeat will be apology enough for me for *ever* having called my honor into question."

He shook his head at me. "You really are a child," he scolded. "This is a waste of effort and there is no benefit to either of us."

"Née maij!" Just as he had barely finished getting the words out I had already fired off a blast of pulsating power his way, mere feet between where we each stood from one another. I intended to make it very clear to him that I was no longer willing to listen to his belittling drivel, all the while attempting to snuff out his mysterious energy.

"Sheiji kalehkt!" He absorbed my spell, causing the blast to fizzle into a puff of hot air. He rushed me, putting his large, clunky shield between us as he closed the distance. "Varjia kijt takhoom!" He fired around it, using its size to hide the angle of his throw. The black energy of the spell was not something I recognized or believed ever to have heard before.

Not taking any chances, I ducked underneath as his blast spiraled over me and off into the distance somewhere. I used my downward trajectory to tuck myself into a roll, displacing blades of green grass on the ground with the weight of my body. I was quick to spring up at his flank, firing off yet another disarming spell; "Née maij!"

The magic was wasted between us as this time he raised his shield, the barrier taking full brunt of the attack. He stepped aside from my roll, drawing a blade this time and lunging toward me with a swipe at my legs. I jumped over his blade with a spin, using the hilt as leverage to project myself upward. Whirling my body around in a backwards kick, I aimed for his jaw, which connected in a loud crack. He stumbled only slightly, the victory of first blood without ceremony as he dropped his shield to catch hold of my leg, twisting as my kick drove him and using the momentum to pull me to the ground. Before I knew it, I had landed abruptly against my hip. I was thankful not to have smashed anything in my back pockets.

Then I winced as I felt a sharp pain shoot through my scalp. I was forced upright by my hair. Along with his shield he had also discarded his blade to snatch up a fistful of my braids, his other hand free to be balled into a fist raised just over my head and reeling back to strike me down. Whether he realized in the heat of battle that he was trying to kill or maim me and had second thoughts, or whether he simply decided he could beat me unarmed was beyond me. Not wasting any time, I reached up and grabbed his forearm, twisting my lower half around in a quick, forceful kick at his legs in an effort to trip him up.

The trip caused his strike to go wild, his fist coming down and hitting me about the shoulder blade, still with impressive force. He was unrelenting of his grip on my hair and yanked me right along with him, his body a considerable weight as he landed on top of me. As he regained his balance, he reeled back once more for another thunderous blow. I was fast to grapple him between his shoulder and arm with my thighs, kicking my legs up to wrap around him like vines up a steel pole. With his other hand still occupied in a fistful of my hair, I used my free hands and close proximity to fire off another blast straight into him.

"Sage hajish kalehkt!" I bellowed. The force of the spell caused a violent rush of heat. Without protectives, Carlyle's armor and body had to contend with the lion's share of the attack. His armor burst rings burning red hot, flying in all directions. His clothing was not spared either, sending ribbons and leaves of fabric, singed, cascading through the air. His belongings in the way of pouches and weapons had also scattered among our battleground. I felt him recoil from the impact, wrenching on my hair painfully before his body recognized the toll. My head reeled with that last tug, the pain temporarily blinding me all the while loosing a surge of adrenaline to reinvigorate me.

Seeming barely conscious, Carlyle sagged into my hold, his grip falling from my scalp. Nearly naked, he lay panting, coiled in my legs and fighting to regain his strength and senses. Even so, he was still very much a threat. There was still fight in me to be had, and I was not about to let my guard down. Untangling one of my legs from his arm, I kicked my heel into his gut hard to open some distance between us, letting my other leg slide out from him as his body tensed with impact. He grunted audibly, the air forced out of him for a moment as he tumbled away. Hurriedly, I climbed to my feet with a few stumbling steps back.

Carlyle pushed himself onto his knees. Slamming a fist onto the ground, he hauled himself to his feet, setting me with a murderous glare. "I drop my sword to fight you on fair terms, and you turn to spells. Underhanded," he breathlessly scolded. He stood straight, eyes on me, body slightly dusted with ash in a spot here or there where my fire spell had gone off. He was solidly built, his torso like a suit of armor all its own with tight muscle rippling under a thick layer of fleshy skin. There were faint scars running the length and width of his strong chest and abdomen, remnants of many battles fought—and won. "If that is the way you want it," he murmured, hunkering down and driving his fingers into the earth.

For the moment I only watched him, his lips formed of an inaudible incantation. I strained to hear, but his words were lost on me. As he chanted, earth and stone began webbing its way up his arms, slowly fashioning a pair of weighty stone fists that sported claws extending several inches. The natural weapons curled up to his elbows, hardening from the loaf and earth into stone. The power of the living soil at his hand, he slammed them together, dislodging dirt and root before stepping forward with a purpose.

All I could do was gasp, unable to hide the genuine fear in my eyes as they danced between the claws hovering high above my head. I jumped back, just out of their reach, hoping desperately to keep the distance. "You said nothing about turning away from spells; cloth and leather against a full suit of armor is hardly fair in unarmed melee!" I retorted, hoping his ego would not blind him to the validity of the point I had drawn. But then, perhaps I should not have acted so rashly. Still, it was no time for regrets.

"To my recollection, you would not stand down. Forgive me for not disrobing, I had little time when you began chucking your powers around," he spat. He brought his arms up, easily handling the weight of the natural earth.

Each finger and joint seemed every bit as flexible, and he demonstrated it by extending the vicious looking claws. "I find no joy in hurting you. But I will find satisfaction in humbling you," he grimly explained.

Waiting not a moment longer, he shook his muscles loose and hunched down, slamming the fists to earth, his breathing becoming wild and frantic. The cool, controlled mask now fell to a wild-eyed savagery. Snarling, he pounded toward me, arms out and ready to pummel me into a limp, quivering pile.

I had all but a couple of seconds as he had spoken to glance around my surroundings, the nearest tree just a dozen paces or so to my right. I sprinted toward it as he rushed me, unable to back out now in late acknowledgment of the risk that I might not get to the tree before he would come within swiping range. Again, my increasingly woeful situation allotted no time for regrets. I committed to my decision, my feet pumping up the thick bark of the trunk in just a few bounding steps before flipping myself over his head to come down in a kick. It was a glorious maneuver, but to my dismay, one he had anticipated. After waiting to strike, he swept my leg with one weighty arm, letting it connect with bruising strength. I shrieked as the bull brunt of force from the swinging arm smashed into my thigh.

Unless I recovered well I would be thrown off balance and suffer his trailing arm, careening at me in a hammer blow down around my head. I flowed with the impact, spinning around just so that the following limb would narrowly miss my head. I felt the air move over me with his earthy arm before landing with a thud on the ground at his feet, awkwardly colliding with my shoulder and collarbone first. I was quick to collect myself as I pushed off the ground with my good leg and swung my arm around at him in a desperate closed-fist backhand, spinning my whole body into the blow to an about-face. My strike connected with his cheek, causing his head to jerk to one side.

Snarling, he surged forward, trying to use his superior reach to pound me to the ground with a flurry of strong jabs and hooks. He was keeping low, practically haunching down, needing a sturdier base to keep from overextending too much with his weighty fists. I steeled myself, the first of his fists clipping the side of my head as I had been turned from him and unable to see. I relied solely now on my fast reflexes to narrowly dodge each sweeping blow, whirling around, bobbing and weaving through every thundering strike that followed before seizing just the right moment to ground myself, balancing over my wounded leg and thrusting my other forth in a snap front kick with the ball of my foot. He took the kick squarely in the chest, causing him to stumble back a pace or so. It seemed that his onslaught had burnt up whatever madness had consumed him, and he was slowly coming down from his rage. Panting hard, his bare body taut and flushed from the exertion of our combat, he steadied himself once more, breathing the fire from his lungs and adopting a more traditional martial stance.

The dizziness caught up with me from the previous nick to the head, simultaneously with the shock of pain that surged up the wounded leg I had dumped all my weight upon. I wavered, gritting my teeth and narrowing my brows, backing up a couple of paces as well. "You attempt to cut me with your sword when I pay no thought to the *possibility* you might have shed your armor of your own accord. Insult my sense of honor no more," I panted. "I am *not* the honorless savage you make of me."

"I never called you a savage," he said simply. "I called you a child. You are stubborn, emotional, and act without consideration for a larger scheme." He slammed his stone palms together, causing a rumble from the impact. "We will finish this," he said firmly. He pushed forward again, this time his posture more guarded, and the strike from his shoulder came without the reckless potency of his rage.

I faded to one side, palming his shoulder in a deflect to counter with my knee which shot up toward him reactively. This time my balance was with my good leg. He let the weight of his arm and the turn of his hip sweep my knee aside, stepping sidelong and closing the distance suddenly to grab me about the middle in a grapple. I felt my body lift from the ground, his arms like steel even without the protection of his armor as they snugly wrapped around my waist. I gasped, legs kicking uselessly and just out of reach. As I was turned nearly horizontal with his surprising lift, all I could do was beat about his head and shoulders, which was hardly the least bit damaging to him.

"Brute!" I snarled, my voice escaping my lungs in a considerably more high-pitched tone than I intended.

He ignored me, puffing out his chest, clenching his arms and at the same time drawing his shoulders back. A proper body lock was more than just a strong hug, in this he proved. He squeezed like a vice, baring his teeth as he tried to crush the wind and life from me. No amount of resistance my body would allot could prepare me for such a tightening grip, my back popping and cracking and my vision blurring. My mouth gaped for the air that was constricted out of me in that moment. I gouged and clawed at his face, his eyes. He tried to angle his head to escape my nails. Refusing to relinquish his hard fought hold, he had little alternative. To escape my hands, he pushed his face forward into my chest to keep free of my scratching, burying himself in my breasts. He flexed his back more tensely, trying to make the best of his hold until there would be no fight left in me to give.

As he flexed into me, I felt my legs fall back within reach of him. With every last bit of strength and energy I could muster, I began kicking up into him, whatever I could reach. I flung my legs against him, finding he would have no real escape; in guarding of his most tender area, he would have to relinquish the hold. With a great surge of strength, he hiked me up, swung from the hip, and delivered me to the ground with a strong throw. I connected with the earth hard against my back, careful to keep my legs raised to protect my back pockets. I could not keep getting flung around like this. Reaching an arm around behind myself, I pulled the fist-sized globe from where I had secured it. As he was lifting his leg to stomp down over me, I flung the trifleberry up at his face.

The orange liquid exploded into him and produced a scattering of glass shards as it broke.

CHAPTER 14
To Seek a Shaman

Carlyle swayed a moment before stumbling back against the ground, his one planted leg insufficient balance in wake of the trifleberry I had just thrown at him. He thrashed about lethargically, crooning with his frustration and outrage. He knew full well what he had been struck with. This bought me enough time to catch my breath, rolling myself over on my side, but with each passing second I was losing my window of opportunity. I had to take advantage. Fast.

"The stones," I gasped breathlessly. I propped myself up with an elbow. "To what constellation do the stones belong?"

"Both... ngghh... Both stones... are Gemini..." he replied through gritted teeth, writhing on the ground in desperation.

"Both?!" I repeated incredulously. Painstakingly, I began to climb to my feet again. "Explain how that's possible if there are only twelve stones to twelve constellations!"

"G-Gemini... is the sign... of *the twins*... Just as the constellation depicts... two figures... there are twin stones..." he grimaced. In an effort to fight against the effects of the trifleberry, he clasped his hands over his ears so as not to hear the questions I set him with.

Having steadied myself on my legs, I stood over him now, delivering a solid boot to his ribs which forced him to lower his hands to protect his body. "How are you able to control the stones?" I demanded.

"...Alchemy..." he gritted.

I brought my boot up from the ground once more, placing it directly over his chest and dug my heel into his sternum. "Be more specific," I said, clenching my teeth now as well. My brows narrowed with my resolve. I ignored the pain spiking up my injured leg, channeling it into willful determination; perhaps even anger.

"Z-Zebadiah…" he stammered. "He is our mentor… he… teaches alchemy… makes potions…"

"*Potions?*" My eyes grew wide. "Do you mean to tell me you have no vessel inside you, that you are able to wield the power of the stones?"

"All that is inside of me… is a concoction Zebadiah had… come up with…" he replied. "And I must drink of it… each time in order to tap into the stone's power…"

"How can you channel the Castle by such artificial means? How was he able to make a potion strong enough to do this?!"

"Not strong enough," he breathed. It looked as though his eyes were struggling to maintain their focus as he looked up at me. "It wears off. A *true* vessel… the very key itself… would be indefinite. And even then… you saw the ritual, with my brother… It wasn't… strong enough to keep."

I could feel my heartbeat quicken with these words he was saying to me. I had never known there were incantations powerful enough to bring new life to deadened soil. I had to learn them. I needed him to teach me; for this *Zebadiah* to teach me.

"I don't know how he made the potion," he continued. "He teaches alchemy… to my brother… My brother keeps the records… I just drink…"

"But I thought you said you teach alchemy to the common folk," I said suspiciously.

"What I *said*… was that I taught the people to *read*… so that they could *learn* alchemy…" he clarified, some of his bite returning to him. "Were you not… *listening…?!*"

He had told me everything I needed to know. The only thing left to do was to meet with this man he spoke of with such knowledge and resources as to create a synthetic substitute to act as the key. In the wrong hands— *Demetrius's* hands—that could be devastating. I was skeptical as to whether such power was wisely entrusted in even Carlyle's hands, though I was certain he would feel the same way about me.

"That was everything I needed from you, short of the stones themselves," I told him, removing my boot from his chest. He gazed up at me with a strange look in his eyes, as if surprised, perhaps having expected more. He remained silent, nevertheless. I welcomed the absence of his commentary.

"I'm going to leave you here now to ride out the remainder effects from that trifleberry, and to gather up your things," I continued. "I can find my own way back to the market. I trust you will not follow me there to make a scene."

I did not know this for sure. I thought to dig out that slip of paper with the duke's seal on it to show him, but reaching back into my pocket, I felt only my brooch. The paper slip was nowhere to be had. I glanced all around the scattered belongings on the ground, that perhaps it might have fallen out somewhere. It was not in plain sight. I decided to write it off as a simple loss, not wanting to be around when the trifleberry wore off. With estimated seconds to spare, I abandoned giving a more thorough search of the area and as quickly as my legs would carry me with one of them injured as it was, I ran. Or, what semblance of a run that I could muster. I limp-skipped, really.

Before long, I was back at the market looking considerably disheveled but no more worse for wear than Carlyle had been when I was through with him. I tried not to take it as a victory by comparison, but I was not above a little silent gloating after the disparaging comments he had made – even if I had only been able to seize the upper hand by using a product of his own brother's alchemy against him. I passed through the hoards of people on the street, each stopping at booths and stalls and coming in and out of buildings. Even if I wanted to call out for Rafe, he would not be able to hear me over the loud ruckus these townspeople were making. It reminded me of the Rogue Musket, the difference being that now I was the most tousled-looking person around.

Eventually I had made my way back to the barber shop where Rafe sat in waiting. Hi-Yoon's cat, Penelope, weaved under and through his legs, rubbing up against him affectionately. I stood watching him a while, his eyes gazing down at the animal to accompany a small crescent smile playing at the corner of his mouth. His elbows rested over his knees as he sat on the ground with his back propped against the wall. I watched as he flicked a gloved finger up underneath the cat's chin, and scratched it dotingly. Penelope nuzzled into his hand. I smiled as I looked at them, losing myself for only a moment. I approached with a renewed sense of calm.

"Hello," I said, coming upon him with my thumbs in my pant pockets. He looked up at me with soft, tired eyes, still kind of smiling. "I was told by the lady in the shop to say that for her. Maybe she's since had an opportunity to say it for herself, though?"

"No, she hadn't," he replied. "Ain't no one even in there but this cat. I came in to check on you and when I found the place empty, I figured I'd wait a while than go runnin' around tryin'a find ya. This place is safe enough."

"Oh? That's strange. Maybe she went to lunch or something," I replied, not lost to the irony of his statement regarding the *safety* of Widowsgrove.

"Maybe. That where *you* go?"

I shifted uncomfortably, passing over his question. "Her name is Hi-Yoon, Rafe. She seemed really interested that you were in town."

My quick changing of subject worked better than I had expected. "Hi-Yoon? *Hi-Yoon* did your hair…?" he asked, eyes widening with surprise. He stopped petting Penelope and climbed to his feet. "Huh! How 'bout that? Woulda never figured her for a hairdresser."

"How had you known her before?" I asked curiously.

"She was the best damn knife play expert I ever seen! The woman could hit a mark with a blade from all the way across a field, no problem! And she always used to beat me at darts…"

I blinked, stunned. "Wow, that's… I never would have expected, um, …How did she lose her eyesight?"

Rafe winced with the question, hesitating.

"I mean, I *assume* she did," I continued, awkwardly. "I'm not sure why else she would veil her eyes."

I suddenly felt a weight push up against my leg. I glanced down to see Penelope, who was now rubbing her furry little body alongside me as she looked up into my eyes and purred. I turned my attention back toward Rafe who was looking down at her now, solemnly. I decided to return the favor and let the issue drop for the time being.

"…Rafe, I need you to take me to see the shaman here," I pleaded.

"I don't know him, sweetheart. I told ya, I don't really pay attention to that stuff," he replied, looking back at me now, still solemn and quiet, as much so as he could be over the sound of the passersby all crowding along the streets and still be heard.

"You've *seen* what I can do," I urged. "There is so much more at stake here than just me. This is not just about what Galvinsglade or my uncle has done either; this is about gathering together the other stones so that they don't fall into destructive hands! *Please!* I know how you can get the information you seek, but you're going to have to take a certain route to get it. It's going to have to be in helping me attain that which *I* seek."

"These stones of yours," Rafe said, his tone searching confirmation.

"Yes. I need to see this shaman. And then I need to go to Fyndridge. I *told* you… I am the key. I can unlock the Castle in the Sky and harness its power to revitalize this earth, this realm of *being*. Maybe even bring our worlds together. I need to devise a team, and if you're stuck with me *any*way, I need you to have a little faith in me right now. So, please."

He was quiet for some time, arms crossed over his chest as he searched my eyes. I felt vulnerable to him. I hated needing help. "Alright," he said finally. "Zebadiah's the guy you want, right?"

"Yes," I said, trying not to come off as overzealous. "I... heard he oversees a grove. In Widowsgrove. I heard going to him would be trespassing."

"Darlin'," Rafe smirked. "Widowsgrove ain't but one *big* grove. And we already in it. We got our passes to be here signed and sealed by the duke himself. All we gotta do is whip 'em out and show 'em to people and we'll be fine."

I decided now would not be a good time to tell him I had lost my paper slip. "Just call me *Bern*, please," I scowled at him.

"I'ma start callin' you *butthead* in a minute here, you keep sassin' me like that!" he retorted, still smirking as he started in on a light stroll in the same direction Carlyle had taken me before.

I felt anxious following him that way. I turned back to look at Penelope, who was seated on her hind legs as she curiously watched us leave. All the while bumping past townspeople along the street, I hurried around him to fall in step at his side. "How do you know which way we're going?" I asked.

"I don't. Not for sure," he said. "I got some pretty good direction sense, though. I think I can get us there without too much trouble. Widowsgrove ain't all that big a place."

"Seems bigger than Fyndridge," I muttered.

"That's because Fyndridge is a dump," he said plainly. "What they got to do on over there for entertainment? Get shit-faced an' beat each other bloody? Them boys ain't seen *real* combat. Classiest thing they got over there's the piano. And what do ya do when the only guy in the whole town who can play ain't even around? About the only thing Fyndridge has got goin' for it are its mines keepin' the place on the map."

The man was full of surprises to me. "You've been to Fyndridge before?" I asked.

"Once. I know the guy that plays the piano at the tavern. We used to play together with this guy Arnie, before he done left to dig out them mines on over there."

I set him with a slow smile. "Boy, do you really get around..."

"Yeah, well, that's just 'cause I'm pretty," he grinned. "Got them rugged bad boy looks to drive the women wild, but not *too* rugged; I like to clean up nice too. I'm a sensitive man. Sensitive men play guitars."

"Do they now," I smirked.

"Yep! When we make it back to my place, I'll snatch up my guitar and serenade ya. I'm prob'ly too old for the likes of you, but I guarantee it'll still charm them pants right off them tight little—"

"Okay, Rafe," I said dismissively. Even so, I could not help but be mildly curious. For all his crass humor and flirtatious advances, I got the sense he truly had my best interests at heart. "…I think I'd like that," I gently added. "The guitar playing, I mean."

My anxieties had all but disappeared for the time being. We left the market walking side by side, in almost perfect step with one another. Almost perfect, in that he did not seem to notice my injured amble.

CHAPTER 15
Zebadiah

Zebadiah's grove was nearby where I had fought Carlyle. It was rich
with lush, green grass and the very same flowers of every color that adorned the
windows of buildings along the street at the market. Thick, tall oak trees competed
with the height of the surrounding wall that separated all parts of Widowsgrove
from the outside world, closing in this little breath of life all but lost on the other
side. We stood before him now outside his shack of mud and sticks, dirt and stone,
the man who lived most simply among all the people in town.

Zebadiah had a long, gray beard with wiry white strands poking out
of it in all different directions. His eyes were deeply set with lines of age like
the golden cracks in a once broken vase made new again. He was remarkably
short, his arms and legs disproportionately small to the rest of his body. Even
so, the sheer presence he exuded more than made up for his slight stature. He
wore ragged brown robes that looked as if they had been cut to size, though
still trailed on the ground behind him. With a jagged walking stick carved
from wood in his right hand, he leaned a bit for support as he greeted us.

"I've been expecting the each of you," was the first thing he said to us.

"Oh, uhh, we ain't who you think we are," Rafe quickly replied. "If
you was waitin' for people, they prob'ly still comin'…"

"No," Zebadiah said. "*You* are not who you think you are as you stand
before me now."

I was intrigued. "Who are we, then?" I asked in earnest.

The much shorter elderly man smiled. "You are the chosen ones. You are destiny running its course."

"I ain't real good at riddles, old man," Rafe said. He sounded apologetic despite his informality. "Don't know what'cha chose us for, but I can't recall us ever havin' met."

"I did not choose you," Zebadiah replied, shifting his weight with the scepter he now moved in front of himself to rest both his hands over. "You are but two of many who will compete for ownership of the stones, and with these stones you will harness the key to unlocking a powerful magic, a great cleansing unlike anything this world has ever known."

"See?" I said, turning to Rafe and feeling validated. "I'm *not* crazy. I know what I'm talking about."

Rafe frowned, furrowing his brows. "I have *never* said you was crazy, where do ya get off on that line a' thinkin'? I'm tryin'a *help* you, girl!"

It was clear I had offended him with the defensiveness I met my convictions with and silently, I conceded.

"You must expand your minds," Zebadiah continued. "You must hone your skills and sharpen your knowledge. There will be many who seek to strike you down; to silence you forever. What you aim to do is a great burden that has been thrust upon you, but you mustn't carry that burden alone. You, girl, will have to trust. You will have to let people in, even at great risk that you would open yourself up to the wrong people. People meant to make up the eleven others, each to activate the stones you gather. That is where your *advisers* must help you along in this journey..."

"My advisers?" I asked, bewildered. "How do you know all this...?"

Zebadiah's dark eyes lit up with my question. "I have dreamed of you. I knew you had finally come from the moment my tired, old eyes focused to rest over yours from when you approached. *You* are what I've trained my pupils for—this *prophecy!*"

"Okay," Rafe interjected, "now all *this* is startin' to sound a little crazy..."

"Rafe—" I started.

His attention was lost on me as he spoke over me now. "We come up on this guy unannounced and now suddenly you're some kinda pawn on a chessboard. This ain't no game!"

"Nobody here thinks it *is* a game, Rafe," I shot back. "We *have* to stop Demetrius!"

"No, little girl, *I* have to stop him! He is *my* case and this is *my* case file," he sternly replied.

My heart leapt with his admission. "What...? But I... I thought your aim was to shut down Galvinsglade, and stop my uncle... What do you mean Demetrius is your *case?*"

"Your uncle and Galvinsglade is only part of it," Rafe said, his brows narrowing sharply over his eyes as he glanced between Zebadiah and myself. "I told you I knew who Demetrius was because he's got a vast criminal history I'm certain you ain't even aware of. He's who I'm *really* after. So, there. The truth's out. It was for your own protection that you weren't supposed to know about it; Orel made that clear enough to me. Then those pirates busted into my home and now I don't know where I'm gonna keep you but *here* if I can somehow convince the duke to take ya in as a temporary citizen while I deal with this great, big mess…"

I was outraged. I could feel my blood boil as it coursed its way through my veins, balling my fists straight down at my sides. "It sounds like I should have been the one asking *you* whether there was anything else I should know about. If nothing else, I certainly feel a lot better having kept things from you too."

"Kept things from me?!" Rafe snarled. "What you ain't been tellin' me, girl?"

A flash of white crossed over my eyes as my rage piqued, and for but a single second or two, I envisioned my fist shooting out from my side and hooking into his jaw. "I'm not your sweetheart," I said, as calmly as I could muster while resisting the urge to do just that. I could feel myself shaking with anger as I tried to get the words out. "I'm nobody's sweet *any*thing. I'm not a little girl. I'm a grown woman, and whether anyone cares to realize it or not, I'm perfectly capable of looking after myself. I've done it longer than people think." Before he could say anything back at me, I abruptly turned my attention toward Zebadiah. "Sir, I'm sorry about all this, but please, what did you mean when you said I would have advisers? Will *you* be advising me, then…?"

"I am not chosen," the old man said, slowly shaking his head. His dark eyes twinkled as he narrowed his gaze, looking me over with a careful smile. "You will have three among you; *one* you have known since the birth of the body you inhabit…"

"Orel…?" I asked, softly. It was more an acknowledgment than a question.

"…One of my very own pupils embarking here, from Widowsgrove to accompany you," he continued, "and lastly, the one who stands beside you now; the other chosen."

I wrinkled my nose disagreeably as I turned my gaze back to Rafe. He looked none too thrilled for the time being as well.

"Perhaps it is true that those who would advise you, you may find to be much akin to the crashing of waves against rocky shores," Zebadiah smirked. "You are stubborn and unmoving. Do you see my analogy?"

"I'll bet it's me," I said cheekily, besetting the short, gray-haired man with a sardonic grin. "I'll bet *I'm* the rocky shores."

"That is a core strength," he said. "It is your willful resolve that will propel you forward and see you achieving your goals. It can just as well be your undoing should you find yourself at odds with the insights of those who would advise you. Just as you must expand your mind, you must also open your ears and *listen* to the words that you hear."

"I wanna know what you ain't been tellin' me," Rafe snapped, not to be forgotten.

"I understand that you have already met two of my pupils," said Zebadiah, quick to speak in part as a response to Rafe. His dark eyes were squarely on me.

"I have," I responded tersely.

"Not for the first time while you was in town though, am I right?" Rafe asked. He crossed his arms over his chest as he glared at me. "That one of the things you been keepin' from me? Had some kinda rendezvous or somethin' while I was asleep?"

"Excuse me, is this a bad time?" came a familiar voice. I turned, somewhat startled not having heard Seth's approach. The tall, robust man glanced between the two of us as he stood carrying a couple bundles of freshly chopped wood under each of his arms. Each bundle looked to be a considerable load, and I found myself guessing whether I would even be able to hold the combined weight by the strength of my back – certainly not with my arms. He was not so heavily outfitted as he had been outside of Widowsgrove, now wearing only a large, loose tunic cinched by his belt and baggy pants that puffed out over his boots. His dark brown hair was matted to his forehead with sweat as loose tresses fell messily about his shoulders.

"Seth Soot," Rafe said, acknowledging the giant of a man with a curt nod. "How's your brother been doin'?"

"You know Car; same gripes, different day. I have not seen him since this morning," Seth replied, his brows raised curiously. "It's... surprising to see you in town, Rafe. Are you the two master Zebadiah said he would be expecting today...?"

"Come, Seth," Zebadiah said, waving him over. "You may bring the lumber inside. There is much to tell."

Seth nodded, walking past us toward the old man's hut. He regarded me with a charming smile and a wink as he went by and I returned him with a nod and an awkward smile of my own. I glanced to my side at Rafe who was seething as he read into these silent social cues, undoubtedly now very much aware that Seth was among the two of Zebadiah's pupils I had met. He could only be imagining whom the other might be. I tried to ignore him as I watched Seth's back, a hatchet fastened over a strap that was previously hidden by his wide frame. He disappeared into the hut through a drape which made up the door and once he was gone from sight, Rafe resumed his angry tone.

"Y'know, it woulda been real nice to a' gone into this a bit more prepared," he grumbled through his teeth.

"The each of you should come inside as well," Zebadiah smiled peacefully. "Once Seth has set a small fire, there *will* be tea."

CHAPTER 16
Disgusting

I carefully sipped my chamomile tea from the stained ceramic cup Seth had set on the table just a moment ago. The sturdy tabletop looked as though it had been a door at one point as it now rested over two thick tree trunks on either end which made up its legs. Zebadiah's abode was quaint and modest. What furniture there was seemed to have functioned as something else entirely at one point or another; even the hearth across from the table looked to be a makeshift ensemble of pieces of furniture no longer identifiable as what they once had been, with the exception of the pot of boiling water that hung over the hearth's crackling flame by the pole end of a battle axe and the old wooden chairs we each sat upon. There was a place to sit for all of us except for Seth who took to standing by the small fire, occasionally stoking it with a curtain rod. This seemed to be his preference, anyway.

At some point as we had settled in, I breached the subject of Zebadiah's alchemy practice. There was a tension that now filled the small, cluttered space among us and it was then that I realized I had touched up on something vital. It was as though the old man had known I would want to know how and why. Just as he had predicted my arrival, he would predict— and plan accordingly—my introduction to his seamless artificial manipulation of the Castle in the Sky's incredible power.

"My potions are harsh on the body," Zebadiah said as he nursed his steeping cup of tea in his hands. "Every partaking is a risk. A sacrifice. For you to be able to use them in any capacity, we must first attune you to their effects.

Otherwise, I do not suspect your constitution alone will suffice in enduring the lingering toxins."

"So how do we do that?" I asked cautiously. I thought back to each time I had borne witness to Carlyle's harnessing of the power. I wondered how many times he tapped into such raw energy by the effects of the concoctions he took into his body. What part of himself was he giving up to be able to do this? It didn't sit right with me.

Zebadiah took this time to dig into a worn cloth pouch at his side. He produced an assortment of shriveled, dried out mushroom caps and stems in the palm of his hand, which he held out to me from across the table. "These are cultivated right here on my land with careful intent. They will start you off on your attunement, but I warn you girl, these are *not* to be trifled with. Any darkness lurking within the deepest recesses of your very soul will be called upon, anything you still keep inside you brought out and laid bare. You will be forced to relive your ugliest moment as your body digests this seed planted within you—and it *will grow.*"

"But, they're just little mushrooms," Rafe said suspiciously, sitting diagonal from the each of us as he clutched his now empty tea cup next to a whiskey bottle of an unknown remaining measure of liquor. "You ain't tryin'a poison her or nothin', are ya?"

I could hear genuine concern in his voice as he inquired about my safety. My nerves had still been rigid all this time, even with the tea to help calm me down. I felt myself soften, perhaps forgivingly, as I looked over at him. He shot me with a stern glare and I bristled once again. Deciding not to regard Rafe with a single courtesy any longer, my eyes instead took to dancing between Zebadiah and his hand outstretched toward me while he continued to speak.

"In light it is a scourge, and as means to an end, she will suffer," Zebadiah replied, his words heavy and slow. "Think not of the pain as scars inflicted, but conditioning gained. It is necessary that she settles this within herself, if she is to face the monsters yet to come."

I snatched up the fungal remnants from his palm and popped them into my mouth with not a second thought to it. Though I could not see Rafe's aura right then, I could *feel* it expand through me, past me, in that moment. I could feel his anxiety projected upon me. My eyes drifted to the quiet Seth standing by the hearth several feet away. He looked very serious under furrowed brows, acknowledging our gazes met with a nod and a wink, though not with a charming smile. I could tell he was nervous for me too. I was beginning to regret my impetuous move. Still, I chewed the dry, spongy substance and swallowed quickly. It had an aftertaste like moldy cheese. I chased it down with the last of my tea.

"Now we wait," Zebadiah said, sitting back in his chair with a wooden creek and crossing his short arms over his chest.

The minutes passed mostly in silence. Having not eaten since that morning, I knew I would not have terribly long to wait, however long it would take for my body to break down the contents of my stomach and release the toxins into my system. And then it hit me. A profound, swirling blackness that surrounded me all at once. It was like a vast rush of wind that blew through me and all I could do was gasp, sucking air deeply into my lungs as the chair fell away out from under me, the room around me and all the faces disappearing. An overwhelming sense of dread quickly started to build within me. It was *familiar*. It was horrible.

I felt the Governor's fat, oily fingers roughly knead my scalp and run along the edges of my tightly coiled braids as he took hold of my head and pulled me into him. My eyes stung with the stench of sweat gone stagnant intermingled with the remnants of fleshly gratification left to curdle from days past. My knees ached as I was forced to rock forward upon them over the hard wood of the floor, no amount of my desperate resistance stopping him from steadily drawing my head closer while he stood over me, smacking his lips.

"C'mon, bitch," he salivated. "I know it's a great, big mouthful to take in all at once, but just let it happen. You got a big fuckin' mouth, so I *know* you can handle it."

I looked straight ahead at the short stub in front of me, flecks of yellowed crust trapped in the crevices of wrinkled flesh saturated in a light, soppy sheen. Wreathed by a vast collection of wiry, dark hairs, it twitched, discharging a single gooey strand to dribble onto the floor. My eyes did not follow, remaining transfixed now on a wriggling, off-white speck tangled up in the moist hairs just above the stub's base. My eyes began to water as the repugnant stink intensified and I retched. Abruptly a hand released one side of my head and I was met with a closed fist smashed into my left cheekbone. It was like an explosion that sent shock waves throughout the whole side of my face, my eye throbbing in its socket and my ear ringing from the force of the blow.

"You're worthless to me if you're gagging already when I haven't even choked you with it yet," the Governor angrily spat. "You got nothing in that mouth of yours, so why are you acting like I've already let you have it? Huh? What're you, *retarded?* You only good for fighting, is that it?"

His fingers raked into my scalp as he grabbed a fistful of my braids with the hand he kept over my head, his free hand cold and clammy, pinching

both sides of my face with his thumb and index finger. He squeezed along
my jawline, forcing my lips to part. I clenched my teeth angrily, my brows
narrowing as he tilted my head back and forced me to look up at him.

"You still have all of your teeth," he said, observantly. "Y'know, most
of the pit fighters don't? Guess you've just been lucky so far, hmm? Maybe
they're getting in the way for you. Maybe your mouth isn't as big as I assumed
it to be, and maybe we ought to make some more room. What do you think
about that?"

I said nothing. I could feel my face get hot, my teeth gritted with my
intense rage. Just the same, I felt helpless to stop him. This was misery. The
tears flowed freely now, due in part to the harsh odor that assaulted my nasal
cavity, but also the result of the overwhelming sense of defeat that washed over
me, carried away by the tide of every cruel word he spoke.

He chuckled suddenly, a gravelly resonance that spiked chills up my
spine, not from inherent fear but a rush of adrenaline. "At least you have the
intelligence to recognize a rhetorical question when you hear one. You know
what that word means, right?"

I resisted the urge to lash out against him as my heartbeat quickened.

"It means I already know you don't think *fuck all* about anything. So if
I'm asking you questions I already know all the answers to, there's no point in
you answering them for me."

He released my face, returning both his hands to either side of my head.
"Now then," he continued. "Let's try this again, shall we? And, no biting. If you
bite me, I swear to the All Mother above that I'll *personally* tear out every one of
your teeth, one by one, before I run it through your bleeding gums."

Again, he drew my head toward him, and again, my body resisted. I
could feel myself go tense, my head fighting against his hands drawing me in.
He shuffled forward a few inches to stand closer in front of me, and when he
did, I could feel him now against the corner of my lips pursed tight, his rancid
wetness sticking against my cheek. *Oh, All Mother, please, please no! No, no, no,
please!* my mind screamed. I let loose a muffled whimper.

"Moaning with bated anticipation, are we?" he drooled. "Come along
then, open up and let's get on with it. Or I might just lose my patience. Some
men like it when women *tease* them, but you know how I feel about it. You
know how it makes me *angry*."

I shut my eyes tight. I could feel him poking against me; my closed
mouth, my cheek. He left his horrible stain.

"You know about the last time I lost my patience and got angry," he
continued. "I'm willing to let it slide since you're so used to men liking it

when you tease them. You're so used to being a little teasing *whore*, but I won't remind you for next time. I know you're a moron, but even the stupidest creatures have survival instincts… and you *want* those food rations for you and that girl of yours—*Lyn*—don't you…?"

I nodded, fighting back the urge to retch again. Every breath I drew in was like tasting it, the air all around me polluted with his sour musk.

"Good girl. Open your mouth."

I wished I could lock myself away somewhere safe, into the farthest recesses of my mind. That I could set aside this moment for someone else to contend with. There could be no one else. The only thing that stood between this man and preserving the stability of all the goodness inside of me, all that was blissful and pure, was me. *Just* me. This had always been my one true purpose in the world; protect the innocence of the Viscountess.

I could feel every inch of him slide into me, hitting the back of my throat.

There's this dream I sometimes have. I am floating in the midst of an endless expanse of ocean, and as I breathe in deeply, the water filters through my lungs as though I were meant to be here. I sigh easily and breathe slow. I am calm.

I could feel moist, coarse hairs prickle against my nose and chin. I could feel my esophagus clench and spasm.

In my dream I have perfect vision through the vastness of aquatic depths that surround me, just as easily as I am able to breathe. I glance around and realize that I am not alone. Dozens of great, blue whales fill the endless void above and below me and from all directions off into the distance. They are each spread so far apart from one another, as well as from me, but I am at the center of them all. Never before had I ever felt so physically small as I did in the presence of these sea giants. The calmness I'd felt before is replaced with awe. There is nowhere to swim, seemingly no surface to emerge from or bottom to lie upon, and certainly not without closing the distance between myself and these whales. All I can do is drift.

I could feel bile rise up in my throat and I gagged and gurgled as it spattered from the corners of my mouth, filling out around that which now blocked my airway, preventing me from drawing a breath. I was suffocating. I was drowning.

In my dream I hear the haunting melody of the blue whale's call, all of them interconnected around me by the deep, droning moans of their kin, but I could not make a sound. Even were I physically capable, I could not bring myself to do so. I simply focused on breathing, in and out, my heart an excited rhythmic beating in my chest. Strangely I was not scared, lost to the depths with nowhere to go. I need not go anywhere at all, but merely subsist in this emptiness with the wonderment that my heart beat among a great many others. I would not be harmed. I was not alone.

I could feel the sharp pulling on my scalp in rapid succession as my hair was ripped forward and back in fistfuls, the only leverage the Governor would use each time he thrust himself into me. I could feel tendrils of dribble fall over me from his mouth with every wheezing grunt he made.

"Fuckin' whore," he sputtered in one final tensed tug. He held my head firmly to his pelvis. I felt his whole body shudder against my face as bitter warmth slid down my engorged gullet. I seized back a swallow. He untangled his fingers from my hair, using my braids to wipe himself off before allowing me to fall backward over the floorboards, a driveling, snotty, soiled mess. His belt buckle clinked as he pulled up his pants.

"You're disgusting," he said. "Clean yourself up."

And then he walked away. I turned myself on my side, retching and quivering, curling myself into a ball as tightly as I could with my arms locked around my knees.

"Hon', can ya hear me?" I heard Rafe's voice, soft and smooth and pulling me back again. I reawakened from my deep, dark memory in this way, curled into a ball on the floor of Zebadiah's hut. "Answer me, darlin'. Tell me you're okay."

It took me several passing moments to realize that I was long and far away from him—the Governor. That I was safe. The wretched taste of him left me, his smell dissipating with it, and I breathed in deeply the fresh air as I opened my eyes. I could feel Rafe's gloved fingers caressing my cheek streaked with tears. I turned my head slightly without raising it off the ground to see three other faces standing over me just behind him. One of them was Carlyle. He and Zebadiah each looked forlorn as they solemnly gazed down at me. Rafe's baby blue eyes were glassy, his brows soft. A bit further back, Seth had visibly been crying. My heart skipped a beat as I had come to realize that they *all* knew my shame.

CHAPTER 17
Sage's Reprise

I decided that I wanted to be left alone for a while. I found a spot outside to lay in the grass underneath an old oak tree. Its trunk curved out to meet with the ground, one of its bigger roots serving as a prop for my head as I gazed up at the clouds, the sun disappearing behind them in the far off distance. Soon it would fall behind the outer wall of Widowsgrove and late afternoon dusk would bleed into the sky. There was nowhere I would rather be but high up among the heavens, captain of my own ship like my noble father, Count Amadeus LaCroix. With the Viscountess a part of me, her memories synced now with my own, I felt grounded enough for a broader purpose than simply to maintain her innocence.

Once my standing was cleared and I proved myself fit to fulfill my duties as rightful heir to my father's estates I would be common no more, but Countess of Fyndridge and Galvinsglade. More importantly, I would further the resources at my disposal in finding the other missing gemstones and gaining access to the Castle. If an earth dweller knight could learn so much of the ancient castlelark tongue and tap into its magic by way of a synthetic agent, I could do so just as well. Rather than mimic the key, the vessel, perhaps drinking such a potion would strengthen the powers already vested in me. I wouldn't know for sure until I learned of their nature. I needed to find out how they were made.

In the midst of my musings I felt something soft and furry firmly nuzzle itself against my cheek. I didn't have to turn my head to look. I knew that it was Penelope, purring softly by my ear, the ear that, were I still trapped within the Viscountess, would not have been able to hear it. I sat up and gingerly pulled her into my lap. She made no resistance, continuing instead to lean against me. I let her settle there within the nest of my legs and I felt a profound sense of peace wash over me. I was a bit surprised she had wandered up this way from the market so freely, but then she was the only cat I had seen within the confines of the whole town. It was all her turf to roam without contention.

"I'll bet you're called 'Penny' for short, hmm?" I said, trying to form any semblance of a smile with my lips as I looked down at her. She looked up at me and mewed, and I brought my fingers up under her chin to gently drag my nails along her jawline. She closed her big, emerald eyes and again leaned into me. "Well, perhaps that's what *I'll* just call you."

"She can't talk back," I heard Carlyle's voice from around the side of the tree. He stepped into my peripheral vision but I did not care to look at him. "…She's a cat."

"You wanna fight about it?" I shot back, noncommittally.

"No," he said. "I'm done fighting with you. Would you mind much if I sat with you a while?"

I shook my head. He made his way toward me, stepping over unearthed roots in the ground before sitting down directly in front of me, bowlegged. I raised my head from Penny to look up at him from under lowered lashes. He looked back at me wearily, having since cleaned himself up from our quarrel earlier in the day. His lip was split, his goatee singed. His jaw looked a bit swollen. I would've liked to have surveyed his body for further damage, but he had outfitted himself once again in another surcoat and new chainmaille armor. The rest of his gear had not been replaced. I found myself wondering how often the knight dressed down like his brother, who seemed not as concerned with arming himself so heavily within the town's walls.

"What *do* you want?" I asked him.

"To talk," Carlyle said. "There were a dozen other truths you could have demanded of me earlier today while I was under the effects of that trifleberry. You could have easily exploited me knowing what you know about me and yet you chose only to focus on what I very well might not've told you about the stones."

"Yeah?" I replied. "So?"

"I took you for the kind of person who fills her own agenda. I guess that's how I take most people: self-serving, eager to be on top at the expense of another… I suppose that's not always the case. You surprised me. It's clear to me now that you perhaps wish to restore the earth as much as we do—as much as *I* do."

I scowled at his words. "I find it fairly contradictory that a man who prefers to keep to himself, who may no sooner inhabit a schoolhouse if he had it his way, would doubt *my* convictions in recovering the stones."

He sighed weightily. "Look, can we start over?" he said, pinching the bridge of his nose between his thumb and his index finger. Conversing with me was apparently giving him a headache. "Zebadiah has asked my brother and me to accompany you and Rafe in your pursuits."

And now I too felt a headache coming on. "He did, did he?" I said, wanting at this point to relieve him of his stones and find someone else suited for their use.

It was evident by his slightly vexed expression that he detected the despondency in my voice. "It still needs to be checked with Duke Archibald, but yes, he did," he replied unwaveringly. "At any rate… I am your knight now. Whether we both like it or not, it will be my sworn duty to protect you. And to advise you."

"*Advise* me?!" I raised my voice in alarm. Penny scampered from my lap with my sudden outburst. "*You* are one of the three Zebadiah was talking about then? Not just a few hours ago you were intending to cut me! Maim me, perhaps!"

"Perhaps," he cut in.

"I don't need your protection," I angrily talked over him. "Now, is that all you came to tell me? Because I sort of want to just be alone for a while if you don't mind."

"And the cat?" he asked with a straight face.

"…She can stay," I replied. I was unable to tell whether he was being serious or not.

"She's probably a more pleasant conversationalist than I am," he said, reaching his fingers out to where she had gone from my sight, back around the side of the tree. She peaked out from behind the trunk curiously, but did not go to him. "…I heard it all."

I fell silent. I knew full well what he was referring to. I cast my gaze away from him to focus on but a single blade of grass a few feet away in the midst of many. Anywhere. I would look anywhere but in his eyes right then. I felt a welling tightness in my throat that made me ill.

"You know something… very personal about me," he said softly. "It's not something I'm proud of. It's not something I can change about myself, either. You didn't exploit that in me when you had the chance. What happened to you was not right. It will not go unpunished, of this, I swear to you."

I didn't know what to say. I just sat there, raising my legs off the ground to pull my knees in toward my chest. I wished he would just go away. My eyes were starting to burn with tears, but I refused to let them fall. I wrapped my arms around my legs in defiance.

"Bad experiences do not break us, my lady. They shape us. You have been cast into the fire and it was expected of you to crumble into ash—but you must remember that *you are still here.* You are resilient like a blade, and hotter flames rear stronger steel."

My heart fluttered in my chest with his words. I liked how he spoke in this way, his words sinking into me like warm water opening my pores and absorbing into my skin, washing me clean. I let down my guard and finally looked up at him. His deep blue, or green, or gray eyes were intense and unwavering, never dropping from mine as he looked hard, straight back at me. I smiled weakly in response to his resilient gaze.

"...Okay," I yielded, my voice since softened with my demeanor. It was all I needed to say.

Seeming satisfied, Carlyle stood up from the ground and regarded me with a cordial nod before turning on his heel. "Alright then," he said affirmatively as he took his leave. "I need to take care of a few things before we get underway."

Before I knew it, Penny had come back from around the tree and situated herself in my lap once again. "What do you think about all this?" I asked her. She gazed up at me inquisitively and allotted me a small chirp in response. I sighed. "Well, I suppose you don't think anything about anything then, do you. Because you're a cat."

She began head-butting my wrist. I lifted my hand over her head and scratched it in compliance.

"You doin' okay, darlin'?" came Rafe's voice, deep and comforting as he made his approach.

"I'm fine," I lied. "Did you pass Sir Carlyle on your way over here?"

Even as my attention was mostly preoccupied with the small, furry creature adorning my lap, I still knew it as Rafe flinched at my words. "Yeah, I did," he said uncomfortably. "He talk to you?"

"He stopped by," I said, meeting his eyes. "You checking to see if I'm okay too? Because I am. Like I said... I'm fine."

His smile looked sympathetic. It was my turn to flinch now. He reached down toward me and offered me his hand. "C'mon," he said. "Let's get on back to Zebadiah. There's some things we gotta do."

Reluctantly I took hold of his forearm. He clasped his gloved fingers around mine as well and pulled me to my feet. Penny hopped from my lap as I rose and ran up ahead of us. We walked for a while in silence. The leg Carlyle had struck had since gone stiff and it was difficult to keep pace and hide my slight limp at the same time. Occasionally I would catch glances from him out of the corner of his eyes and he would smile faintly at me. I hated that I felt so awkward about it. I hoped he hadn't noticed.

"Hey, uhh, I also wanted to tell ya that I'm sorry," he said softly. "I didn't know what you done went through and I—"

I pushed the palm of my hand against his mouth. "Shhhh!" I said, in an attempt to distract him from my leg just as much as his own apology.

I kept it against his face. He offered no resistance, totally unprepared for my sudden bid at playfulness and his head went back. It took him off balance for a second or two, and he had to readjust his stride as he walked alongside me. He was not a man who would be outdone. I could feel his tongue slip past my fingers as he messily licked my whole hand. I pulled back for a moment, shocked and amused, before wiping his own spit across his face in a gentle smack.

"Augh! Butthead!" he exclaimed.

"Slobberface," I retorted.

We each fell silent again, smirking and grinning, and for a short while my mind was taken off the unsavory elements of my past and the humiliation I felt that he now knew. That they *all* knew. Still, the feelings returned and before long I was somber all over again. He seemed to realize, placing a heavy hand around my shoulder and giving me a little squeeze as we each walked on.

CHAPTER 18
Seal of Salvation

No sooner had we made it back to Zebadiah's hut than Rafe and myself were given instructions; tasks we each needed to complete before we would be allowed to leave with two of the town's inhabitants in tow, one of whom was among the duke's personal guard. I left with Seth just as the sun was setting behind the outer perimeter of the wall. Rafe was to remain with Zebadiah, who would give him personal briefing while Seth and I would help Carlyle attempt to convince Duke Archibald to relieve him of duty.

"By the time we make it to the duke's estate, it will be dark enough that he should be out and about," Seth said reassuringly. Neither he nor Zebadiah had brought up my earlier episode, for which I was unnerved as I was grateful. I decided it best not to dwell on what he must have thought about me and focus only on the task at hand.

"Why is it that Duke Archibald only comes out at nightfall?" I asked curiously.

"No one knows," he said. "Except Zebadiah, that is. But he refuses to talk about it. According to Rafe, he wasn't such a night owl back before the Great War. Or even shortly after establishing Widowsgrove as a safe haven, supposedly. Car and I didn't come here until long after things had changed in him, and that's when we came to know Zebadiah. He took us in with the other of his pupils and trained us to do our outside research and perform alchemy to use his potions. As Car likes to sometimes put it, we're kind of his guinea pigs."

"I see," I replied. "Did… Rafe's son train under him with you, too?"

"Oh, no," he said with a slight chuckle. "He was always very much like his dad in that he never paid much mind to this sort of stuff. Car knew the guy better than I did. He trained alongside him to become a knight and fight in the duke's army. The walls weren't completely built then, so we as a town occasionally had to defend ourselves more actively. They were battle buddies. That's how we know Rafe."

I furrowed my brows as he spoke, taking much longer strides to keep up with the mountain of a man as we walked. "So where is his son now, then?"

Seth slowed his pace a little, clearly somewhat disturbed by my question. "Oh, ahh, Rafe never told you...?" he asked uncomfortably. "He, uhh, ...well, he died in combat a couple years back."

I suddenly felt a little ashamed I had not realized, or thought to ask about his son more in talking with him. But then, he never brought the subject of his son up himself. I quickly resigned myself to the thought that maybe it was best I never had.

"Rafe hasn't come into town since then," he somberly continued. "Not sure if you noticed it, but things are a bit... *awkward* between him and Car. I'm guessing he probably hasn't told you anything about all that either, has he?"

"No," I replied. "But, yes, I *have* noticed. What's going on there?"

"It's not mine to tell, my lady," he said firmly, though not without his usual charm. "I don't know whether I should have even said anything about Rafe's son. I mean, I guess if we're all traveling together you would have found out one way or another though, right? But this, I'm thinking you ought to take up with my brother or with Rafe. You are, I suppose, kind of leading this expedition... aren't you?"

I don't know why the last of his words made me feel so coy, so suddenly. "I don't know, *am* I?" I dodged. The very thought of acknowledging this kind of responsibility set my heart to racing. I wondered whether I was even equipped to handle such a title as 'leader.' I picked up pace as I walked. "What do you suppose Sir Carlyle would have to say about that?"

He walked a little faster to match, and soon I was once more trying to keep up with him. "As I understand it, Zebadiah appointed him as your adviser. What he has to say about your leadership will only be as important as *you* think it is, and everyone else will follow suit."

"That's a whole lot of faith to put in one woman... whom you only just met," I frowned.

"Just as I have faith in you, I too have faith in my brother's ability to set aside his dated, impractical ideals in favor of doing what is truly right," he replied. "You have Zebadiah's backing. That alone is voucher enough, but I had a feeling about you even before I returned to him last night when my brother and I first encountered you. When I spoke of our findings and had mentioned you to him, Zebadiah said that the potions we'd made... the meager work we had accomplished... *all* of it paled in comparison to the real thing. The prophecy he spoke of. *You.*"

"Me," I repeated dubiously.

"You are the key. We were simply able to make faulty copies on the meantime. Before we had you."

It was a lot for me to take in. "How were you able to *make* those 'copies' I needed to be *attuned* to in order to use? And if I'm the key, then why is it something I should even need?"

"*May* need, not should," he corrected. "We don't know whether you'll need to utilize a consumable potion as of yet, but it never hurts to know you'd be able to if for whatever reason, you found you had few other options. And in due time, I'll show you what I know. For now, let's just focus on figuring out what we're going to say to Duke Archibald."

"...Alright," I conceded.

Before long we had made it back into the town marketplace. The shops were beginning to close down, the stalls on the streets sacked of their produce and the bustling crowd that once filled the area dwindling in number. The shadows cast by nightfall had steadily crept up the walls of the surrounding buildings and as we walked, patrolling guards now carried torches much like those I had seen along the inside perimeter of wall closing in the whole town.

"The duke's estate is on the other side of town from Zebadiah's grove," Seth said as he allotted the occasional guard we passed by with a polite nod. "I would have suggested we buy a carriage to transport us there if it weren't for the curfew."

"There's a curfew?" I asked, somewhat surprised.

"This is a safe haven for a reason," he replied. "There are standard rules and regulations in place spanning all of Widowsgrove's inhabitants. The town guard are exempt from this, of course. By the time we reach Duke Archibald's estate we will need to request a waiver from him to be out past dusk on our way back home. That way the guards don't bother us. Sort of like the one you and Rafe got when you came into town, only different. It would have an hour expiry as opposed to the one you each have that grants you pardon for your whole visit."

"I see," I said, wishing I hadn't lost my paper during my quarrel with his brother.

"It also doesn't exempt you from trade, obviously," he smirked, accompanying his smile with an otherwise cheesy wink. I was beginning to feel as though this was his signature of sorts. "Not that you'd be able to anyway, with all the shops closing down at once. I'll bet it's felt pretty nice though, having people waiting on you and being handed whatever you want or need just by flashing them a slip of paper. Only other time I heard of the duke granting his seal like that was with Zebadiah, and he only used it once for base necessities—whatever he needed to work his magic on his land."

"Sir Carlyle mentioned owning a few plots of land in town," I said offhandedly.

"Yeah, he got that on his own though. My brother's pretty good with trade. He's gained his modest wealth from the people in town who rent out his few homes. Also the duke made him a knight, so, there is that. But hey, you can just call him 'Car' around me. I don't care much for formalities. Especially when applied to someone I'm so close to. It's weird."

I smiled in response. "It seems your brother has taken to the title rather well."

"It's just another excuse for him to bark orders," he shrugged. "We're only a year apart, almost exactly, but since he's the older of us he's always felt he had authority over me even since we were little. It's just now he has something tangible to hold over my head while he does it. I'm bigger than him though, so I can still whoop him!"

"I wouldn't doubt it," I laughed. "But does size really have much to do with it?"

"It helps," he grinned. "Granted you're a little on the petite side comparatively, but as lovely as you are, I'll bet you could throw down with the rest of us."

"I appreciate your vote of confidence," I replied. And I did, quite a bit. I found that to be far greater compliment than being the recipient to his flirtatious nature, which I wasn't sure yet how to take.

I had done enough walking to break in my new boots and shake off the stiffness in my leg which only throbbed with pain the longer we went without stop. I took it in stride, knowing we would reach the duke's abode soon. Once we had arrived, I found myself standing before an elegant black gate as tall as I was with slim steel bars and decorative accents engraved into the metal. Seth easily peered over, his eyes scanning the lush garden on the other side.

"He must still be inside," he said, nodding toward the tall building made of stone beyond that. I noticed his eyes were fixed on one window in particular, draped by a red velvet curtain which blocked all view inside from behind the glass pane. Vines lined every stone brick having long since staked their claim on the walls like vascular veins tracing a body built for power.

"How do we let him know we're here?" I asked.

"He already knows. I saw him pull back the drapes in that window there."

My brows furrowed with his response. I saw very few minute details at all in the night, even with the aid of lit torches all around to keep the town's streets and buildings reasonably visible. I wondered how the patrolling guards managed to light the torches so quickly. Suddenly the front door of the building burst open. Inside was oddly pitch black. Out into what little light there was stepped the form of Duke Archibald.

"Seth Soot," he said, acknowledging the much larger man with a curt nod. It was as if he had not even noticed me yet. "You're past curfew, son." The last of his words were more a condescending expression than a term of endearment.

"Your Grace, my apologies for the intrusion," he bowed. He barely cleared the gate with the gesture, his height keeping him in considerable line of sight for the duke's disapproving eyes. "I am here on Zebadiah's behalf to ask that you release my brother from duty for a prolonged mission spanning more than just a couple of days as you have allotted us in the past, the details of which I was told would be of great importance that they be for your ears only to hear…" He spoke very cordially, his voice robust.

"The knights are members of my personal guard," Duke Archibald replied, coming up to the gate. "If Zebadiah should need men to embark on some kind of journey, he would be better to do so using the town guard, those whose exclusive responsibility it is to protect the people, as this is a people's matter. Of this, he has my expressed permission, but no more than *five*. As for Sir Carlyle, well, it's inconvenient enough that he leaves my court for Zebadiah's little expeditions on top of his off-duty work at the schoolhouse. All knights must always remain on call to serve me. Zebadiah has requested he be exempt from this when the purpose of his… *shamanism*… calls for it. I granted him this exception, but I must have all twelve knights at my side and replacing Rafe's bastard was difficult enough. Return to the shaman now with my regards, and I will give you a pass so that the guards know you are on your way back home. Is that understood?" His eyes were strange, perhaps glowing. He never once acknowledged me and I did not like the manner in which he spoke of Rafe's deceased son. I decided it was time I made my presence known.

"Your Grace," I spoke hesitantly. His eyes immediately turned toward me from around the bars of the gate. They pierced me, viciously. He looked startled. "With all due respect," I continued, picking up the pacing of my words as if to speak over the noise of his uncomfortable gaze. "I, umm, I *truly* believe you will want to hear Seth out on this one. This is not just a matter of the people, but a matter of great importance concerning you, Widowsgrove, this whole continent, and *all* others in the world! This is a matter of the *Castle in the Sky.*"

He was glaringly silent for a moment. I could tell Seth was holding his breath beside me, bracing himself for the duke's reply. "I see, well, that just changes everything now doesn't it," he said scathingly. I couldn't tell whether he meant it or not. "That is to say… *you being here* changes everything."

I stared at him another passing moment, unsure of what to say.

"Well I gave you my seal, did I not?" he said, reaching a pale hand through the bars expectantly. "Present it to me, and you may have anything you wish. *Even* one of my knights."

My heart altogether leapt and sunk within me. Seth surveyed my expression. He knew something was wrong even before I said it.

"I… I lost it."

CHAPTER 19
An Unfortunate Turn of Events

"Your Grace, would it not be possible to overlook her misplacing of your seal?" Seth pleaded, trying to reason with Duke Archibald from the other side of the gate which divided us from him. Why would he not simply just open the gate to us? "Should she be faulted in her honest ignorance of our customs? Rafe must still have *his* seal..."

"Then Rafe should have been the one to accompany you here," the duke replied, unwavering. "What is he doing in town right now, anyway? It was my understanding he was this girl's escort, and would keep a close eye on her. Am I to consider he may have been *dishonest* with me?"

I wanted to tell him to consider my fist in his face.

"Your Grace, she has been in constant company between the each of us; myself, Rafe, my brother *and* Zebadiah," Seth urged. "She's been in good hands."

"*My seal* has not been in good hands. All anyone need do is display it to any resident in Widowsgrove and they know they are to obey command and relinquish belonging. *I* keep my seal at all times, otherwise! And now it has gone missing. Someone *else* has it if she does not; it could not have disappeared. Until it is returned to me, she *will* be detained."

Duke Archibald's words pumped blood to my heart, forcing it to race in my chest. Coming here was a horrendous mistake. I would *not* be a prisoner again. The very thought spread over my head like a darkness which dimmed every lit torch along the inner perimeter of the town's walls and every other light and post throughout all the buildings and streets. Like the bottom of a great warship sailing overhead, it blanketed me in shadow.

"What… What *is* that?" Seth said bewilderedly.

It took me a moment to realize the looming darkness was not an imagined effect of my panicked mind. Both Seth and Duke Archibald looked to the blackened skies above, and slowly my eyes followed upward as well. My blood ran cold as I caught the familiar off-white lettering, crudely painted across the hull of the ship lined with cannons. With the massive vessel almost directly above us, I was unable to see all of the messily splattered shapes that formed words even if I *could* read. I didn't have to, to know what it said: *The S.S. Beulah.* Demetrius had found me again.

I was startled sober by a piercing mechanical screech. "*Detective* Rafe Edgewood," followed the chilling, familiar voice, low and husky over a sound amplifier of some kind, coming from the ship. "Detective, I *know* you've sought refuge here, in this town…"

I could hear doors and windows open from down the street leading up to the duke's estate. I turned my gaze to Seth, who was looking back at me now with severity. Duke Archibald paid no longer mind to us, still transfixed on the hovering sky ship above us. The longer we stood in waiting, the more activity I could hear around me in the shadows. Clinking chain links grew in volume as the duke's knights drew nearer from locations unknown. My adrenaline surged.

"Who is that?" he asked, directing the question my way as he regarded me with far less animosity.

"Demetrius," I answered him. He offered no inference that he knew of whom I spoke.

"I have twenty men manning twenty cannons," Demetrius's voice boomed. "All ready to fire away upon the whole town until not a single building is left standing—and yet they've held their fire. Do you know why that is? …Don't you see that no one else needs to die? Give me the girl, and I will leave the rest of you in peace. No one else needs to know about her *or* about *you* and what you've done, Detective. You have one minute."

The duke finally opened the gate. By the time he stepped out toward us, his knights were stopped short before us and beginning to form a circle. "What is the meaning of this?" he demanded, his eyes darting between Seth and me. "Who *is* she? …Who *are* you?!"

"The escaped Viscountess of Galvinsglade," Seth replied in astonishment as the realization finally dawned on him. Carlyle had not told him, after all.

I could feel Seth leave me, if not by physically backing away then by his own aura receding. It was hard to tell in the dark, and with my heartbeat thumping through my ribcage and shortening my breath, the panic set in full mast. I glanced around through the dusk at many faces which now surrounded me, each of their features lit by brandished torches. It was clear they knew who I was by Seth's description.

"I am Abernathy LaCroix," I said, steadying my voice as best I could while I spoke. "I *am* the daughter of my late father, Count Amadeus LaCroix, but I am *not* who you think I am."

"Rafe, what have you done?" Duke Archibald spoke under hushed tone, then once more, loudly; startlingly. "What have you done?! Seize her! Seize her, now!"

The knights immediately moved in on me. As their unfamiliar faces drew nearer I did not see Carlyle's among them. I had no other choice. "Réii ma!" I chanted, casting an arm up over my head.

The light burst through me in a beam of glowing white, forcing back the night shadows and ripping into the ship high above. I could see everything in close proximity as clear as day, up to the very details of the knight's surcoats, identical but for rips and tears, smudges and wear to tell each body apart. All the knights were without helmets just as Carlyle had always been, and each of them with their hair cropped short with minimal facial hair just the same. The light mimicked the light of day, but was soothing on the eyes. Everyone around me paused, transfixed; all except for Duke Archibald himself who let forth a strange sputtering hiss through his teeth and recoiled back behind the gateway, stumbling for the sanctuary of his home. I took my only chance with what seconds I had left to spare.

I bolted as fast as I could, projecting my will skyward, that the light would remain bound in this way even as I picked my injured leg up over my tired leg and with every ounce of strength I had left to spare, carried myself long and far. Haphazardly, the knights began trailing after me with the duke's last instruction perhaps barely fresh in their minds. I knew my stunt had stunned them but that they would catch up with me before too long. My mind raced frantically. I had to find Rafe. We had to leave this place. There was no time. All I could do was hope that Demetrius would see my signal and hold his men back from firing on all of Widowsgrove. As I carried myself out from beneath the shadow of the ship, my vertical light followed up through the bow and the spherical sails which kept it aloft, until it had finally pierced the sky. He had to have seen it now, if not before. No firing yet, as I raced by townspeople hanging in the doorways of their homes and watching intently but saying nothing.

"*There's* our lovely girl," came Demetrius's smug, smarmy voice through the amplifier overhead. "Won't someone down there *catch* her for me so I don't lose my patience and get angry…?"

I pumped my legs furiously. If only I could reach the town gate, my only exit. There was no way I would reach it before the duke's knights caught up with me or before I would be intercepted by one of the more daring inhabitants who paid heed to his warning. If only I could lead the ship away from Widowsgrove, I would terminate the light and they'd lose me in the surrounding deadwood forest. *But, then what?* the Viscountess in me thought. *He would only attack the town until you submitted yourself to him.*

I slowed my pace, a dent in my iron resolve. It was hopeless. I wondered what Rafe was thinking from the other side of town and whether this was still all a part of Zebadiah's prophecy. What could he be saying to him? I turned down a narrow alleyway, panting breathlessly and stumbling over my feet. I caught myself on the stone wall now before me—a dead end. I whirled around, placing my palms firmly against the cool bricks, pressing my back up against them in a half-defeated daze. The alley was narrow, a few wooden doors lining the walls as they led into different buildings that were all connected here. The power from the key within me lit it all up well, broadcasting where I was, the place where I had just about given up.

The knights and even a couple of guards and townspeople rounded the corner. I was trapped. I could bolt for a door on the off chance it wouldn't be locked, but where would I end up? Where would I go from there? I stood with my back to the wall behind me, looking over each of the faces staring back at me, all of which appeared morbidly fascinated to downright angry. I was no longer welcome here.

"I knew we shouldn't have let *you* in," one of the guards said. My eyes traced the source of the voice to the same man who had instructed me to step back from the gate entrance into town when Rafe and I first arrived to Widowsgrove.

I was unsure of what to say. I scowled, resentfully. "It was never my intention to compromise your homes by being here," I said, choosing my words carefully. "Just… let me pass. If I can leave town, I can lead the intruders away from here."

"*You* are just as much an intruder here, *girl*," the guard spat.

I was getting awfully tired of people calling me 'girl.' I said nothing in response, only gritted my teeth with disdain.

"She's some kind of witch," a knight in the front and just a few feet away from me said as he slowly inched closer, one foot after the other. He and a couple other knights crouched low as they made their approach, each one of them standing at the ready to strike me down. "Bad enough as it is we got Zebadiah and that creepy barber shop lady here," he continued. "You people only bring trouble."

A few townspeople in the back shouted their unintelligible support, bidding for my head on a stick. This was a much darker side of Widowsgrove once absent in the wakeful hours of day. As they all slowly approached me, my dread piled high.

"Take her!" another of the knights shouted. The mob quickly moved in on me, weapons and shields drawn.

"Née ma!" I chanted. The skyward beam of light around me abruptly went out, cloaking the alleyway in pitch darkness. It would take all of our eyes a few moments to readjust to the absence of a light source. Even the few torches a couple of the guards had brought with them were no use, blurred into obscurity by the sudden change.

I could hear frantic rustling all around me, followed by angry shouts and gasps. Suddenly the sound of a door opening drew my attention. A second later I was snatched forward by my forearms and spun off my feet, two heavy arms wrapped tightly around me. A small yelp escaped my lips before it was constricted out of me. I was quickly carried away by force, kicking my legs back against my assailant as hard as I could for the surprisingly short span of time I was transported. Finally, the sound of a door now closing resulted in the muffling of noise from the angry mob.

"All Mother almighty, why do you always *kick?!*" the strained voice of Carlyle gritted close to my ear. I immediately stopped struggling, and when I did, he set me down.

We were in what looked to be some kind of storage room with various crates and boxes all throughout the vicinity of what I could see through the dim lighting of a lantern set over a small desk. I turned to look at him. He was hunched over, rubbing his shins.

"Sir Caryle?" I said, breathlessly.

"I don't think they noticed. Follow, quickly," he replied, straightening himself out and seizing up the lantern from the table.

He walked briskly across the room around stacks of the crates piled high as he was tall. The light from his lantern dimly flickered as I followed him around a corner and up a flight of stairs. I was careful not to stumble or make much noise, but still I had to know.

"What is this place?" I asked under hushed tone. "What business had you to take care of, before?"

He started to say something but was drowned out by another

startlingly loud mechanical screech.

"People of Widowsgrove," I could hear Demetrius's voice echo over the stirrings of the town, "and you, especially, detective… I am giving you one minute, *once more.* If you do not produce to me that girl, your town is forfeit. I must assume since her light went out, you've captured her and are ready to turn her over to me! That would be the wise choice… I'm waiting…"

I stood before Carlyle now, his features illuminated by dancing golden rays cast up his face as he held his lantern to sway gently by his chest. His joyless expression pierced into me and set my heart racing. I could only imagine the thoughts going through his head.

"I am your knight, my lady," he said.

"I lost the duke's seal," I replied gravely. "You are still his to serve."

"I am burdened with greater purpose." His voice was heavy as he spoke. "By a turn of fate I've been appointed as your adviser, and as your adviser I speak to you now, but not as your knight—you must turn yourself in to him."

My heart sank. "I know," I said.

"I will not compromise the children or the schoolhouse," he continued. "I will not compromise these people. I know you lost the seal. Even as a member of the duke's personal guard, my loyalty lies with the people, as should be with any form of governing. It is only what's right. The gilded duke serves *himself* enough that he can stand to let go of a lone bodyguard for a while. I don't care what was on that piece of paper; I am your knight."

"…You are my knight," I repeated, apprehensively.

"The clock is ticking," Demetrius's voice boomed from overhead.

The sound of the door bursting open from downstairs wrenched my attention away from Carlyle's face.

He drew it back to him, clasping his heavy hands over my shoulders and dropping the lantern. Its flame snuffed out as it hit the floorboards. "There's a ladder leading up to the roof. Go, now. I'll hold them off," he said urgently. "And then I'm coming after you."

I looked into his eyes through the darkness, now vaguely aware of a square open space in the roof as it lent what little luminosity hailed from a moon blocked by airship. Even then I could make out his captivating gaze, interrupted only by his mouth. I don't know why I found it so inviting. Perhaps it was the comforting scent of sandalwood that came off his body as he held me. It was less than a second after he spoke that I leaned in to kiss him. It was less than a second after that, that he released me and pulled away. I was uncertain whether my lips had even touched his or if he had known through the darkness what I had done. He left me standing there alone, to race down the stairs and intercept those of the mob that had broken in.

"No sign of her in here," I heard him shout after them.

I gathered up the broken pieces of my composure and clambered up the ladder, through the square opening onto the roof.

CHAPTER 20
Pain, Truth, & Choice

I did not have to stand out on the rooftop long, having recalled the beam of light to serve as a beacon for Demetrius and his men to take me. I barely even caught a glimpse of Rafe running down the street toward me as I was being whisked away. He had drawn his rifle from his back and knelt down to take aim, presumably at the pirates who held my arms while they forced me up a rope ladder leading onto the ship. In that fleeting moment I remembered the duke told him to keep his gun put away. It was clear that he had forgotten, or something. He did not fire. Perhaps he could not get an open enough shot with me wedged between them. Either way, he was gone from my vision all but a few seconds later as I was brought over deck and thrown to the floorboards.

I hit the wooden planks with a sharp thud. Immediately my eyes focused on a pair of black boots partly hidden beneath the falls of a black cloak. I trailed my gaze upward. Even with Demetrius's hood pulled down to cover most of his face, our eyes met from my position on the floor—but then this was the way of it, almost far back as I could remember with him. That simply would not do. Cautiously, and without averting my gaze from his, I climbed to my feet. He may still have towered over me, but I was mad enough in the brain and weighty enough in the heart not to allow this to intimidate me. He knew.

"Take us up," Demetrius ordered, his eyes never leaving mine. His burnt skin had healed over his left eye, leaving only the blood red of his right to stare me down.

"Aye, Cap'n," the each of his men conceded in perfect housebroken unison. On top of playing fetch, it seemed they took well to other commands as well. They left us standing there, staring silently at one another. The others of his crew seemed disinterested, simply going about their business in seeing to it that the ship was prepared for a swift retreat.

He was expressionless. I could not read him from his gaze alone. Even so, I was certain he could feel my burning contempt. I hoped it scorched him like the fires he had set to my father's ship. After another passing moment, he slowly extended his right hand, gloved to the elbow by the metallic, machinelike carapace I was so bitterly familiar with. "Come with me to my quarters," he said. "Let us talk somewhere where we will have a bit more privacy."

"What, am I a *guest* now?" I said dispassionately. I ignored his hand and moved past him. I knew exactly where his quarters were.

I steeled myself as I walked steadily toward the keel end of the ship, the mast consisting of spherical canopy sails filtering the cool breeze of the night to whip my braids about my shoulders like cords of rope in a game of Double Dutch. Demetrius stayed at my side, his cloak billowing out but never far from his body as he pulled it in close around him. We passed by many others of his crew along the way, but there was no sign of Gertie, his right-hand man. As we approached the door to his quarters, he quickly stepped ahead of me and opened it to my immense surprise.

"Ladies first," he slithered from under his hood.

I could feel myself bristle with disdain, a whole body reaction run through to my bones with his hypocrisy. "Really? You don't think it's a little late for the gentleman act?" I seethed.

"The door locks from the outside," he replied coolly. "Or, don't you remember? Can't have you pulling a fast one on me in my own home. It would be *inconvenient* for me to have to break it down…"

Demetrius's personal space was just as I had remembered it; a wicker loveseat padded by the same plush pillows as before, a heart-shaped double bed further back in the room, a deep oak desk opposite the wicker chair, another smaller, painted wooden chair opposite that, and a floor rug taking up the majority of space from the room's center. Everything was in soft pastels, all the furnishings a result of his involvement with the woman for which he named his vessel. A twinge of disgust pricked me like a needle sunken into my heart.

"Why don't you sit down," he said gesturing to the loveseat.

I made my way over to the wooden chair instead. It seemed at first to make little difference to him as he silently followed suit, sitting across the desk a bit to one side, indicating he may have wanted to sit close beside me. I didn't want him within moment's reach.

"So, you want to talk," I said joylessly, seated with my legs apart so I could jump up quickly if it came to that.

"Ironically, I do," he replied with a small crescent smile. "That's the one thing I appreciate about you… You offer insights into your *better parts* where they either cannot, or don't. Most men prefer their women talk less."

"And you know what I appreciate about you?" I asked, crossing my arms over my chest with a crescent smile in turn, to challenge his. "If nothing else, you're remarkably consistent. Each of your *parts*, while no better than the next, are equal parts confused—I was *never* your woman."

His smile faded. There was a spark in his eye as I was yet unable to get a reading on him. At the very least, I knew I was getting to him.

"So we can do this any number of ways," Demetrius said, steely-eyed. "You can submit yourself to me willingly and readily, and do as I tell you. Consider this a second chance… as well as my *forgiveness*."

"Forgiveness?" I said incredulously. "Forgiveness for *what?*"

I could feel Demetrius's energy shift darkly as I questioned him. "… It's alright," he reassured, perhaps more to himself than me. "You don't know you do anything wrong. It's not as if you purposefully defied me when I gave you simple instructions that still you were ill-equipped to follow. You were weak and fragile, and so you deviated from the plan. I should have had the foresight not to entrust you with such tasks."

"What are you even talking about?" I asked shakily. Sorrow suddenly overcame me to match my anger as the words left my lips. How quickly he could turn the table on me. His self-righteous denial of his own wrongdoing was inconceivable. I felt as though I were staring into a black abyss as I looked at him, and he back at me through his one red eye, a lone window into a warped soul.

"Your father's ship was to burn and so were they all. That was the plan we agreed to, and you failed," he said. "It cost me my flesh and my blood. It cost me my *eye*. It was all for you, and you ran from me!" His voice picked up volume as he smashed his iron fist against the table between us. I flinched back, involuntarily. "Which brings me to the other way we can do this," he continued.

I already knew. "You would keep me, then, as your prisoner," I said. The words were bitter on my tongue. I could feel my throat well up with my disdain.

"You carry the key inside of you now," he replied. "I would keep you for as long as it took to gather the other stones with you as the vessel to unlock the castle."

"Gertie reported back to you, then," I said. "How's his arm?" Asking the question as more of a shot, I didn't actually care.

There was a slight snarl to accompany Demetrius's smile as he curled his upper lip and bore his teeth. "Yes, you and that detective who's been inconveniencing me as of late did a fair number on poor ol' Gertie. He seems to think we should cut the key out of you and be done with it."

"So why not just do *that*, then?" I asked daringly. I hoped he wouldn't call my bluff.

He was silent a moment as if processing what I had just said, mulling it over though his expression remained the same. "…Because the Viscountess is still in there, somewhere. Because she's the closest to Lyn any one of us may ever get to, ever again."

My heart skipped and then sank at the mention of the innocent one I'd loved and lost. *Lyn…*

"I fell in love with the girl I watched through the crack in the door, cleaning her uncle's study. Her simplistic beauty… her *purity*… It drove me to distraction during my sessions with Doctor Acanthus LaCroix. Your uncle, Acanthus—he and I were on a first name basis before long. He even went so far as to tell me a little more about *himself* for a change…" Again, his upper lip curled into a smile, a sinister one that chilled me through. "And do you know what he told me?"

"Obviously not," I said, consciously aware now of my heart beating inside my chest.

"He was so wracked with guilt, he stopped smoking his cigars," he sneered, leaning in goadingly. "He spoke of it all. How the Viscountess was only four years of age when he made the choice that brought *you* into being, the facet of her existence which most plagues me. How he burnt the end of that cigar on the back of that innocent child's neck! He spoke of his resentment for your father, Amadeus, how though *he* was the elder brother, your grandparents favored him. I *suspect* he had feelings for your mother as well. He never said so, but it would not surprise me. I'll bet that only contributed to the malice he harbored for your place in the world, and why in a moment of weakness he *branded you* for life."

Involuntarily, my hand rose up to meet with the back of my neck, my fingers gliding over the raised flesh where the mark of my birthright served as stark reminder for how I came to be, like a phoenix risen of the ashes. I glared at him, catching my emotions and grounding myself in that image as he spoke.

"I wish Acanthus had never branded you," he continued. "I wish I didn't have to *go around* you to get to the Viscountess in all her servile purity, or what's *left* of it after your negligence resulted in Lyn's death."

I shot up from my seat. "My negligence?!" I shouted, infuriated. If there was any anxiety or sadness I felt in being in his presence after all we had been through, it was washed away in a moment of vindicated rage. "Just as Lyn was a part of me, the Governor of Fyndridge is a part of *you!* I did everything that was demanded of me, went to every length I could to protect her, and *still* he took her from me! I will not carry that guilt any longer; not when I know now that it was driven into me by *all of you!* By Roland, by the Governor, by *every part* of you!"

He was on me now like a flash, the table between us flying to one side as he crossed toward me with his iron fist loosed fingers around my neck before tightening in a vice grip. I was thrown to the floor, the chair once behind me also knocked out of the way somewhere as his full weight came down upon me, pinning me in place. He leaned in close, forcing my head to one side as he shook with volatile rage all his own.

"You *pervert* me," he leered, his damp, hot breath shaking its way through his teeth and into my ear.

I could feel the cold metal of his fingers cutting into the circulation of blood to my head as they dug at small veins running the length of my neck. "P-Please…" I choked.

My mind flashed back to years ago, how he laid along my body as he did now, his hand not gripped around me but caressing my jawline down my neck and breast. He touched me lovingly then, kissing me tenderly along the other side of my face, my neck, and bosom, in between the sweet nectar of his spoken words which inundated my mind; 'I *love* you,' over and over again to follow each softest kiss. The words came fast and hungry, drinking me in and washing me down; 'I *love* you'… 'I *love* you'…

The memory had come and gone like the morning sun shining through dark clouds passing, only to be shrouded in gloom once more. Through the corner of my eye I watched his demeanor suddenly change. I could feel a shift in his aura, a blackening sickness that grew with his dissonance before finally he was overtaken. He forced my head to turn so that I was facing him directly as before, still gripping my neck as his point of control. My heart stopped. An ugly, sinister grin accompanied a crazed look in his eye. I knew this look all too well as no longer was I denied passage by Demetrius, but by someone else entirely now inhabiting his shell.

"I've missed you, Berny," the Governor hissed.

CHAPTER 21
Burning the Sails

I'll never forget the look on his face as he hovered over me and kept me pinned to the floorboards. His hood had fallen away to reveal the full extent of the grooves and lines of gnarled flesh that coiled up and around his head, leaving him bald. He stared down at me, full of sadistic cruelty with his one bloodshot eye like an intruder gazing through the window into a home he would soon break into. He would soon *rob* me.

"You are resilient," he said to me tauntingly, no longer Demetrius in tone, but the Governor who now spoke through him.

"Like a blade," I muttered through clenched teeth, Carlyle's words still fresh in my mind as I was reminded of what he had told me.

"I will *break* you," the Governor replied.

"You do not break me," I shot back. "Only shape me. And breaking me will not *fix you.*"

I had to stall somehow. As I lay there, I could feel the ship move as it had only just begun to take off into the sky and far away from Widowsgrove. I had a plan, but I could not use my power against him, not before the S.S. Beulah would carry us back through the canyon and over the desert. How this massive vessel managed to maneuver through the canyons to come upon this town surrounded by the thicket of a dead forest was beyond me. It must have been no easy task. I knew he would leave them alone if I escaped then. We just had to get far enough away first.

The Governor clasped a metal fist around my braids, tugging my head back as he moved his knuckles behind my neck. "Well I'm bound to wanna get my rocks off again, that's true," he sneered. "A temporary fix is still a fix… and you need to be put in your place."

"Like you put *Lyn* in hers?" I said, straining against him.

"Lyn," the Governor harrumphed. "Lyn O'Bannion. I always found it interesting, the way we're all linked like this to one another… I found it especially interesting how Lyn's namesake is the same as the Viscountess's mother. *O'Bannion.* When I first learned about it, I thought it was absurd."

"Why," I asked, though my inflection came out more in the form of a demand than a question.

The Governor hovered over me, hesitating a moment, eyeballing me with disregard. "You better just watch your tone, girl," he spoke, gruffly.

There was that word again, wrapped in condescension. *Girl.* I did my best not to bristle as he continued.

"Rose *lost* her family name when she married Amadeus. None of you were born O'Bannions – if she really did marry him. Amadeus was a fool, but a man deserves more respect than that."

"Is that why you're called 'the Governor,' then?" I carefully asked. "You're a man, so you deserve more respect? And beyond that, he who governs the lives of others, so you deserve *most* respect…?"

Abruptly, he reached for my groin. I jumped out of my skin with his seizing touch and a small gasp escaped my lips. He was rough, kneading through my leather pants with his fingers and clumsily beginning to unfasten my belts from their buckle. I immediately fell silent, amazed at myself, how small this man could still make me feel.

"It was time for you to shut your filthy whore mouth," he chuckled gutturally, tugging the belts down around my hips with his one free hand.

I could feel the cold steel from his other against the back of my neck as he tightened his grip around my braids. My heart was racing. I felt humiliated and degraded all over again as I stared up at the ceiling, suddenly paralyzed and just as helpless as I always had been. Why did he have this kind of power over me? It was sickening. Maddening. I hated myself for it. All I had to do was wait for the right moment. It was hard to judge when that moment would be, or whether I would even have the strength to do what I was thinking once that moment came. I felt the ship's movements with my backside to the floorboards, the wood reverberating with each slightest turn the whole of the ship made as it steadily climbed in altitude.

These terrible minutes passed slowly as a dagger turned in my sternum. I grimaced through him fondling me, violating me. Each moment in his arms was the embrace of a sarcophagus lined with nails, an iron maiden piercing my soul and bleeding it bare. I was but a husk as I lay there, dry. I felt his wet spittle against my cheek and it was all I could do to keep my sanity from fracturing. I couldn't take this any longer.

"Λογία þovis!" I bellowed, casting a pulse of white light and energy to fill the room.

I felt it rock out from my body through my chest and with a split second of pressure I was cemented flat to the floorboards with the kickback. Demetrius's body took the full brunt of the force, the Governor contorting Demetrius's face with surprise, perhaps also pain, as he flew up and off me before landing with a loud crash behind the toppled furniture. I was on my feet before I knew it, stumbling towards the door with my loose belt clattering my buckle all about my hips. I flung the door open, quickly catching it and slamming it shut. I turned the lock and closed him inside.

From there, I did my best to act natural while walking hurriedly. The Governor or Demetrius would soon catch his breath and realize what I'd done, but I knew if I ran across the deck unescorted one of the deckhands would know that I was not let out. I kept my head down, meeting the eyes of no one and making my way anxiously to the bow end of the ship. I felt all eyes upon me, though I would not return them. My heart was fluttering around inside me like a moth in a lit lantern made of glass. I did not get very far.

A piercing mechanical screech jolted my senses and a small gasp escaped my lips. I don't know why it surprised me; this was something I had been expecting in the minutes to follow. I ran—just as Demetrius's voice came in over the ship's intercom system—as quickly as I could, one leg stronger than the other as my boots hit the floorboards in rapid succession.

"My key is getting away!" he announced frantically. I was unable to tell whether the Governor's link was still intact, by his words. "Grab her! Bring her back to me now, now, *now!*"

Ahead of me was an expanse of black starry sky as I came upon the ship's end. We had cleared the canyons and were now far from Widowsgrove, sailing through the heavens with cool winds sweeping back my braids. I was poised to take a plunge, the key's magic glowing inside of me and ready to deliver me from my captors. I passed cabin windows and pillars, netting and rope, and just as I thought I would make it to the nearest edge in a valiant leap of faith, I felt something slam into the side of my face. Everything went black for a moment as my backside once more came in contact with the floorboards. Then the pain. My eye socket ignited in a tiny explosion of reactant nerves that quickly spread across the rest of my face. I rolled myself over on my side and cradled the point of impact, my brow ridge and cheekbone fractured. I cried out in agony, and through the rise and fall of my heaving despair I could hear the hoarse, wheezing laughter of a familiar foe.

"How yeh like them apples?" Gertie sneered, standing over me. "Figgered rather'n shootin' yeh and waste Susan's bullets, I'd see if I still got a good swing in me even though yer detective man 'bout done shot my arm off!"

He gave me a solid kick to the ribs around my backside. I grimaced with the sharp pain from his steel-toed boot, now consumed with rage as I blinked my eyes, opening them wide trying desperately to regain my vision. For the moment, all I was able to see was static before me. I heard what must have been a wooden plank drop beside me, the object Gertie had struck me with, before feeling arms around me tugging my body upright and dragging me somewhere to another part of the ship. I grunted and snarled, convulsing and jerking, but try as I might, the arms which now encased me stayed their iron grip. I was thrown down a flight of stairs, the edges of each step cutting into me as I tumbled over them, hitting my head against a cluster of barrels below.

They had thrown me into the ship's cargo hold. My left eye was still throbbing and my vision was blurry, but I managed to make out several other crates and barrels all around me in this dark room where the only light shone in through the open door above. Outlined were the imposing body frames of Demetrius's men, each of them gathering behind Gertie and his horrible gleaming ingot teeth. Painfully, I stood. I clutched the sides of the barrels around me for support. My whole body shook with pain, anxiety, and a surge of adrenalin to wash it all away so that I could deal with this *now*.

"The Cap'n promised us we could 'ave our way with yeh if yeh wasn't gonna play nice," Gertie gleamed sinisterly.

He made his way down the stairs slowly, his stubby legs falling into each lazy clop. The other sky pirates were close in tow. Some were cracking their knuckles and rolling their shoulders. Not Gertie. He clutched his injured arm as it dangled limply at his side. He seemed to pay it no mind, his eager eyes transfixed on my person. These men were going to hurt me before they turned me back over to Demetrius, and Demetrius was going to let them, if not the Governor. None of that mattered now.

"You want to take me?" I breathed, exhaling my shaky nerves. Steadily, I regained my calm. "You're free to try. Just know this… I *will* fight each one of you, and you *may* break me down… but not before I've left my mark. It will serve as a reminder from this night and every other; a missing finger or two, an eye, perhaps an entire limb. You'll *know* you faced me 'til the day you die, however soon that may be."

Gertie sneered. "She got a mouth on 'er. Let's show 'er 'ow to use it," he said.

"Réii ma!" I chanted, raising a hand to call up the energy inside of me. It pulsed with light, filling the room.

Five men came rushing down the stairs, spilling out around Gertie who just stood there watching.

"λογία þovis!" I shouted, thrusting my hand forward and channeling every bit of power through palm to fingertips in a mighty blast that sent the two nearest assailants spiraling into the far wall on either side of the stairs.

The other three were upon me fast, the man closest to me winding his arm around in a closed-fist punch aimed for my head. I caught it with a swipe of my forearm, waxing full circle to pin his whole arm between my bicep and my side. With his arm locked, I counterattacked in a straight punch to his nose. I felt the cartilage crack, his head snapping back with the strength of my blow. Having forced him off balance, I swept his leg out from under him by knocking my heel against the back of his knee. He tumbled to the ground as I released my hold on his arm just in time for me to use my other leg on the next man, whirling around in a back kick just as he was raising a plank over his head in preparation to strike. My foot hit him squarely in the sternum, folding him over like a collapsed windbag. Unfortunately he was the bigger of the men and remained on his feet.

Pain immediately shot up through my thigh to my hip and I staggered. My injury from my previous fight with Carlyle was slowing me down. I cursed him silently, just as a metal rod came down around my head. The last man to attack had been waiting for the right moment, seizing the opportunity to take a cheap shot like a true sky pirate would. I fell back against the barrels behind me, feeling a warm wetness meet with my brow and then trickle down the side of my face. Blood. The larger man I had kicked before had straightened himself out by then. His eyes were maddened with rage. I felt two heavy palms clasp around either side of my head.

"λογία þovis!" I shouted once more, blasting him away from me before he would have a chance to retaliate. His large hands ripped away from my head, loosening a braid

By this point my heart was pumping so much adrenaline through my veins the pain I now felt was minimal, but my vision was blurred. I was tired and dizzy. I knew casting the key's magic so frequently straight through my body was expending much of my energy. *One last time,* I thought.

I aimed my open palm at the man who struck me with the rod. "Ζεῦ þovis!" The light all around me popped and fizzled out, enshrouding the room in shadow as before. Nothing happened.

My heart jumped into my throat just as I felt the bar come down around my extended arm with a loud crack. I shrieked in pain, withdrawing it to my chest and cradling it with my other. The man laughed through the darkness, winding back for another fast blow. This time I caught it with my right arm—my good arm—as it painfully smacked against my palm. I closed my hand around it and thrust sharply into his face. It was his turn to shriek. I was uncertain as to what I had struck in the absence of light, but I felt the rod wedged itself between bone and cartilage as the man fell away from me to writhe unseen on the floor. I glanced up toward the stairs where a bit of light still shone through the open door. Gertie was standing there, pointing his gun at me as more of Demetrius's men began to fill out around him.

"Guess ol' Susan 'ere will jest need teh shoot'cha, then," he muttered, clicking back the hammer.

I mustered every last bit of strength I had, sprinting toward him and up the stairs. My boot missed a step on my way up and I tripped just before him, grappling him awkwardly around the legs. The gun went off with a loud bang, the unseen bullet splitting splinters in one of the stacked crates of the room. He fell backward against the stairs with a wheezing puff. From there I felt hands, fists, and boots all upon me. I wildly thrashed while grabbing for Gertie's gun, trying desperately to cease the vicious onslaught upon my backside and all about my head. The gun went off again, this time pointed directly above us and loosing dust and splinters from the wood in the ceiling.

I had lost count of how many men were around me, struggling and clawing and grabbing at my braids and fitted clothing. I felt myself being raised with arms around my middle and over my chest as we all fought on the stairs. They tried to throw me back down, but I resisted. I kicked out in front of me, landing my boots wherever I could hit. I bit into someone's hand as he held me from behind. Grinding my teeth into flesh, I drew blood. I tasted dirt and oil on him. He released me.

"Réii ma!" I chanted, once more filling the room with light, temporarily blinding those closest to me.

Wasting no time, I stepped over Gertie and rushed up the last few steps and out of the cabin. I came face to face with Demetrius and several more of his men, now armed with a variety of weapons and standing at the ready.

"You've lost your chance," he said. I could tell it was truly him in the way he spoke.

I gazed up at the spherical sails holding the ship aloft, the night's stars shining brightly through the slightly transparent sheets that made up each mast. I had resigned myself to a final decision, once and for all.

"No," I panted. "You've lost yours."

His stare was made of stone. "Cut her open. Get me that key."

"Sage hajish kalehkt."

My words came slow. It felt as if the Viscountess in me had spoken them herself right alongside my careful enunciation of each part from the incantation. Raising my hands above my head to clasp together in a single sweeping motion, I called forth a fiery hurricane of raw energy, twisting upward from my body and penetrating the sails like a massive volley of arrows. In mere seconds the flaming holes my power had caused expanded as they burned away at the billowy fabric, the cords and ropes holding it all together quickly coming undone. In a matter of minutes, the S. S. Beulah would be in free fall. Every man aboard the ship broke out into a panic.

"You fucking bitch!" Demetrius shouted over all the commotion, stepping toward me and cupping my head in his hands. He was hysterical with grief. "You *stupid* fucking bitch! Why do you do this to me?!"

"You still have a stone, Demetrius," I said calmly. I could barely be heard over the shouts and cries of the sky pirates as they all ran the length and width of the deck like ants under an eyeglass. "Or, at least one of you does. I guess I'll soon know who."

CHAPTER 22
Countess of the Clouds

I clung to the folds of a black cloak under the water, soft light dancing over my skin in sync with the surface waves somewhere high above. My braids had risen and fallen around me as I felt my body ever slowly being swept away by a peaceful current. I heard the sounds of blue whales, their haunting melody reverberating in deep, long sighs though I could not see them through the cloak, my face buried in the chest of a familiar stranger. I felt a hand over my head, gently stroking down the back of my neck as I listened to those ghostly sounds.

"Why keep me?" I asked, my lips unmoving as my voice came in the form of an echoed resonance in my head, my thoughts passing unto him. "You've found Beulah—"

"I've never loved her," he interjected, his voice also echoing in my mind. "Not like I did, you. I just needed her."

"You've found many others before her," I thought aloud, in this way. "Many others alongside me. Why? Why could I never be enough for you?"

"…I just needed them too," he replied, still stroking my hair, pulling me close and holding me securely in his arms as we drifted through the nothing and the everything.

"But how can you say you've ever loved me at all when you hurt me the way you do?"

"I don't know," he said. "I don't mean to."

"I just want to forgive you," I continued. "I want to be free of you. Of this! I need to set myself free, and can't, while I carry this heaviness in my heart."

"You may need to kill me," came his whispering echo as he tenderly stroked a floating braid back behind my ear. "You are far gone. Forgiveness would be a hard won battle for you, and killing me may be the only way to rid yourself of that weight."

"I wish there were some other way," I sobbed.

I felt his lips against my forehead in a gentle kiss. "I know," he said. "I do, too. It was never my intent to instill in you so much rage and anguish, and I'd take it all back if I could. I just can't help... the things I need..."

"I know you can't help it," I replied, nuzzling into him. "Maybe that's why you have to die. Maybe it would be better for us both."

I could feel his weary smile. "Maybe."

The ghostly sound of the whale calls grew, and as they did I peeked out from behind the folds of his cloak. The gargantuan creatures swam so close, dozens of them crying out to one another, to *us*. They were more daring now than I had ever before dreamed.

"It would be easier to forgive if only you admitted to the things you have done," I pleaded, urgency turning over in my mind like an anxious array of static. "If only you knew it was wrong."

"I cannot," he said. "*I cannot face that.* But at my core, you must know I want peace for you. If peace be my gift to you in death, then it is up to you to redeem it..."

The blue whales were drawing nearer still. The static in my head grew, and with it the otherworldly sighs turned to moans and dull screeches.

"*Please*," I helplessly urged. "I don't understand how you not only refuse to acknowledge my plight, but *deny* what had happened between us altogether!"

"The guilt," he replied. "It would swallow me whole."

And with that, so then did the endless waters, suddenly swirling around us and into oblivion, blue whales and all swept into the nothingness. It was as if a frozen star had opened up right then and there, parting me from him and transporting me to a time long past and a place within the deepest recesses of my waking memory. I knew I was dreaming. I recollected another conversation in the midst of my slumber, this time one I knew I once had. The darkness which engulfed me now expanded into light, and I was seated outside the Rogue Musket with my back to the side of the building...

"I trusted you to keep her safe when I couldn't!" Roland sobbed.

"Roland, I'm sorry," I replied solemnly. I felt an overwhelming sense of guilt in alignment with my own grief that I remembered so well. "This time *he* took her anyway. We had a deal; he would leave her be, so long as he could have me instead. I loved her just as you did. You *know* that."

He heaved a sorrowful sigh and met my eyes for the first time since I told him the news that Lyn was dead. His blue eyes once bore the sunny skies of a cloudless day on the shore of an ocean, but now all I saw was gray. His sadness streaked his face like heavy rain, his skin made puffy around the cobalt crescent scar under his left eye from the coal mines whence he worked, though this time no crescent smile played at the corner of his mouth to match. He sat with me in the dirt outside the tavern, looking at me intently with a curious expression on his face.

"Why do you have to fight, Abernathy?" he asked, wiping off his nose and his eyes with the back of his hand.

The question startled me. Enough so that I let slide his use of my name when he knew full well I didn't like it. "What do you mean why do I *have* to?" I replied. "We're all a team, so we must operate as *one*. My participation in the matches increases our chances—"

"They were never meant for you," he responded sternly, cutting me off.

"What's that supposed to mean…?" I demanded, bewildered and somewhat annoyed.

He looked away from me, silent for a time before gathering his thoughts enough to speak again. "Do you know what I loved most about Lyn? …She was feminine, and she was innocent. She was pure. When she looked at me, she knew I could look after her and keep her safe. She would never have to fight anything or anyone so long as she had me right there to protect her. She called me her 'hero,' and she was my 'tenderheart.' She understood me. But more importantly, she understood *herself*. She understood that she was my woman and I was the man."

"…I don't understand what that even means," I said, angrily.

"See, and that's just my point," he replied. "You're actually pretty. Some might say you're even beautiful, and—"

"What's that got to do with—?!"

"Just listen," he continued, ignoring my rapidly building annoyance. He looked very serious. "Why would a beautiful woman want to risk jeopardizing her appearance in a fight? Do you know how many times I've had my nose broke? About as much as Kael's had his eye busted up."

"Well that's just because you're both *horrible* at ducking and weaving," I interjected. "If you were half as good at that as you are at throwing a punch—"

"Lyn never knew anything about that sort of stuff," he said, cutting me off again. "But she'd know what it meant when I say that I'm the man and she's my woman! Abernathy, you're a difficult woman to approach. You up and leave town for days at a stretch like you're some kind of soldier or mercenary or something, with your little bow and your quiver and all these supplies that the men use, and you wear men's clothes tailored especially to fit you since they don't make women's clothes like that *for a reason* and then you go and sign up for pit fights! That was the last straw for me."

"Why?" I frowned. "Why's all this such a big deal to you?"

Roland sighed exasperatedly, his eyes now dried. "You know, I'd just— Maybe I'd really like you to be my woman too if you acted… more womanly or something, that's all."

"So that's why I'm so hard to approach, then?" I glowered. "Because I'm not *feminine* enough for you?"

"Not just me," he said. "All the guys. And not just that, either. It's hard to think of you as any sort of romantic prospect. Hell, about the only thing feminine about you is your body, and that's why the Governor pays any attention to you at all."

I reached over and slapped him across the face with no particular force behind the blow. Even still, he looked stunned for a moment as I climbed to my feet and stood before him. "There. That 'feminine' enough for you?"

He stood up too. I almost matched him for height. "I don't hit women; you *know* this," he said, baring his teeth angrily at me. "But you're about as tall as a man."

"It's the boots," I shot back. "And probably also the backbone. Maybe if you had one, you'd be a little taller yourself."

"Working in the coal mines is the most dangerous work we got out here, Abernathy!" he yelled, a few inches from my face. "More often dangerous than guard duty outside these walls! What do you mean *if* I had a backbone? Damn it, we got guards patrolling outside the perimeter of the town walls; why don't you just leave it to them?!"

"The town guards aren't the ones who found Blythe out in the desert," I said coolly. "*I* was. The Governor gave me his express permission to be out there. Why is that not okay with *you?* Why is my participation in the pit fights so wrong to you?"

"It just is," he replied. His words were thick with resentment.

I stared him down, his blue eyes ablaze with icy resolve. My own resolve was none the lesser. I was not about to back down from this. "When I speak of your backbone, I don't mean your willingness to put your body in the way of physical harm," I affirmed. "I think you're afraid of bettering yourself, and that's why you need a lover who's under you, *stagnant*, so you don't have to worry about growing the hell up. I think the very notion that a woman could be better than you at *any*thing drives you mad because you're so insecure in yourself in what you think it means to be a man that you feel you need to hinder the growth in another. A bigger man would rise to the challenge within himself to surpass his fears; his limitations… but you writhe in them and then expect me to join you. *No*. I'm busy."

I watched him go as cold as his gaze, his severe features softening into a numb distance between us. He stood so close, yet drifted so far as I became aware of an aura around him dulling in color and receding into him. He stepped back from me, stony and despondent.

"You should watch the things you say," he dispassionately warned. "Something *else* bad could happen to you…"

I gasped suddenly, taking air into my lungs as if snatched from the brink of death. My body shot upright involuntarily with the oxygen now filling my airways. It was not until a moment's passing that I realized I had woken from my dreams. As my vision focused, I realized only my right eye was able to open. I felt the seat beneath me jostle around with each bump and groove along the dirt path, aware of my surroundings as being the inside of a carriage—*Rafe's* carriage. I pulled back the curtain and glanced outside the window. Sure enough, I was able to make out the side end of a horse's body in scorching broad daylight, its strong ebony legs powering onward at a quick and steadied pace.

"Surely you must remember Mercedes," a familiar woman's voice softly spoke.

I turned to face Hi-Yoon, draped elegantly over the opposite seat of the carriage with her soft, deft hands resting comfortably in her lap.

"She remembers you," Hi-Yoon smiled. Her small red lips parted ever slightly though not as to reveal her teeth.

"The horse?" I asked, a bit at a loss.

"Did Rafe not tell you she had a name?" Hi-Yoon replied. "No, I suppose he would not have. That would be very much like him. Penelope is just 'gray cat' to him, after all."

I was startled by a furry object hopping up into my lap with a short 'mew' as it then began to settle itself. I looked down at Penny who kneaded my legs once, twice, then lowered her little body to be seated across me.

Hi-Yoon's smile warmly grew. "She has taken to you well," she said. I sensed the faintest hint of expression behind the black lace that still concealed her eyes.

"How did…? Where—?" I stammered.

"We are on our way to Fyndridge," she said, knowingly. "You likely would not be able to see him without poking your head all the way out of the window, but Mercedes has allowed Rafe to ride her for the time being while your knight and his brother have taken to marching behind the carriage. They say it is a safety precaution, in case of an ambush. *I* say their needless expending of energy in this desert heat will give them each a stroke... *especially* the one in all that metal armor."

I stared at her wordlessly. They were all here. We were on our way to Fyndridge. I was uncertain how to process this information.

"How long had I been out?" I asked.

"We only found you earlier this morning," she said. "The sun was just barely rising off the horizon... and *you* were barely falling. It was Rafe who first spotted you in the distance, slowly floating right out of the sky."

CHAPTER 23
From Sand to Stone

It took me a little while after I had lost consciousness to remember the events that transpired in the S.S. Beulah's final moments. Anything not bolted down to the whole of the ship fell away once it entered free fall. This included myself, Demetrius, and all of his men. He embraced me seconds before our feet left the planks, the winds carrying us both with his arms secured tightly around my waist and my shoulders. I struggled to be free of him, even as we each plummeted headlong toward the earth far below us. The oxygen changed rapidly with our tumbling descent. I passed out.

I told this to Rafe.

"Well we ain't seen nobody else but you and some pieces from the ship you was on," he said, seated atop Mercedes swaying left to right with her every step.

He cast his baby blue eyes out over the rolling sand dunes far ahead and all around us. As I walked beside Mercedes with my slight limp in an effort to loosen my sore muscles in spite of my bruised bones, I got the feeling he didn't want to look at me.

"You know, you never explicitly said you would do this for me," I said, looking up at him. "…This quest for the stones, I mean. I wanted to thank you for that."

"Yeah, well," he started, avoiding my eyes. "It ain't just for your sake and I know savin' the world is prob'ly important n' whatnot, and Zebadiah seems to have a good head on his shoulders for what we're s'posed to be doin', so I just figured… Why not?"

I smiled absently, dissatisfied. He still wouldn't look at me. I decided to fall back my pace, allowing the carriage to pass by where Hi-Yoon remained and Seth had taken my place. I synced my step with Carlyle, who would have no breaks from his trudging armor-heavy trek. His face was pouring with sweat as he stoically tailed the carriage.

"Rafe won't look at me when I'm talking to him," I said quietly, doing my best not to sound like I was sulking.

Carlyle offered me a sidelong glance. "He doesn't like seeing your face all busted up like that," he replied. "It bothers him. He thinks we should have done more to keep you safe, and with you looking the way you do, I can understand why he'd avoid eye contact. Don't take it to mean he doesn't like you anymore… It's just hard on a man's sensibilities. I'm not happy with it either."

"Oh, really?" I said combatively. "You seemed awfully liberal with your attacks when you and I faced off with one another."

He turned his head to look me over as we continued to walk, his expression at first steely before his eyes met with mine, the one I could presently see out of with my left eye being swollen shut as it was. His gaze softened in that moment and once more he looked away.

"I would never have done that to you," he solemnly spoke. "I would never have taken it so far to have hurt you like that."

"To have bested me, Sir Carlyle, you would have had to," I retorted. "And with my wounds I *still* escaped that ship on my own. Besides that, you pulled *your sword* on me. You attacked me with everything you had. You can't tell me you wouldn't take it this far!"

He said nothing, but exhaled gruffly. He focused on the path before us, looking out straight ahead toward the back of the carriage. I kept in step alongside him feeling more alienated than before. We continued on in this way with the silence between us disquieting and long lasting. My thoughts drifted back and forth between him and Rafe.

"How come Rafe's all the way up there and you're all the way back here?" I demanded.

He looked at me like I was the dumbest creature alive. "That's *Rafe's* horse. This is *his* carriage. Someone has to be leading the way to make sure we're headed in the right direction. And someone has to cover our backs… Something you're in no condition to do right now. You really should get back in the carriage, my lady."

"Are you *advising* me right now, then?" I replied snottily.

"My lady—" he started, through gritted teeth.

"Why are things so awkward between you two?" I interjected. He looked somewhat taken aback. "It's something I'll need to be made aware of *as your lady*. Rafe told me you preferred not to see him if you didn't have to, and now we're all traveling together. Did you know he has a portrait of you hanging up in his weird cave-house? He obviously cares for you. What do you have against him, exactly…?"

He sighed weightily. "I… I could never— …You have it all wrong, my lady. It is *he* who should hold me in contempt. Not the other way around."

"Why…?" I asked, surprised by his admission.

"I can't speak to him. I can hardly look him in the eye. Two men in my battle group were injured and I could only carry one of them on my back at the time. I chose the man least injured… the man with the greatest chance of survival. I left his son to die."

I hung my head low at his words, focusing on the bit of sandy earth before the each of my footsteps. "I'm sorry," I mustered. "I didn't know."

"I do not accept *any* apology," he growled. "You ordered me to tell you, did you not? I'm simply fulfilling my duty to you, my lady."

"Stop calling me that," I said. "*Bern*. My name is Bern."

"As you wish," he curtly replied.

"It is my wish also to call you by name before title," I said, looking back at him. "If we are to travel together, I see little point in adhering to formalities between us."

His expression remained unchanged. "Very well. Could that be why you tried to kiss me last night before your *boyfriend* whisked you away?"

My heart leapt, then sank. I felt myself go cold. "That… That was an accident," I replied, flustered. "I was confused. I don't know what came over me, but it meant *nothing*, and I thank you for not taking advantage of me in my moment of weakness. Just as I could have once exploited you and chose not to, you could have done the same to me…"

He looked at me out from the corner of his eye, but said nothing. My anxiety mounted and with it, so did my resentment of him coupled with my resentment of his silence.

"…Because I *don't* like you like that," I added. "And Demetrius is *not* my 'boyfriend.' Not anymore."

"Did you know you talk in your sleep?" he asked.

"Yeah, a bunch of meaningless drivel," I shot back defensively. "What's your point?"

"It's not all so meaningless. As your adviser, I need to be made aware of a few things too… and I heard you talking to him. You were dreaming. It sounded to me like you're still attached to this man. Tell me; do you *love* him…?"

I hesitated a moment before answering him, my throat welling up to join my heart. "I loved him, once," I said. "I think a part of me always will. It all hurt so bad. I've given myself so much closure. I would never, *ever* go back, and yet… I can't keep the door completely shut."

"Then whatever closure you feel you've given yourself still isn't enough," he remarked. "And it's a disconcerting thing when… our *leader*… is held hostage by the enemy."

I could hear the slight grimace in his voice as he uttered his recognition, and perhaps also acceptance, of the position thrust upon me. His tone felt more warm than begrudged as he spoke, as though his very aura were reaching out for me in a protective embrace in spite of him.

"I suspect he still holds you hostage, even now," he continued. "The part of you that matters most, at least. *Bern* – we need your head on the objective at hand. I overheard Rafe speaking with the witch, Hi-Yoon, about a detour he intends to take us on the way to Fyndridge. As your advisers, we must make decisions on your behalf when you are unable to act… but you have since awakened, and he should be keeping you informed."

"Witch?" I exhaled, aghast.

"Maybe you should talk to her first. In the end, this call is yours to make," he said. "Although, since it is your desire to discard formalities, allow me to say that I will not bring up the kiss again if *you* don't bring up how you could have exploited me as if to hold it over my head what happened. In fact, don't even reference it at all." He paused for a moment before speaking again, his face contorting in a twitch. "…And keep your boots on."

I said nothing but nodded my affirmation. My mind was now preoccupied with Rafe and his apparent usurping of engagements. I quickened my pace, starting in on him as I moved ahead of Carlyle and hurried alongside the carriage in hot pursuit. I *would* meet his eyes with my own.

"It is all necessary, my lady," Hi-Yoon's voice crooned around lifted curtains. I slowed my step and turned my head to face her though I could only make out her small red lips and subtle smile. "Come. Rest inside the carriage awhile and allow Seth to speak of his findings."

I looked ahead toward Rafe, who seemed altogether oblivious to my conversation with Carlyle as well as Hi-Yoon's gentle voice now beckoning me. I gritted my teeth and narrowed my brows but begrudgingly decided upon rejoining her, flinging open the side door and stepping up with my good leg. Once more, Seth extended a hand to me. I took hold and clambered into the damned moving container and shut the damned door behind me, falling back into the seat alongside him and opposite Hi-Yoon. I gazed at her coldly.

"You're a witch?" I asked plainly.

"A *sorceress*," she calmly replied. Her smile grew. "It is how I managed to procure Rafe's carriage for him—or rather, how I was able to communicate to Mercedes the rendezvous point she would need to bring it to. Luckily he had left her saddled with it since you both left her all alone two days ago, the poor dear. You should have seen how parched and famished she was!"

"There was not much we could do about that at the time," I retorted, suppressing my guilt and trying to remain on her as the subject at hand. "Is that how you were able to leave Widowsgrove? Sorcery?"

"My lady," she giggled. "I was only *teasing* you. I am an alchemist, just as Seth is. I left Widowsgrove by presenting the Duke's seal to the gatekeepers. Oh, and I do apologize for that by the way… I understand it put you in a bit of a bind. As I have said, it is all necessary."

"So it was *you*, then," I muttered disgruntledly.

"Listen," Seth chimed in, planting a firm hand over my shoulder and drawing my attention to him. "All you need to know is that with the right components and the right incantation, we too can communicate by the power of the stones and even track where others may be! So turns out that one of Rafe's old companions carries a stone… we're just not sure which. When we linked ours up with hers, we were only able to decipher its whereabouts and whether it was in the possession of anyone at present; this girl, Tigerlily. Rafe recognized her voice. You should have seen the look on his face when she spoke to us from the other end," he smirked, letting his hand drop. "She sounded awfully surprised, too. Apparently she didn't even know it housed such a power."

"Once we meet with her, we shall find out which of the gemstones she possesses," Hi-Yoon smiled. "It is unlikely that her alignment is such that she is able to harness its power, having gone so long without stumbling upon its properties even once. She *was* able to communicate through it however, and *she is not alone.* We heard other voices on her end before the link broke." Hi-Yoon's smile faded. "Without the use of a vessel—the *key*—all we have to go by are the potions we consume which turn us into such, for a short time."

"Regardless," Seth started, "we still need the corresponding gemstones to do anything at all. And on that note, where on your person might yours be, my lady?"

Processing everything the each of them had told me, I had finally begun to relax for the first time since I had woken. I fished my brooch out of my back pocket and brandished it to them, on one side my family crest, the sapphire gemstone securely fastened on the other.

"Ahh, so there it is," Hi-Yoon gleefully rang. "I felt it while I was pickpocketing you for the duke's seal, but seeing it now, I am glad I opted not to take that *too* knowing what it is!"

"How exactly had you managed to escape from Demetrius's ship?" Seth inquired. "A man like Demetrius... What I heard, you'd think he'd want to confiscate your gemstone the moment he got his hands on you; disarm you of your powers from the get-go. Why didn't he?"

I sighed wearily, clipping the brooch to my bustier. "He was more focused on... other things."

CHAPTER 24
Rendezvous

We arrived at an oasis where a lone caravan appeared to have been parked for some time. Sand collected around its large wooden wheels to where it would need to be dug up before they would move again. The sun had long passed over the horizon and in a few short hours, would set. I thought I might have been hallucinating as I took in the view of crystal waters reflecting sunlight off its still surface. My esophagus tightened briefly, loosening an empty swallow. I thirsted.

Two tall trees stood adjacent, one from the other, their bristled green leaves jutting out in all directions like an unruly head of hair would crown a couple of lithe, statuesque women. Between these trees, a long beige sheet had been tied as a makeshift hammock. Beside it, I noticed a fire pit made with branches sticking out of the sand at clumsy angles. Hot coals filled the divot in the sand glowing orange and red as a metal pot dangled from the branches a few feet above it. I was surprised Rafe's contact had managed to set camp here out in the open for such a long while, yet also somewhat perturbed in all my time walking the desert never having stumbled upon this location myself.

A small, slender woman stepped out from the stationary caravan, her head tilted to one side so that her just barely shoulder-length hair fell around her prominent collarbones. Her eyes were large and bright, her whole face splotched in freckles which trailed down the sides of her neck and over her bare shoulders and arms. With the back of her hand she brushed loose strawberry-blonde tresses behind one of her markedly large ears. It was the girl from the portrait on Rafe's wall.

"Rafe!" she squeaked, bounding toward our carriage with the enthusiasm of a squirrel to an acorn. A long silver chain jostled loosely around her neck, disappearing into her noticeable cleavage as she made her approach.

Rafe slung a leg over Mercedes and hopped down from her saddle, turning just in time to catch the woman's arms around his neck. He wrapped her up around the waist and gently lifted her off the ground in a warm embrace. "Hey there, darlin'," he spoke softly, just loud enough that I could hear him from within the carriage. "Did ya miss me?"

"O'course I did!" she beamed. "You gotta introduce me to your friends! Then I can introduce you to my fiancé and my cousin when they get back from scoutin'. Basically we have a *lot* of catchin' up to do, in general."

Fiancé? I thought, skeptically. I wondered how she was going to find a reverend to sanction a marriage all the way out here, in these harsh times.

Both Hi-Yoon and Seth opened the doors of the carriage from either side, my perch at a window falling away from me as Seth reached over with his considerable 'wingspan' to push it ajar. As Hi-Yoon stepped out onto the sand, he was not about to step over me in following suit.

"After you, my lady," he said with a charming lilt in his voice, gesticulating with extended open palm.

I complied, easing myself from the carriage and sinking my boots into loose sand as I settled my footing. I stepped around the carriage just as Carlyle marched on past me with not so much as a glance. I scowled up at his back but followed silently, Seth following closely behind me. I felt like a squirrel myself, between the two towering brothers. We each stopped a few feet short of Rafe and the woman, both still embracing, Hi-Yoon smirking somewhat from around the other side of them.

"I'd like y'all to meet the girl dearest to my heart," Rafe said, nodding to the woman slight in stature. I felt an odd twinge of ache in my chest with his words that I could not place. "Tigerlily here has been a friend to me when I needed one most. Me n' her go back a ways."

"Happy to meet you guys!" she said, breaking away from Rafe to extend a hand to me first. "You must be the escaped Viscountess I've heard so much about! You got sent away from Fyndridge, right? To Galvinsglade?" She snatched up my hand and gave it a vigorous shake much to my discomfort. She smelled sweetly of citrus. "I don't know how you managed to flee from *the town of thieves* intact, but by the looks of you I'd guess it was no easy task!"

"I, uhh, ...my injuries are not from Galvinsglade," I replied, abruptly reclaiming my hand from her firm grip.

"Oh, well I suppose they wouldn't be what with Rafe being there to rescue you n' all," she said, casting her eyes in his direction and shooting him a nauseating wink. He responded in likeness with a smug grin.

If I hadn't been so painfully aware of the dryness in my throat I would have opted to leave them all there to the oasis so that I might continue the journey to Fyndridge alone and on foot.

"Don't *degenerates* roam rampant from inside the town's walls?" she continued. "Me n' my fiancé encountered a few of 'em since we been out here! Pretty scary…"

"Yes," I reluctantly replied. "They *are* scary."

"Just how *long* you n' yer fiancé been out here exactly?" Rafe inquired. "You done set'cherself up real cozy by the look of it."

"Not long," Tigerlily replied, turning back to face him. "We got attacked a little while back n' lost our horses… Been stuck here ever since."

"Degenerates?" Seth asked.

"Nah. A couple a' subterrans," she corrected. "Strange for them to be wanderin' around on the surface, wouldn't ya think?"

"Not necessarily," I interjected. "They've gotten more bold as they continue to run out of resources… so far as to create traps, ensnaring the unafflicted."

"Oh?" she piqued, raising a bushy brow. "Who told ya that?"

"I speak from experience," I replied, recalling my encounter with the two subterrans who briefly captured the Viscountess in me. I turned my gaze on Rafe, somewhat testily. "So turns out, I'm not too bad at rescuing *myself*."

He paid me a brief uncomfortable glance out the corner of his eye before turning his attention to the others. "Guess I oughta finish up introductions n' all that," he said, ignoring me. "Tigerlily, I'd like ya to meet Seth Soot n' his brother there, Sir Carlyle Soot… and behind ya over there is Hi-Yoon Bao."

Tigerlily followed his indication of each person with her eyes. They each nodded back at her, all remaining silent and still but for Seth who stepped forward to take her hand into his.

"The pleasure's mine," Seth said with a grandiose bow, bending far forward to level his gaze with hers. He kissed the back of her hand, his short beard grazing over her slender fingers.

I watched Tigerlily's face as she beamed her bright eyes and admittedly infectious smile at him. I studied her features, the creases in her complexion belying her youth. It wasn't until then that I noticed the whiskers lining her cheeks and trailing down her jawline into a bit of a light beard. The hairs appeared fine, though coarse enough to grow outward from her sun-kissed skin. I blinked my eyes, startled by this discovery. Surely she knew about it herself, not that there was much to be done to hide it stationed at an oasis nestled among desert dunes. Still – why would she? It didn't seem to be something that bothered her, at least in the way that she carried herself.

"We have a cat, too," Hi-Yoon chimed. "Penelope. You will meet her when she no longer wishes to be shy. And the horse; she is called Mercedes."

"Well it's certainly nice to see some new faces 'round these parts that still look normal!" Tigerlily grinned.

"Where's the stone?" I asked. All eyes fell on me. I realized I may have sounded somewhat forceful in my tone. I tried to relax my posture a bit, cracking an apologetic smile to the best of my ability. "We really should at least see whether it can be identified."

"Oh, yeah!" she replied. "I keep it on me always. More for sentimental reasons n' anything… Never knew it was *magic*…" She brought her hand to her chest and clutched the silver chain around her neck, pulling it up out of her peach tank top. On the other end of the chain, a deep blue gemstone was set into the base of a pocket watch. It filled her palm as she held it out.

"*I* remember that stone," Rafe exclaimed with moderate excitement. "There's a lot a' nostalgia attached to that little piece of jewelry there. Remember where ya got it from?"

"How could I forget?" Tigerlily smiled. "Before Widowsgrove had walls put up around it, back when the foliage wadn't all burnt and dead 'round those parts? Now the river's all dried out…"

"Was awf'ly fun catchin' them fish try'na swim upstream, bare-handed, with you," Rafe smirked. "Never woulda known it. That big ol' rock we found in that catfish's mouth is actually worth somethin'. Didn't even believe in none a' this stuff more'n a couple days ago!"

Tigerlily let loose a musical giggle. "I just thought it was pretty. And it smelled good! That's why I kept it all this time. It's always made me feel like you were close by my side; and wadayaknow? You really were!"

I felt vaguely detached listening to the each of them carry on as they reminisced of happier days. An inexplicable melancholy washed over me as my eyes fell over the faces of my travel companions, all of them unaware of whatever it was that I felt in this moment, no more so than myself.

"You were never far from my thoughts, darlin'," Rafe gently reassured her. "I couldn't have reached you without Sir Carlyle usin' his stone. I don't got one, and I don't really know how they work. All I know is that it pointed us in the direction of the next nearest one and *you* happened to be it!"

"The stone corresponds with my astrological alignment," Carlyle added. "That is how I am able to use it… and only while supplemented by alchemy. After that, I established a connection with the purpose of seeing if anyone was in possession of the stone we were looking for. I can do this, regardless of whether the carrier is aligned. If the carrier is *not*, then he or she would not be able to reopen the connection once it is closed. That being said, Bern," he continued, turning to me. I was almost startled by his manner of addressing me. "I have it on good word that you were supposed to hear back from a contact in Fyndridge once he acquired the stone there—correct?"

"Yes," I replied. "To my knowledge, he still hasn't."

"The only time he could have done so without you knowing would have been while you were unconscious and not with us… but we found you *as* you were falling out of the sky, and we made it to you before you reached the ground. Someone was always watching you after that, and we would have known if your contact opened a connection with you."

"She *fell* from the *sky?!*" Tigerlily interjected.

Rafe raised a gloved hand to one of her freckled shoulders to hush her. "I'll fill ya in about it later, sweets."

"What this means," Carlyle continued, speaking over them, "is that there was a very short window of time in which he could have tried to contact you without any one of us ever knowing about it. I think we ought to go on the assumption that he never has… and if that's the case, then we may have a bigger problem on our hands. Someone *else* could have discovered the stone before him. Perhaps a known enemy."

"The Governor," I thought aloud, my heart sinking into my stomach.

"We won't know before we make it into town; and even then, we still need to figure out how we're going to get over, *or through* those walls undetected," he said gravely.

"It shall not be an issue in my hands," Hi-Yoon smiled, her long sheer gown sheerer than ever under direct sunlight, hugging her willowy form and leaving little to the imagination. How she intended to scale a wall taller than the tallest building in Fyndridge dressed like that would be anyone's guess, blindness notwithstanding.

"You, uhh, sure you don't want to leave that up to me n' Car?" Seth muttered, his voice deep and husky with apparent discomfort.

I hadn't registered it before he spoke that he had been visibly blushing in Hi-Yoon's presence this entire time, fighting a losing battle with his own eyes as they dragged back and forth between her pronounced curves and the desert sand. He was not quite so flustered under the shade of the carriage's boxed walls. It then dawned on me that she may have remained in the carriage through dusk to daylight, having only now emerged.

"I have faith in 'er," Rafe said. "Ain't nobody else seen 'er use them hands of hers but me, and I'll tell y'all right now, blindness ain't never been in the way before."

Hi-Yoon's laugh was like honey gently being stirred. "I retrieved Mercedes, did I not?"

I felt Mercedes' eyes burn like a couple of headlights. I felt her watching me.

"Oh, All Mother, they're back!" Tigerlily shouted suddenly.

We each turned to look in the direction Tigerlily had cast her gaze, the desert dunes spanning as far as the eye could see. I was unable to tell north from south, having not watched the sun in the time I had regained consciousness. In the distance, the figures of two men came over the horizon.

"Dragonfly!" Tigerlily bellowed, her high voice carrying farther than before. "Kael!"

Kael? I gasped.

As the figures drew nearer, I began to make out their features. The man called Dragonfly hunched over slightly with Kael's arm draped around his broad shoulders. He wore a long black braid that coiled down his chest. His hair was pulled very tightly and close to his scalp. The man, much taller than Kael, may well have been wearing a potato sack, his ragged clothing playing contradiction to his bejeweled ears and bushy brows, each pierced with golden loops more than I cared to count. His face was angular and rugged, a stubbly beard blending with the dirt which darkened his already deep complexion. I noticed two hilts of what looked to be swords, or perhaps long daggers, peeking out from around his back as he ambled toward us.

I would have thought Kael to be seriously wounded if not for the goofy smile plastered across his face, partially hidden underneath his jet-black hair as he dazedly hung his head. From what I knew of Kael, I immediately presumed he was drunk. I felt shocked, not expecting him to be the cousin of whom Tigerlily had spoken, his long, jet-black hair falling over his familiar face in an unruly crow's nest, his skin darkened with the sun's unforgiving branding upon him and the dirt of the earth from travels long past which served only as indication enough that he had seen his share of nights slept in the open desert. Whatever atrocities he had been through, he seemed okay now, jovial even, as his eyes met with my own. Immediately his face lit up and he began frantically waving his free arm in greeting. He pulled away from the other man, a mere several yards from me before calling out my name with glee.

"Bern!" he exclaimed. "I'm hallucinating for real this time… Is it you?"

I made my way toward him in response, arms outstretched to receive him. He was considerably shorter than me but what he lacked in height, he made up for in hard, sculpted muscle. Clumsily, he wrapped me up and locked himself around my waist, lifting me from the ground an inch or two.

"I'm as real as the oasis," I smirked as he squeezed me.

"I've never seen you like this," he replied, setting me down but not letting go. "What happened to you…?"

"Never mind that," I said. "What are you doing out here? How long had you been away from Fyndridge since…"

My thoughts trailed off. My memory was sketchy at best, having experienced only bits and pieces of that first night escaping from Demetrius's ship as I did my best to shield the Viscountess in me from whatever she had to face. It was then that I'd lost her, rekindling my connection to her after stepping through the portal between worlds.

"Never mind that either," Kael interrupted, tearing from my sudden divot in thought. "There's something real funny I gotta tell ya!"

"Kael…" the one called Dragonfly said, his tone a warning. His voice was deep like Carlyle's with a booming cadence like Seth's. He was shorter than each of the brothers, though considerably taller than Tigerlily or Kael. "I'd like to not get into this now."

Tigerlily strode over to him and reached up her arms to delicately run her palms over either side of his neck, lacing her fingers to crown at his nape. "Get into what, my dashing dragon?"

"What I don't want to get into," Dragonfly gritted. "…My lovely lily," he added.

"Perhaps another round of introductions are in order," Hi-Yoon suggested.

"I'll go ffirsst," Kael slurred. "So there we were—"

"Damn it, Kael, please…!" Dragonfly pleaded.

"—just raiding this subterran's hole in the ground, right?" he continued, ignoring Dragonfly's request.

Tigerlily snapped her head around at Kael with a gasp, turning back to meet Dragonfly's eyes, elated. "You found a subterran hole?!"

Dragonfly huffed his protest but said nothing, looking helpless and annoyed as the rest of us stood still and just listened. Occasionally our eyes met; mine with Seth's, Seth's with Rafe's or Carlyle's, and each of us only looking at Hi-Yoon who must have felt our eyes upon her because she shrugged.

"Well, anyway, we found a whole *lot* of liquor!" Kael beamed. "But that's not all. You guys ever hear about 'the order of social senses'?"

"The *what?*" I blinked.

"The order of social senses is the order by which you perceive others and make judgments on them be they conscious or subconscious. The first sense you use when perceiving someone is your sense of sight; you follow me? You see them, you acknowledge them; maybe they're really hot—like Bern. Or this *other* tall drink of foxy lady…"

"Hi-Yoon," Hi-Yoon said.

"Right, like Hi-Yoon," he continued, swaying a little to one side and staggering to keep his balance on his own. "So anyway, your second sense is hearing. Inflections in speech help build familiarity and set the tone of conversation. Some people have shrill voices, others, deep and sultry; they *all* play a role in how a person is received. Then there's your sense of smell, which comes third—"

"Does any of this have a point?" Carlyle grumbled, arms crossed over his chest.

Kael raised a hand excitedly, pointing a finger to wag just short of Carlyle's face as he stepped toward him. "Yes!" he replied. Carlyle flinched back in annoyance.

"Yessirr, it *does* have a point! You ssee," Kael slurred, "you may notice cologne or perfume, or in some unpleasant cases, body odor. Even if you don't notice a detectable smell, pheromones still remain an active agent and that triggers the subconscious. Next would be your sense of touch and this can come from a handshake or other friendly gesture. With a handshake, you may notice if the person engaging your social senses had a nice, firm grip or lay limp between your ffffingers."

"I *hate* that," Seth murmured.

"The very last sense you should use for judgment when interacting with others, which is typically only reserved for intimate situations, is your sense of taste… but sometimes people step outside the order of social senses. For example, when me n' Dragonfly were exploring the subterran hole, we found a couple of their carcasses that had been left a while and the smell was so foul, so pungent, we could *taste* it."

Dragonfly's face grew pale in that moment, presumably with the memory of what they both had experienced. He looked as if he would soon be sick.

"You remember the Rogue Musket, right Bern?" Kael went on, his glazed eyes dancing over me. "Bunch of sweaty, dirty men all cooped up under one roof never produced very pleasant smells, but we always got used to it after a while. There was no getting used to *this*. Normally taste is supposed to be the last social sense in the lineup, but with a smell so bad it jumps to first?

...I felt *violated*."

I could not help but feel a little angry, somehow, at his choice of word. I reminded myself that he was only trying to be funny in light of past events.

"Y'all find anythin' down in that hole more'n booze?" Rafe inquired.

"Weapons? Some supplies?"

"Yes," Dragonfly muttered weakly. "We found bones. Human remains. Some ragged clothes and belongings here and there, probably from nomadic earthdwellers *like us*... but nothing usable."

"There were no marks on the bodies," Kael added, still swaying slightly. "I mean, beyond their own disfigurements, that is. Looked like they died of natural causes. They certainly hadn't been poisoned by the booze, that's for sure. I drank *plenty* of it and I'm okay!"

"You risked your life for a drink?" Tigerlily squeaked.

"Don't be silly; it wasn't *a* drink. I checked them all, just to be sure." he replied.

I felt somewhat appalled by his recklessness. There was something markedly different about him than back when I'd last seen him in Fyndridge. I couldn't quite place it, but it made me leery.

"You know what this means, though, right?" Dragonfly said, regaining his composure. "The subterrans are *dying off*."

CHAPTER 25
Reassurance

"Bern…" a faraway voice soothed me.

I opened my eyes. The darkly dressed Ovocula stood over me alongside the white and pastel-clothed Gwendolyn, each girl smiling down at me. They were surrounded in white light.

"Where are we?" I asked. "Is this a dream?"

"Sort of," Ovocula grinned. "It's like an astral projection, but from the inside out. In other words, we are inside of you. You fell asleep, so we thought we'd come say hello."

"Hello, miss lady Bern," Gwendolyn smiled sweetly. She curtsied with a familiar naïveté.

I seemed to be laying over nothing. I tried to stand, but all I could do was float into an upright position as though my mind were read by forces outside of my body's control. "Why come to me now, of all times?"

"Kael wants to die," Ovocula said matter-of-factly, in an almost dismissive tone that made me wince. "The things he endured on the S.S. Beulah were too much for him, and now he's lost his will to live. That's why he drinks whenever he can, without thought to implication. I wonder how much time he even spends being sober these days. You know he's not the same."

"*What* had he endured?" I beseeched them, my eyes dancing between them both under narrowed brow.

"I've spoken quite a bit with our uncle," she continued, changing the subject. "I've done my best to help him to understand your feelings; the

Viscountess's too, since I know the each of you were never in a position to tell him these things yourselves. I thought it would help… but it didn't."

"What…?" I breathed. "*What* things? Where *is* the Viscountess? What happened on that ship after *the first time* I fought off Demetrius's crew? Tell me!"

"What miss Ovocula *means* to say," Gwendolyn chimed in, "is that you have not the presence of mind to speak with him rationally what with all your rage—and mister uncle Acanthus is in the business of rationality, you see! I should certainly know, for all those times I had found myself eavesdropping on his shrinking."

"Shrinking?" Ovocula blinked.

Gwendolyn blinked back. "Oh, um, shrinkage? That thing psychiatrists have."

"All Mother mercy; psychiatrists are called *shrinks*, you amoeba!"

"Wait," I said, my heart suddenly skipping beats in my chest. "How were you able to eavesdrop on my uncle's sessions?"

"I cleaned his study at times, in Galvinsglade," Gwendolyn replied. "He would leave his door cracked open, sometimes enough to where I could see inside. I met a man with a number of personalities… It is how I met Roland."

If there were ground beneath my feet, surely it would have opened up right then to swallow me whole in accompaniment of my heart's descent into my stomach. "Lyn?" I welled. "You're Lyn…?"

"We wanted to tell you sooner," Ovocula said, her tone seeming apologetic. "*Much* sooner. You were preoccupied with other things. I took it upon myself to hide her away, *change* her, so nobody would notice. Not even you."

"I got to choose my name though," Gwendolyn smiled. "Gwendolyn Amber Rose O'Bannion sounded pretty. I wished to keep the namesake of our mother, Rose O'Bannion. I also chose Amber, since amber is the gemstone for Taurus!"

"You aren't even a Taurus, though," Ovocula murmured. "You're an Aries; a ram! Or, an ewe, rather…"

"Ewes like bulls!" Gwendolyn enthusiastically replied, still smiling.

"Please!" I interrupted, my emotions weighing upon me with an urgency I could not ignore. "What was I *so* preoccupied with that you thought I needed to believe my *most treasured* connection was lost to me forever?" I could feel the sting of tears beginning to form around my eyes with my distress.

"Bern," Ovocula calmly replied, "I'm sorry, but if you did not truly believe your innocence had been stolen from you, how were we to fool everyone else into believing it too…?"

Gwendolyn drifted toward me, her striking gray eyes locking with mine as she gently cupped my face in both her hands. "I am not so weak as you think me to be, miss lady Bern. I know you tried to keep the Viscountess safe to make up for me, but I think the part of you who could *truly* use your help… is miss Rivkah."

I leaned my face into her cool hands, shutting my eyes for a moment to just feel her. She smelled of lavender. Everything did. "I do not know Rivkah," I admitted, somewhat perplexed by the suggestion.

"Demetrius had her tongue cut out," Ovocula gravely informed. "He wished to *silence* her as punishment for the Viscountess's silence. You didn't notice how she would not speak…?"

"Tell me where the Viscountess is," I said.

Gwendolyn pulled away suddenly, her fingertips gliding from my face as she and Ovocula began to recede into the white nothingness which surrounded us. "She is with miss Rivkah, my lady… and that is where we too shall be."

My heart sank. I knew there was nothing I could do to make them stay. I would soon awaken, alone in the desert. "You've never called me '*my lady*' before…"

"You are no common woman," Ovocula smiled, their forms fainter with each passing second. "Not while the Viscountess rests here with us. *Within you.*"

I awoke just then, realizing I had dozed off in the sand far from the rest of the group. The sun was down, the light from the stars and moon high above illuminating the rolling dunes far into the distance. Another light source shone several yards away from the caravan site—a fire. I turned to Carlyle's steady approach.

"Hey, is everything alright?" Carlyle asked, his voice a gentle cadence as he came upon me from behind.

I pivoted my body so that I could face him, sinking my fingers into the cool sand beneath me. He stood there before me, his appearance taking me by surprise dressed only in a simple white shirt and tattered brown pants. The gentle breeze swept through strands of his short brown hair and rustled the fabric of his clothes. He remained still, like a sturdy sculpture with both his bare feet planted firmly upon the earth.

"Yeah. I'll be fine," I replied.

"I'm not asking how you'll be. I'm asking how you are."

I winced. He was stony; unyielding. "I hate that question," I said, knowing full well that I could not escape him. "Do you know how when people say 'hi, how are you' in passing, it's like a regurgitated gesture? No one *really* wants to know how that person is doing; it's just what's polite. When I was younger and people would ask that, I would just say the 'hello' part to test whether they'd notice that I didn't answer the question. No one ever noticed. It was a telling private experiment."

I paused for a moment, dropping my gaze from him to think. My eyes fell over my slender fingers, partially buried, as I unconsciously lifted them and felt the sand grains fall, slipping from my hand. It was almost like a soft powder. I was nervous. I often fidgeted when I felt nervous.

"When people ask me how I am, for real, though," I continued, "and they don't let me get away with it… I don't know what to do."

"Tell the truth," he said.

There was suddenly a great weight in my chest to accompany my truthful admission. "I am slowly dying inside."

"Alright, we've got a chief complaint," he said, stepping toward me. He crouched down beside me, and I could feel him looking into me. I could not bring myself to look up at him as he spoke. "Now I need to deduce the mechanism of injury. Why do you feel that you are slowly dying?"

"That's a simple question with a very complex answer," I replied, my eyes welling up with tears. I kept my voice as steady as I could while I hid behind my hair. I let the braids fall over my shoulders and wreathe my face. I couldn't allow him to see me cry. "You're asking me to confront something in myself and I was going to be just fine and do that thing where I go off by myself for a while and drown out the noise in my head until I'm so sleepy that I just can't hear it anymore."

For the time being, he didn't say anything in response. He just sat there with me and allotted me time enough to collect myself, steady and calmly waiting.

"You're a very special kind of person," I said finally, after a minute of silence. "I feel cared for by you, and that means a whole lot to me. I wish I could express in words. I suppose what it boils down to is that I'm just so lonely. I'm usually okay with it. I don't know why it's so difficult for me to even say."

"Well, you have a lot of friends and acquaintances," he replied. "You seem to have an entire slew of people willing to literally bend over for you. You've reached mild fame around the continent in your pursuit of the lost gemstones. I would say that what you're looking for is something more encompassing than friendship. Recognizing what you want and pursuing it is the fastest way to initiating an escape. You tell me you're dying. I don't want to hear that. If I were to diagnose you, that would be a pretty scary answer. Do you know how we treat scary, 'priority one' distress calls?"

Finally, I found the strength to look up at him. "Tell me how," I said, glancing over his mouth, his eyes, the whole of his features resonating a stalwart resolve.

"The three miracle drugs: oxygen, fluids, fuel. This is going to sound pretty hollow, but until you find what you're looking for, you need the three. Keep breathing, remember that it's okay to cry, and get moving. You can beat this, and you don't need help doing it. The Bern I've spoken with isn't someone who can't figure herself out, she isn't someone who lays down and lets herself waste away. The person I've gotten to spend the last few evenings picking brains with is only short on a little confidence. Something she ought to have in spades."

The tears came like summer rain, streaking my cheeks as I gazed at him through glassy eyes. I smiled apologetically, my lips parting to make room for my teeth. "I can't remember the last time I let a man see me cry," I laughed.

"Crying isn't a sign of weakness," he softly smiled back. "It means you're having a healthy emotional response to something that's causing you harm. You don't need me to play life coach. Before you knew me you had everything well in hand, even if it wasn't ideal. You're shaken up because you're on the move and because you're pressured by your pursuers, and on top of all that you and I have met. There are strong feelings between us. These feelings aren't any less valid outside of a relationship. I care about you, Abernathy. Just because we aren't together doesn't mean I have not come to want the best for you."

He put his arm around me and pulled me into him. Everything was all running together now, my eyes, my nose, my mouth; an indignant reminder of why I hated crying. I was a mess of colliding emotions and every one of them were painted over my face. "The feeling is mutual, Carlyle. I want all the happiness in the world for you. I'm very lucky to have met you."

"Good, then if you want me to be happy you'll not swallow your emotions. You'll take the right lengths and the right time to heal yourself. There isn't weakness in feeling. There should never be shame in wanting, and there certainly shouldn't be guilt in longing. I want you to go to sleep smiling, because when I met you I was blown away. I want you to realize that the only thing keeping you rutted is that you're too guarded—I should know. You will learn to trust again, and then you will learn to love again. Bad experiences do not break us, they shape us. Remember? Hotter flames rear stronger steel?"

"Yeah," I said, still smiling. "I remember. Thank you."

"Good," he replied, slipping his arm out from around me and climbing to his feet. "You hadn't come back for a while when you said you were going off to be alone. People were starting to wonder if you'd fallen asleep over here or something!"

I smirked, wiping my eyes off my knuckles. "Or something."

He extended a hand to me. I hesitated a moment, looking vacantly at his empty palm before glancing up at him, confused.

"What, got a problem with my hand over my brother's?" he inquired, raising a brow.

I placed my hand in his. His palm was rough and textured like that of a fighter's, considerably larger than my own though not as large as Seth's. He pulled me to my feet. "Sorry," I said, a little embarrassed. "I thought you were handing me something. I didn't think you would be one to help me to my feet."

"It's true that Seth is more about charm and courtship than me; he did not take the same vows that I have, after all," Carlyle said. "It's also true that at one point I was guarded as you. Still am, in lots of ways. That doesn't mean I wouldn't carry you in my arms if that's what it took, and you were unable to be helped to your feet."

I walked back with him toward the caravan. Everyone was sitting around the fire with bowls in their laps; even Penny who shared Hi-Yoon's lap with a bowl had come out from hiding, stopping to look up at me for just a moment before resuming to lap up the remnants of stew that once filled it. My eyes fell over Rafe, who still would not look at me. Instead his fixation was with Carlyle who returned his gaze, both men nodding to one another as though some form of reconciliation had transpired between them in my absence.

"Welcome back, my lady," Seth greeted me with a grin. "The lovely Tigerlily made some wonderful stew for us and we saved you a bowl! You've got to be hungry by now, right?"

Tigerlily energetically sat upright from resting her head over Dragonfly's barrel chest. "Ooh! I'll fix some for ya!"

"There's no need," I said. "I'm not hungry."

"Ya really gotta eat somethin', Bern," Rafe interjected, finally turning his attention upon me. It was short-lived, as his eyes caught mine for only a mere second before he cast them down at the bowl balanced over his legs. "Gotta keep up your strength. Seth's been drawin' extracts 'round the campsite fer them potions he been makin'; maybe he has somethin' supplemental you could use?"

"Nothing in the way of meal replacements," Seth replied. "She should eat. I drew berry more n' anything else."

"You make any more trifleberry, then?" Carlyle asked.

"Yeah, a few baubles. Resources are scarce, though. They're normally pretty durable unless forcibly coming into contact with warm skin, but the

chemicals are weak in this batch. Gonna have to apply more force behind a
throw to get 'em to thermally interact and explode."

Carlyle frowned, almost irritably. "I don't know what any of that means."

"Not to worry; I follow, and am even learning a few things
accordingly!" Hi-Yoon chimed in, stroking down the back of Penny's coat
as the friendly feline nuzzled into her, finished with the bowl. "Zebadiah
is a prolific alchemist and teacher to have come up with combining such
properties to replicate the effects of the gemstones and key."

"Y'know, *Alasdair* talked about that stuff once," Kael said, his words
clumsily falling from his mouth with a drunken cadence. Everyone was silent.
I turned to look him over, an empty bottle in hand as he returned my stare
with faded expression. His eyes were glazed and distant. I wasn't sure whether
he was even looking at me or looking past me. *Through* me.

Tigerlily stood, appearing somewhat spooked. "I'll… get that bowl
filled for ya," she said, reaching over the fire pit for the pot of remaining stew.

"I said I'm not hungry," I snapped at her a little more forcefully than I
meant to. I did not tear my eyes from Kael.

"Just feed whatever's left to the horse," Dragonfly suggested. "I'm
certain the beast could stand to have a little more. We'll have quite the journey
come sunrise."

"You were always making plans for our group with him, or with
Roland," Kael said, continuing his thought. "Me n' Blythe just kinda went
along with whatever you all decided, and even mister voice of reason, Orel
himself, seemed to follow suit. I never fully understood what the big deal was
with the key or the stones. He filled me in about it when we stowed away on
board that bad man's ship on a *hopeless* rescue mission."

Tigerlily frowned. "Kael. Don't."

"Come, my lily," Dragonfly softly urged her, standing to clasp a hand
around her slender shoulder. "Let's let them catch up. It's been a while since
they've seen each other." He began to lead her away to the caravan despite her
open protest.

Hi-Yoon wrapped Penny up in her arms like a swaddled babe,
standing alongside Seth who turned to his brother.

"You should get some shut eye while you can, Car," he said with a grin.
"I want to take full advantage of this watch shift—before you change your
mind and suit up again."

Carlyle nodded, sparing me one last solemn glance for reassurance as
he took his leave with Hi-Yoon and Seth. Rafe remained, taking the pot off
the flames presumably for Mercedes. I kept my eyes on Kael, feeling my brows

involuntarily narrow with his words. I could not hide my malcontent.

"Tell me what was so hopeless about the rescue mission, Kael," I demanded, taking on a more dire tone.

"That man," Kael softly replied. "D-Demetrius? I watched him kill Alasdair. *Slowly.* I… I just don't understand why he wouldn't tell the man what he wanted to hear; why he couldn't have just told *me* everything you all discussed and not just useless bits and pieces so I could tell *for* him! Since he wouldn't!"

I could feel my heart rate rising. "It would have compromised every—"

"I don't care!" Kael shot, his glassy, droopy eyes filling with tears and spilling out over his cheeks. "I know there's plenty I don't understand, but what I do know is that *nothing* could have been worth what Alasdair went through! I'd have told the minute he started ripping out his teeth…"

I flinched back. A cold shudder ran through my spine.

"I'd have told even before that, when he bent back his fingers," Kael continued. "When he gouged his eyes later and cut off his… his…"

"It don't matter," Rafe said. "It's in the past. Now we gotta make sure what he gone through ain't in vain."

"That's just it," Kael snapped back at him, turning his listless gaze in his direction. "*None* of it matters! None of *this* matters; what we're doing, being out here and collecting some stupid stones! I have… I have *no memory* of what went on after what happened to Alasdair. Ended up in this desert with my cousin and her man, and we've been together ever since, and it's all been incredibly *pointless*. Enjoyable, generally speaking, but pointless. And now I'm out of booze."

"The stones mean the restoration of the entire planet, Kael," I anxiously replied. "We can't just give this up when we've come so far."

"At whose expense?" he quietly asked. His voice was a hoarse whisper. "Alasdair's? When Demetrius was through with him, he made a shallow slit in his neck and let him choke on his own blood for a while—before almost severing his head completely. At Roland's expense, maybe? He beat him half to death and then had him thrown off the side of the ship. Or maybe he did it himself, I don't know."

"Roland may have had a stone on him at the time," I said. "If Demetrius didn't discover it on him and seize it, first."

"So what?" Kael asked, chucking his empty bottle to the dying flames.

I cast a sidelong glance to Rafe, discouraged, who returned my look with a sympathetic nod. It was a simple acknowledgment, but it was what I needed. "The stones can slow down the descent of a carrier whose sun sign –

in astrology – correlates with the stone on hand. Roland could still be alive somewhere. He kept it from us for all this time. We'll know for sure when we find him, or Demetrius's body."

There was a long pause before Kael spoke again. "All Mother; I need another drink," he exclaimed, climbing to his feet on unsteady legs and ambling off without another word.

Rafe had also stood and made his way toward me. He stopped in front of me and gave me the longest look he'd ever given me. His eyes were soft. "Life is really scary sometimes baby doll," he said, his voice sweet. "I live it everyday too. But you're strong and beautiful and aimed. You're gonna change the world, even if it's just someone you care about. You're gonna be great. You don't even know yourself how great you're gonna be."

He allotted me one final nod. Then he left me there to ponder.

CHAPTER 26
Attack on Fyndridge

"This might have come in handy forty some odd hours ago," I griped, awkwardly holding the clunky wooden longbow much larger than I was used to.

Dragonfly knelt beside me, readying his sleeker, wieldier crossbow to be loaded up and poised for our first clear shot upon Rafe's signal. "It's only as handy as you are good with it," he responded, returning me with a sidelong glance.

I continued to fumble with the bow. "I'd be much handier with something not quite so large. This bow is built for bigger people. You're big. Why can't you just let me use the crossbow?"

"Same reason Tigerlily's old boyfriend won't let you use his rifle," he replied. "That's my backup bow. I'm *allowing* you to borrow it. I don't know you too good yet, 'cept what little Kael's told me about you. If your shooting's as sharp as he's said it is, it won't be that much of a problem."

I grimaced a moment before speaking again, picking up on Dragonfly's strange addressing of Rafe. "Tigerlily's... old boyfriend...?"

"She says it wasn't like that," he sighed. "I guess it probably wasn't. He's much too old for her, anyway. Still. There's always been something up with their friendship. It used to make me feel kinda uneasy, in a way. I guess jealous."

"I suppose I know what you mean," I muttered.

I looked out into the distance where the outer walls of Fyndridge met with the stars, just barely seen over the scale of a sand dune obstructing most of the view. We each laid low, Rafe a bit of a ways in front of us. I could scarcely make out his gloved fingers along the trigger of his gun. Unseen to us was Hi-Yoon. I knew he was watching her intently as she advanced on the wall, cloaked by the dusk of early morn.

"What ever did your ex do to get you to love him?" Dragonfly inquired, his question catching me a bit off guard.

I recovered swiftly. "He made a bunch of mouth noises at me that sounded pretty. And then I believed them to be so."

"Ah, he spoke *lies* to you," he said. "Do you know how I got Tigerlily to love me? I gave her what I said I would. I followed up. You should always have reason to trust someone before you take them on their word."

"I imagine that she didn't trust you at first," I replied, somewhat resentful of his insinuation that I was naïve, however indirect it might have been.

He smiled, perhaps proudly. "I can only imagine the courage it took her, for in our tribe she is what's known as *two-spirit*."

I had no idea what he meant. "Why would she need courage for that?" I asked.

"She is a special kind of spirit. It is part of what drew me to her. There are people in this world who don't like what's special, and rare. A better question might be – why do people hate?"

"Because they're bigots and they don't even know it," I replied flatly.

My mind trailed back to the Viscountess in me; how an aristocratic society of privilege far removed from famine and despair had shaped the sheltered girl into a woman filled with fears and prejudices, a sense of entitlement that I too fed off of in wake of my time spent in her body, inhabiting her consciousness. It was not until I was able to really look at myself—at *her*—that I managed to overcome it.

"There! That's the signal!" Dragonfly exclaimed, reaching around the quiver to his back to retrieve a single bolt which he proceeded to load up into his crossbow.

I followed his eyes to Rafe far ahead, his arm extended high into the air as he balanced his rifle on his opposite shoulder. He did not look back at us, slowly lowering his raised arm to fall about the firearm in preparation to shoot. Hurriedly, I reached around the quiver on my own back to snatch up a couple of arrows. I held them each between my knuckles as I struggled against the draw weight of the bow. My eyes danced all along the outer wall of Fyndridge, scanning for signs of movement from patrolling guards. I wondered what Rafe was seeing that I was not, but whatever it was, Dragonfly seemed to see it too. My anxiety built in my chest.

Suddenly what looked to be Hi-Yoon's silky garments began to flutter up the wall as she scaled it with shocking precision. I was startled by the sound of Rafe's rifle which followed, the light from the blast exploding into the air high above – the signal.

My arms quaked as I held back the string of the bow, pressing the backs of the two arrows into it with all my might. I shakily lined up my shot with a number of guards who suddenly began to spill out from around the side of the wall where the gate entrance stood – the other way in. They headed toward Rafe, who stood in plain view. Just as Hi-Yoon disappeared over the other side of the wall, Dragonfly loosed a bolt into the nearest approaching guard. It flew past Rafe and struck the man's shoulder. I steadied the string against my cheek and felt it whip into my skin as I let my two arrows fly. Only one hit its intended mark, pinning a guard's leg into the ground as he was forced to take a knee. The other zipped past him unseen through the darkness.

Rafe used the butt of his rifle like a bludgeon against the tagged men, beating them to the ground. As he made short work of our marks, Carlyle and Seth jumped into view from behind four guards who remained standing, each of the brothers shield-bashing one man apiece. Seth smashed a trifleberry into another guard's face, knocking his cap from his head. As I fumbled to reload the longbow I continued to struggle with, Dragonfly had already loaded another bolt into his crossbow and fired it off, successfully disabling the final guard with a penetrative shot to his weapon arm. He dropped whatever object he had wound back to strike with, the glint of a blade flashing before falling to the sand. He agonizingly crumpled with the rest of the defeated guardsmen, but not long after Rafe had knocked him out with another one of his cracks upside the head, compliments of his rifle.

Carlyle held up his shield with a look of agitation contorting his features. My arrow was stuck in its surface, a little off from the center. "So which one of you is trying to kill me, the desert chieftain or the warrior princess?"

I swiveled the bow around my back to meet with my quiver and tried not to look so distraught. I couldn't help but to scowl, both mortified and somewhat indignant. "I told him to let me use the crossbow," I grumbled, closing the distance with an anxious stride.

Dragonfly steadily followed alongside me. "Maybe you ought to just stick to using your powers from here on."

"No!" Seth barked. "We've been over this. It's too risky."

Rafe stepped up to the one conscious guard who had been struck with Seth's trifleberry. He knelt down in front of him as he writhed and moaned, unable to stand. "How much time do we have on this thing?"

"Hard to say," Seth replied. "The batch was weak. Usually not much more than a minute or two."

"Better make this quick," Carlyle barked, snapping the lodged arrow in half and pulling it from his shield. "This guy's fiancée and that little alcoholic should have slipped through the gate by now."

"How many more'a you we gotta deal with?" Rafe demanded, staring the guard down.

"S-Six others on duty right now," the man replied.

"Where they at?" Rafe snarled, his usual slow southern drawl all but lost for the time being.

I thought about what it could mean for him if something had happened to Tigerlily in there, while we lingered out here. He was not the calm and collected man I first met; not in this moment where stakes had run high.

"Two… went to w-warn the others…" the guard stammered. "Went to w-wake the men off duty a-a-and tell… the Governor… Others patrolling th-the other side of t-town…"

My heart skipped, then dropped at his mentioning of the Governor.

"Let's hope Hi-Yoon got to them first," Seth grimaced.

"Was a loud shot," Carlyle darkly frowned. "I'd be surprised if every man, woman, and child in Fyndridge wasn't awake by now and wondering what the All Mother above is going on."

"No," Rafe said, rising to his feet as he slammed the butt of his rifle into the guard's temple, knocking him unconscious too. "The sound ain't gonna carry that much farther back through town. I know where the Governor sleeps."

"Me too," I added. My blood ran both hot and cold.

Dragonfly was the first to break into a sprint. "Come," his deep voice carried. "Let's hurry."

My boots pumped loose sand to funnel up around my knees as I had broken out into full tilt movement. My braids lifted from my back as I ran, head down, following closely behind Dragonfly as I watched his footwraps blur with sweeping dust. I heard the sound of metal links collide and clunky armor thud as Rafe and Carlyle kept pace at my backside, a quieter, lesser outfitted Seth coming up on my flank. We each moved with an efficiency that should not have surprised me; these were highly trained, seasoned men after all. When we reached the gate entrance, Hi-Yoon was there to greet us. A felled guard lay at her feet whose body served as a makeshift doorstop.

"Tigerlily and Kael are on their way to find the one called Blythe," she calmly stated. Her hair was just as perfect as ever, the veil over her eyes intact, the folds in her dress uncreased.

"Good… ya took care of one'a the guards," Rafe spoke. He sounded somewhat winded. "That means they still got—"

"Five more after this one," Hi-Yoon interrupted him, her small red lips curling into a subtle smile. "I took care of them. No one else seems to be aware of our presence. Should a townsperson have awoken to the sound of your gunshot, not a one of them seem to have cared. None of the lights in the buildings have come on. Not for a fleeting moment!"

"How do you even know that?" Carlyle blinked, completely aghast.

Hi-Yoon's smile tilted into a crescent grin. "These old eyes of mine no longer see, and yet still they are able to detect changes in the light around my person; part of why I wear this sheer veil. I find it serves to facilitate that for me. I am uncertain as to why. Perhaps when we find this Doctor Orel Fischer, he might be able to—"

"Oh, All Mother," I gaped, slowly stepping over the guard wedged against the gate bars as I ducked around and into the town looking straight ahead.

My path was illuminated by the torches from overhead, all along the inner wall. It was there that I saw it—scattered about the ground and building rooftops, the debris from a plummeted ship that would never again sail—the S.S. Beulah. I continued to walk, the liquid fire that coursed through my veins to ignite my resolve now turned to ice, freezing my lungs. Every drawn breath was sharp like an icicle penetrating the snow of my heart. I knew the others had realized something was amiss as well, even Hi-Yoon, whose awareness of her surroundings relied solely on her hearing and what I now knew to be a presence of light.

I barely became aware of a light source of my own as it slowly expanded from my chest, my gemstone brooch, growing ever larger like an aura to encapsulate me and carry me forward. I clutched the brooch tightly. My pace steadily quickened as I passed by concaved roof after collapsed wall, each structure fallen under the weight of ship breakage in greater concentrations. I passed scattered remnants of barrel and twisted metal, stepped over what was left of a captain's wheel and a crudely painted letter 'S' over splintered wood, all that remained of Beulah's terrible honorific. I wondered whether my allies still followed behind me as I approached the Rogue Musket, the tallest building in Fyndridge discounting an abode of the Governor himself. The light from my brooch pulsed, starting up a faint buzzing in my head.

Rafe's gloved hand abruptly came down around my shoulder, startling me out of an apparent trance. "You are not the detective here," he warned under hushed tone, tearing my attention away from the Rogue Musket. "Do *not* go in there. You leave this part to me, n' Hi-Yoon'll escort ya to Blythe.

Tigerlily n' Kael woulda found 'im by now!"

The light around me pulsed again and again. The buzzing grew louder, like a sharp static.

"My lady," Hi-Yoon said, coming up beside me and taking hold of my wrist. It was the first time I'd heard a sense of urgency in her voice. "Let's let these gentlemen handle this one. We are needed elsewhere."

I had no idea what either one of them were on about. As the static buzzing continued to grow in volume and became more jarring, my eyes trailed downward to rest over what looked to be a silvery cigar case strewn on the ground. A lone cigar had fallen out of it; that familiar brand of cigar which resembled the mark of my noble birthright decorating its paper sleeve – that four-pointed star within a diamond, the curved line running through it. I touched a hand to the back of my neck, my brows narrowing with outrage.

"I thought he'd quit a long time ago," I said softly.

Carlyle and Seth each stepped forward, shields raised as they cautiously inched toward the tavern door. The light was engulfing everything. The ringing white noise was becoming deafening.

"Go, Bern," I could barely hear Carlyle say as he turned back to me. "Go help your friend. We've got this."

Got what? I gritted. They were all acting strangely. I had to find out what this was. I wrenched my arm free of Hi-Yoon's grasp and elbowed my way past Rafe. I acted as a battering ram, shoving past the brothers and barreling through the door. The light flashed.

My hand was weighted with the handset of a radio transceiver balanced over my palm, its cord coiling around my back to connect to the heavy box casing harnessed to me, as I stood with confusion in a grungy hallway. It screeched with electronic static as the distortion of a man's voice came through the line. Demetrius stood before me, his metal arm wrapped tightly around my uncle's neck from behind. Gone was his cloak as he stared me down, covered head to toe in his ugly burns now bare for all to see. His grin was as gnarled and twisted as the healed flesh stretched across his tall, muscular form. Blood poured from my uncle's broken nose as he swayed unsteadily over his knees, his greasy hair once slicked back now falling all about his visibly distressed face.

"Answer it," Demetrius glowered.

CHAPTER 27
The Grey Matter In Between

There's this dream I sometimes have, an out of body experience as I watch myself playing with little dolls made of glass and porcelain. I am four in this dream, and it is just after the exact moment upon which my cognitive awareness had been conceived. It is the earliest memory I have as the day I became Bern, post-gift opening and pre-celebration of the birth of a young Viscountess. I watch intently like a spider on a corner of the ceiling. The young girl is immaculate: rosy cheeks, big honey brown eyes, fiery red curls in a crown of controlled chaos that gently cascades around her slight, ivory shoulders. Her floral pattern dress is neat and though she lay on her knees with the palms of her tiny hands pressed to the waxed wood floor, she is poised as can be. Even after my uncle pressed a lit cigar into her neck, the ashy crater it had left would not be enough to break that poise. Not while she was paralyzed with the pain.

I remember how startling the sensation had been, like awakening from a daydream of peaceful reverie to the sudden sting of a hornet. It was almost as if my feelings were hurt before I was, the shock of pain triggering an emotional response first that only then grew with the lingering pulse of burning agony. When I would fall and scrape my knees my mother would tell me how sorry she was, wrapping me up and cradling me in her arms. It was nothing she had done wrong; no matter how attentive a parent is, they are powerless to stop *every* ache, *every* prick of pain. Looking back, it isn't difficult for me to see how 'sorry' worked so well to alleviate whatever self-inflicted harm I had gotten myself into. I felt my mother's sincerity. I felt her desire to take all that ailed me and wash it all away in her love. *I'm so sorry you're hurt,* she would say, and with that I would be cured. Even if the physical pain took longer to subside, it made the wait that much less difficult to endure.

"Nigger cunt," my uncle spat, slipping the cigar he had just used to burn me with back into the corner of his mouth.

He leaned back in his armchair while my young, underdeveloped mind processed what he just did to me; what he just said to me. I understood what neither word meant, nor how they applied to my person, but I understood at that tender age the hatred with which he spewed. It was ugly and vicious, two words which might as well have been one wherein the fragile mind of a child knows not a collection of syllables from another. Loud, sudden noises frightened me. A soft resonance like floorboards creaking under the weight of stealthy footfalls to cut through the quiet of night frightened me more. My back was turned to my uncle when he burned me, so I wasn't sure whether he was even the source of my pain at first, but somehow I knew it with the three syllables he spoke; that dark and sickly rasp with a spit to it that ripped the silence.

"Here I am. *Stuck* here keeping an eye on you while Amadeus is probably sticking it right now to your whore mum," he dripped with disdain, my eyes fixed on the top of his head and his thinning, graying, slicked back hair as I hovered undetected. "I tried so hard. Did everything I could. Rose should have been *mine* and you should not exist. Amadeus takes *everything* from me."

I stole a quick glance at myself; the little Viscountess beneath me. She was so silent, not even a whimper as her body quaked. I remember the fear.

"Mother always liked him best," he continued venomously. "I was her son. Her *first—son—*! Amadeus had everything handed to him while I worked so hard just to keep my head above water. All that effort I put in for Rose, and she barely acknowledged my affections… How difficult it is to find roses in full bloom in these dark times, much less keep one alive long enough… Gave her one every day for a week, left on her pillow, in her mandolin, within the binding of one of those damned insipid romance novels she reads…"

His words trailed off. The girl once paralyzed began sniffling and trembling, flooding back into my mind a sea of memories of when she used to be me as I watched them both from above.

"…But, it's no matter," he muttered darkly, seeming not to notice beyond his raving rant. "She's just another one of *them* anyway, and even if you are my little brother's daughter, you're *hers* just as well. If I'd been born in my father's time I could just take her if I wanted. I'd buy her up and then she would be mine and I wouldn't need any *fucking flowers* for her to just ignore anyway."

He stood from his armchair, towering over the trembling child I once was, raising a hand to the cigar in his mouth to take a deep drag before letting out a cloud of smoke. I remembered this so vividly, the dream a mere wrinkle in time for an actual occurrence in my life I'd do my best to bury away. He stepped toward the girl and dropped the cigar over her so that it landed just in front of her, smoke still rolling. I remembered watching the still-burning embers skip off the smooth surface of the floor as it connected, although I could not clearly see it now from the ceiling.

"I don't know why your parents continue this charade. It's not as if they could ever be wed, even if the war had never happened at all and we weren't left in the situation we're in now. Someone of your kind, a blood noble. The very notion turns my stomach."

I became aware of a door somewhere only after it had swung open, letting in a gust of air. A stout bespectacled woman, short in stature, began making her approach. My uncle stepped over me to raise a foot above the cigar. He hastily stamped out the ashes with his fine black leather loafers.

"Acanthus, my darling," the woman cooed as she came up beside him and wrapped her pillowy arms around his thin neck, an awkward display given their stark difference in height. "We're about to begin the celebration! I was sent to gather you up with the birthday girl!"

My uncle shrugged her off him, visibly uncomfortable with her contact. "Madame Beatrice," he greeted her, clearing his throat.

"Just Beatrice, please," she eagerly, almost desperately replied. "Or Bea!"

"…Beatrice," he conceded. "Please, give me a few moments if you will; the *birthday girl* got into my cigar box and decided to play with one like she does with her little dolls. She burned herself."

"She what?!" Madame Beatrice showily exclaimed, her voice rising. "You mean it was lit? How did she manage to *light* it…?"

My uncle paused. "She… Never mind that," he flushed. "You have such lovely eyes, my dear."

Madame Beatrice gasped with delight. "Oh, Acanthas—" she started, longingly moving in on him again for another affectionate embrace.

He stepped around the child, evasively. "Um. If you could be so kind as to *use* those lovely eyes to find an ointment for her; surely we must have something. I wouldn't want Amadeus to think I'd been negligent, it just, it happened so quickly you see!"

"Oh," Madame Beatrice sighed. "Yes, yes. I shall see to it at once." She

turned on her heel to see her way back out. "And before I forget! When I was
laying out the silverware and arranging the seating for tonight's meal, I placed
you next to me! You'll know where because I put down your handkerchief!"

Even from my space on the ceiling I could feel my uncle's cringe.
"Thank you," he called after her, and then she was gone. His attention from
there resumed on the girl. It is then that my dream cut off. I normally find
myself awake and confused and horribly distraught.

Just as my mind had trailed to a memory of a dream of a memory, it
also brought me back to the brink of a psychological break; the reality of my
time spent on Demetrius's ship where he had locked the Viscountess in me
away. I remember where I was that it happened, transported from the desert to
the ship's holding cell I would then break out of, laying siege to the ship and
conquering all in my wake. I would face Beulah herself, defeating her, aiming
to choke the life from her body before I would be wrenched back from that of
the Viscountess, whose body I commandeered for the duration of that time.

The Viscountess would not be successful in finishing what I'd started,
but my efforts to save her would not be in vain. On one of a great many days
and nights I spent locked in chains, some in a white jacket which forced
my arms to hug around myself, I would overhear a conversation take place
between my uncle and Orel much like the one they had that would send me
back through the portal between worlds. I would learn more about myself in
this exchange than any other time before it…

"I need you to disclose to me *everything*, Doctor Fischer," I heard my
uncle's voice, distorted only slightly through the vent of the padded room that
had become my home. "You know that Demetrius was an old patient of mine
for many years… He locked you both away while he and his hooligans ran
amok. You were caged up with her for the better part of a day, and I want to
know what you observed…"

"Observed…?" came the shaky voice of Orel.

"What did she *do* while you were alone with her?" my uncle barked.
"What did she tell you?!"

"She… She talked to herself, sir. She spoke back and forth, as if she
were more than a single person. I thought it was just one other at first, but it
seems that she's taken on many different personalities at once! It was startling.
I… I wasn't sure what to believe; whether she was acting out, or if she really
did feel there were others simultaneously residing within her."

"Not simultaneously," my uncle replied. "Usually, that is. I've discovered
in my sessions counseling her that she takes on these personas, one at a time,
as a means of *hiding* herself all the while dealing with a situation which causes

her stress. I've had most success in speaking with her while she is pretending to be another girl; Ovocula, she calls herself. Though, never have I witnessed her taking them *all* on at once. She's grown to be quite the little performer."

"There's... more..." Orel strained. "She was a-able to convince Blythe to release her; each p-personality she displayed to him at once."

"Blythe...?" my uncle inquired. "He evaded capture? What was he doing outside of Fyndridge to begin with?"

"He was assisting Kael, s-sir. Kael and Alasdair."

There was a pause. Even through the vents I knew my uncle must have been scowling now as I listened intently with bated breath.

"They should not have stowed away into Galvinsglade," he weightily sighed. "They should not have breeched security with Demetrius and his... riffraff."

"Sir?"

"...She should not have escaped."

With a loud and sudden bang which pierced only my right ear, I was delivered from my memories and returned to the present. The transceiver continued to spark and fizzle with radio interference, reverberating against my back as I carried it around my person.

"*Answer* it!" Demetrius shouted, repeating himself.

A rain of ceiling plaster fell over his broad, scar-burned shoulders as Beulah stepped around from behind him with a smoking gun; Gertie's pistol, 'Susan.'

She did not appear how she had when I faced her the time I laid waste to Demetrius's followers, sky pirates and asylum orderlies alike, spanning both realities I had come to know. When I had broken the Viscountess out of captivity as well as Gwendolyn, Ovocula, and Rivkah, the castlelark witch had smooth skin like ebony. She had plump lips and a wide button nose, brow ridge absent of hair over her violet, catlike eyes. Her strong bones were all the more prominent than if she had any hair at all, but then, she was bald with not so much as a lash from her lids. The only part of her visage that remained the same was the round curvature of her body, visibly flabby in the absence of her rich, flowing robes replaced now by the scrubs of an orderly.

The skin on her arms, now a pale ivory, faintly drooped as she kept one raised to point the gun toward the ceiling, the other bending elbow outward so that her free hand rested comfortably over her hip. Her once plush, full lips were thin and pursed tight in a slight frown that seemed to make up the features of her face at rest. Her sandy brunette hair was thin and lifeless in straight strands down her back, with thinning brows to match. I imagined she had the kind of face which prompted whomever had been caught in her stare to build a dam around their thoughts, that her stream of contemptuous judgment could not flow in. In general, her face fought a losing battle with gravity much the same as her body, her pasty sagging features showing signs of age to compliment hateful abandon.

I raised the handset of the transceiver to my lips which quivered with anticipation, the looping cord stretching to accommodate me as I swallowed hard, barely able to think much less comprehend the situation. "H-Hello…?" I stammered, tense and resentfully shaken.

The static interference dropped, then picked up again as the man's voice came through more clearly now. Though straining my good ear to hear him, his voice was finally recognizable as belonging to Orel. "B…ern…?" he said, his transmission broken up by the persisting white noise. "I'm trapped… the Rogue Musk—… downstair—… *help!* Don't come… all cra—… *all* of them!"

"What?!" I pleaded. "I can't… I can't *understand* you! Orel?!"

More static. "Tell Detecti—… Edge—… *they're all crazy!* Don't…"

His voice was completely drowned out now, lost in an electrical void. I turned helplessly to my companions, but my eyes met only with Rafe's, however brief his quick glance was with his rifle aimed steadily at our three adversaries. Beyond him, the banging of a metal door which could only have been Carlyle and Seth on the other side. I realized it must have locked behind us—if we had even truly used it to begin with.

"Don't even think of opening that door," Beulah said, regaining my attention as she clicked back the hammer of the pistol and pointed it toward me. "Bullets are harder to come by than the firearms that shoot them *or…* decent footwear." She let her eyes drop to my feet for a moment which caused me to shift uncomfortably. "I've already wasted one bullet as it is, just getting you to pay proper attention to *my love* when he's speaking to you. I suspect that's part of why he left you for me."

"Because you're bad at managing valuable resources?" I dryly remarked. "I can see the connection; he's bad at that, too. Incidentally, I think I'm beginning to realize my self-worth."

Beulah scowled. "In ragged clothes like those? I can only guess how many consecutive days you've worn that *poodle skirt* without a wash. At least you haven't soiled yourself this time… otherwise I'd be smelling you from here. And *that hair!*"

I glanced down at myself, realizing I was back in the clothes Orel had given me to make my escape in, the shoes a half size too small now broken in by constant wear, the hideous embroidered beast along the hemline of my large, poofy skirt, and the same buttoned blouse, though missing a couple of buttons and torn in places much like the skirt which shown through bits of petticoat underneath. The whole length of my body was splotched in dirt from time spent battling the elements while on the run.

"You know, I really didn't take you for the fashionable type," she continued, crossing in front of Demetrius and my uncle as she spoke. She kept the pistol pointed straight at my chest. I could sense Rafe's tension from behind me, though further back, the frantic banging on the metal door had ceased. "I suppose you thought deviating from your mother's hand-me-downs would've helped you to *blend in* better with the hipper, younger, *whiter* girls."

"We got more coppers on the way," Rafe warned, finally speaking up. "Our boys outside are lookin' for another way inside as we speak. I may not be able to let 'em in with you pointin' that little piece at me, lady, but mine's bigger. What're you thinkin' this is gonna do to you when I pull my trigger? With you lined up, I can waste you *and* that deranged monster behind ya usin' one bullet—if y'all wanna talk managin' resources."

"Set that rifle down, detective," Demetrius snarled from around Beulah. "It would take less than a second for me to twist the old shrink's neck until I hear the pop."

"*Do* it," I urged darkly.

Rafe stood, aghast. "What in the—?"

I took a step forward, closing some of the distance between myself and Beulah for a moment before she flinched, taking a couple steps back.

"You should do it; I want you to," I repeated, feeling strangely detached. Though I could not see his expression from behind Beulah, I felt my uncle's anxiousness mounting with my words. "I already know about how he conspired with you; how you worked with him to make me into his little psychology test subject. These walls are thin; either you didn't know that, or you didn't care enough about it. Perhaps you just assumed I was *too crazy* to understand what was happening to me, like I wouldn't figure it out later, given enough time. You aren't manipulating me any more. *Neither* of you."

"Shut *up*," Beulah spat. Her arm began to tremble slightly. "You're just a mental patient here, now. You don't know as much as you'd like to think you do."

"Bern, don't," Rafe pleaded, trying to gather my attention. I didn't care. I wasn't in the mood to play it careful anymore.

"He battered me," I snarled. "He put me in a cage, and he broke Doctor Fischer's arms, and blackened his eyes, and locked him up right alongside me. He did these things, and my uncle condoned it. Now you've got the doctor locked in the cellar with all the medicines, and *I'm* the crazy one? What about when the patients need their prescriptions; is that when you intend to let him out of there?!" I was nearly shouting by this point.

"Bern!" Rafe interjected, forceful in his tone.

I continued, ignoring him once more. "Now *you're* being manipulated, Beulah; though not by much, I'd imagine, since you delight in the suffering of those under your care. Still, manipulated enough that he's influenced you to wear a *wig* to hide your *shameful* disease."

Another deafening bang rang through my right ear as Beulah pulled the pistol trigger. I felt my heart spike painfully in my chest as the bullet pierced into me, drilling my breast and out through my back, undoubtedly damaging the casing of the radio transceiver. I did not feel my body collapse into a crumpled heap on the floor. The last thing I saw before I blacked out was Rafe as he stepped over me before staggering backward with the kickback from his rifle blast.

CHAPTER 28
Black & White

In much the same way Lyn and Ovocula had come to me by infinite void flushed all in white as if we were paint splotches on blank canvas, so had a woman of lean stature and caramel mocha skin, the bouncy black waves in her hair recognizable as belonging only to Rivkah. She came to me in corduroy overalls, tidy and crisp in the absence of soot from the coals she was purportedly always covered in from her work aboard our father's ship, the Wild Rose.

"I don't think you should be in charge anymore; you're too biased," Rivkah stated very simply and without pause for thought. She sounded self-assured in her diction. Her voice was like mine.

"Biased how?" I inquired, my once assertive tone wavering in conjunction with my disposition. "In what way?"

"Beulah was never black," she informatively spoke. "And it's interesting to me that you had to make yourself *white* just so that the Viscountess could have a *safe space* for her to feel superior to everyone else!"

I didn't understand her. "Wha-What are you—?"

"Everyone else, when they see you, what they see is *me*. So why can't you see me too?" she sighed.

"I-I don't even *know* you," I shot, defensively. "I only met you just once on Demetrius's ship when I broke you and the others out of his imprisonment!"

"Bern," she continued, "you were born so that we could all be strong. The Viscountess was born of us *all*; after Lyn had to be masked and hidden away… You've never known me because I've been buried beneath every one of you! You aren't even consciously aware of the *shame* ingrained in you, that's how bad it is."

"Shame…?" I repeated.

Rivkah's deep honey brown eyes shone the weariness of a vagabond in rags uplifting the wealthiest of kingships. "I worked aboard the *Cap'n's* ship, our father's vessel. I got my hands dirty for him, for our way of life, and the whole time I'd been drawing out plans of my own for building *my own* ship; my own way apart from the sheltering confinement of the parents who worked to protect us from the oppressive nature of the world. I didn't *want* to be sheltered any more. And I don't want to be stuck playing this circle charade any longer, either, with all of you."

I wasn't sure how to feel with her words. "When I met you before, you spoke not a word to me…"

"How could I?" she said with weighty regard. "Demetrius had silenced me. And before that, you had come to replace me, then Lyn, and then Ovocula. None of you *ever* spoke to me; just amongst yourselves, until the Viscountess came along. She was the one who acknowledged me in the beginning."

"I'm sorry," I resignedly shrugged. "I want… *integration*. What can I do to help?"

"I want you to understand that when and if that happens, it won't be the each of us being absorbed by you, but you being absorbed by *me*, and I want you to be okay with that. We all inhabit one body, Bern. We each have our own memories apart from one another, and different perspectives because of this… but as our thoughts become one, that body will be mine. It's the only one we have. Those outside of us might never accept that, but what chance do any of us have if even to you, white means good and black means bad? We are one half our mother… and she was *beautiful*."

I felt a deep heaviness take me. "Why…? Why did she have to die…?"

"You *know* why," Rivkah answered, sorrow concluding her words. "She was the wrong color in the wrong place."

I awoke.

I awoke looking down at myself, my pastel blouse drenched red with my own blood as I lay in Rafe's arms, tanned by the sun. His skin played stark contrast to my own, much darker in shade as my arms lay limp at my sides while he held me close. The left side of my head rested on his shoulder in the backseat of a Mercedes speeding down the road with its red headlights blaring in the night. Carlyle had taken the wheel in the front seat beside his brother who frantically directed him. Though they shouted at each other, and occasionally Rafe too, their voices were faraway in my state of delirium.

Hi-Yoon's ivory hand reached over me to tap at Rafe's forearm. It was only then that I became aware of her presence in the vehicle, to my right, and Penny's too, perched over her lap. I somehow knew intuitively that she was trying to get Rafe's attention, having seen that I had stirred from my slumber. I could not move my head to look at her. I could not feel much of anything. I was *so* very tired.

"Quiet!" Rafe shouted over the calamity of the brothers that he himself had been a part of just moments before. "She's awake. God almighty!"

All Mother almighty, I thought to myself.

"You holdin' up alright, darlin'?" Rafe asked almost pleadingly, his southern drawl shaken by the vibrations of his Mercedes speeding along the road, or perhaps his own shot nerves. He raised his gloved hand in front of my face. "How many fingers I got up?"

I saw three fingers. "Forty-two," I said.

"You're just bein' ridiculous, now," he replied, his body relaxing against me slightly. I realized then how tense he had been.

"Ridic... ulous...?" I wheezed. "Or cr-crazy?"

"She should not be straining herself to speak," Hi-Yoon scolded. "Stop encouraging her!"

"Uh'm okay," I reassured. I suspected my words would not be convincing.

"I never once thought you was crazy, little girl," he soothed, brushing a couple of braids back from my face. For once I took comfort in the fatherly manner in which he addressed me.

"Not... so little..." I said, breathlessly. "Uh'm all... fuh—... fully grown...!"

"Turn left up here," I heard Seth say from the front passenger seat.

I felt lightheaded and dizzy. "Where... we goin'...?"

"Carlyle's takin' you to a hospital," Rafe replied, his voice soft as if trying to get me to lower the volume of mine as well. "They're gonna take real good care'a you."

Carlyle said nothing in response or acknowledgment, seeming focused on the road in front of him. I felt the car turn sharply, shifting my placement a bit on Rafe's shoulder.

"Every time you blink, your eyelashes beat against my neck," Rafe said, changing the subject.

I was too tired to push for more information right then. I began fluttering my lashes, rapidly opening and closing my eyes. He rewarded me with a light chuckle to my satisfaction, and kissed the top of my head. I smiled weakly as I began to feel myself drifting.

Suddenly Hi-Yoon began snapping her fingers in front of my face. "No, no, no, no!" she shouted. "You cannot fall back asleep! You need to stay with us."

"Th-There's no way... H'yoon is... really blind..." I agitatedly murmured.

"Maybe she *oughta* be talkin' right now," Rafe said. "Tell me about them stones again, sweetheart. How many we got now?"

I felt a twinge of pain in my chest, separate from whatever pain I might have felt from the entry point of the bullet, or the exit wound in my backside. "D-Does Orel still have his...?" I sputtered. "He used it to call me..."

"That big ol' clunky radio set you been luggin' arou—?"

"Yes," Hi-Yoon interrupted him. "Yes, Doctor Fischer still has it."

I was beginning to doubt my own powers, and the legend of the Castle in the Sky altogether. My skin was dark, like Rivkah's. Just as much as the Viscountess had been a manifestation of us all, Rivkah was all of me.

"The others have your friend," Hi-Yoon continued. "The rest of the patients are being taken into protective custody by Rafe's department, from both asylums. A few arrests were made, your uncle included."

"Wha—... What of... D-Demetrius...?" I strained.

The car came to an abrupt stop. Both Seth and Carlyle flung their doors open, Seth rushing into the building we pulled up in front of while Carlyle circled back to whip open the passenger door on Rafe's side.

"Pass her off to me," he commanded, seeming to forget himself in the dire urgency of his diction. As my gaze wandered toward him, I realized his full attention was just on me, his own lightly tanned skin splotched with blood, indicative that he had helped transport me once before. "Seth's getting some hospital personnel out here to help us, but it might just be best to meet 'em halfway."

I felt Rafe struggle to lift me up around the waist, moving me over his body with tentative care like an oversized porcelain doll. I had bled all over him by now. I felt Hi-Yoon's soft hands around my calves, assisting in getting me into Carlyle's strong arms.

"Phew," Rafe exhaled. "I'm gettin' old for all this."

Carlyle gathered me up as a babe in a cradle, curling my deadweight body so that my bottom drooped lower than my legs or head, one of his arms wrapped under the back of my knees while the other supported my neck. He walked hurriedly, but steady; much steadier than Roland had carried the Viscountess in me through the Fyndridge mines the last time she, or I, had been injured—distant memories, though foggy, I now had to my recollection. I could feel my skirt billowing with his stoic stride, but I was far too weak to feel the shame of immodesty on top of my sordid state.

"I… n-never cared much for dresses…" I wheezed pathetically.

"You'll have dozens of years ahead of you to continue not caring for dresses," Carlyle curtly replied.

I heard the rattling of metal over concrete and the drumming of footsteps upon the pavement growing louder. "Here! Put 'er on here!" I heard a husky voice say. Before I knew what was happening, Carlyle had stopped abruptly and with one swift motion, had set me down over some kind of bed on wheels. As I looked up, I briefly caught a glimpse of Seth's face among several others; dark complexions all around me, each man or woman dressed in starkly contrasting white uniform scrubs.

"We need to get an IV in 'er, lickety-split. She's gonna need at least four blood transfusions," one of them said.

"Where's Doctor Fischer?" inquired another as I felt the bed begin to move, my view of the night sky from laying on my back quickly transforming to white ceiling panels as the hospital personnel crossed the threshold into the building.

"He came from where she come from," a particularly dark-skinned woman replied whose scrubs had 'Nurse' stitched into the breast pocket, which I was glad to find that I was able to read. "They all just gettin' in from one of them LaCroix funny farms. They been herdin' 'em in like cock-eyed sheep!"

"Word has it they neglect their patients," one woman of similar complexion responded. "Treated bedsores the size of your head from at least a couple of them coming here."

"This is Count Amadeus LaCroix's daughter," I heard Seth say, warningly.

"That rich white man from overseas?" the first woman gasped. "The man who done run them places before…?"

I grew agitated by how they carried on as if I were not even there, but by this point it was a struggle simply staying conscious much less speaking another word.

"They all from outta country," a man chimed in. "At least the father's side. Never seen what she look like before; don't think they ever run her pit'cher in the paper. I ain't never woulda believed she a Negro too!"

The more they carried on, the more disillusioned and rattled with anxiety I felt. From there, it was all a whirlwind of chatter and prep work with predominantly dark faces hovering over me, sticking me with foreign objects, and pumping me with fluids.

"So she some kinda royalty, then?"

"Not nowhere in America, she ain't."

"How's it that her daddy married her mama? He's white!"

"She outta wedlock. I seen it in the papers."

I felt a piercing sharpness running through my veins and up my arms. The searing pain ripped me from my state of lethargy and I gasped and shrieked.

"Sorry, baby," one of the nurses said, giving my hand a light squeeze. "All the blood come out the freezer. Ain't never any time to warm it enough 'fore it go into you."

"She come to?" a voice from another part of the hospital responded to my cries. I hadn't even realized the bed on wheels had come to a stop. "We typed her blood; we still need a name."

"Legal name is Rivkah Abernathy LaCroix," came Rafe's voice, also somewhere near.

I wanted to cry out for him. I didn't know where everyone else had gone; Seth around me just a moment ago, Carlyle and Hi-Yoon nowhere to be seen or heard. Everything was happening so fast. I was sobbing with pain and anxiety now, my breaths raspy and wheezing; my chest on fire and sharp tingles all down the whole of my backside. I could feel my entire body, and it was pure agony.

"No, her father never married," I heard him say in response to a question one of the nurses had asked him, which I did not hear in between my own gasps and sobs. "And I ain't a blood relative; I'm a detective with the police department. I been workin' on a case concernin' the LaCroix asylums for the past couple'a years. I can't discuss any more'n that."

Never married...? I thought. It was a lie; it had to be. As many of my father's textbooks the Viscountess in me had read, I knew how sheltered I was on certain matters pertaining to law and the functions of society; how any reportings on my family had been hidden from me. I tried to recollect photographs I may have seen of my parents on their wedding day; nothing came to my mind. Still, this had to be a lie. *All of it.*

"Doctor Fischer, thank goodness; there you are!" someone exclaimed.

"I apologize; the police held me up for questioning," the voice of Orel resounded over the sounds of my own hysteria.

I gritted my teeth, holding in my immeasurable pain in order to contain myself enough that I might talk to him, if just for a moment.

"Viscountess; howd'youdo," he greeted me, coming upon me as he pushed his glasses up the bridge of his nose before strapping a clear plastic cup attached to tubing over my mouth and nostrils. He was no longer the sight for sore eyes I'd last seen him in—except he too shared the similar ebony complexion of those around me. "I know this all must be overwhelming for you right now," he continued, "but you will be given a serum that will teleport you back to your world. Do you understand me?" His tone was calm.

"Back... through the portal, then...?" I wheezed.

All the pain I felt lifted from my body as I made my descent once more.

CHAPTER 29
Purgatory

I remember sitting with Blythe in his chamber at the Fyndridge asylum, my hair unbraided and untamed like the mane of a wild lion, though not the fiery red I liked to imagine it was. It was black as the coals I had come to be so accustomed to, my skin dark to where I did not know what was dirt and what was me; at least this is what I told myself, even just recently having washed myself clean.

My arm was around him as he looked up at me from under his tufts of wispy blond hair and lashes unusually long for a boy. He had a haunted look to his Aryan blue eyes speckled brown, like deep watery pools spilling over with the sorrows they failed to contain. I recalled having met his willful sadness with irritation in the beginning, calling to question what he possibly had to feel so horrible about. My demeanor softened as he spoke.

"I owe you my life, you know," he whispered hoarsely, shifting his position over his mattress where we each perched with our backs to the corner wall. "I don't think I'd have lasted another day out there on the streets."

I watched his eyes wander from mine and across the room, where his collapsible table display of sheep figurines—stuffed animals, handmade cotton swab manifestations, and other sheeplike paraphernalia—were all set out, his only worldly possessions he had accumulated over the course of his residency at the asylum. At the right end of the table, a dirty lamb doll with button eyes, torn in places and losing its stuffing, sat upright and proud; the eldest among its inanimate brethren. It was the one item he had on him, tucked safely away in his pant pocket when he wasn't clutching it to his chest to sleep amid newspapers and cardboard behind alleyway dumpsters. This was how I found him.

"Well, the homeless shelters wouldn't take you," I replied, shifting uncomfortably. I still don't understand why, but I couldn't just leave you out there either. It was going to be this, or the slammer. I'd rather know you were safe with the looney tunes in here than sharing a bunk with some kind of… murdering rapist." The last of my words hung in the air like a lynched man. I wanted only to look away, but the sick cold feeling in the pit of my stomach froze me and I was still.

As Blythe sat before me huddled under my arm, I watched his face change like summer rain to winter snow. "I was… I was so in love, once," he said, his already pale complexion fading into white. He looked as though he may vomit.

I slipped my arm out from around his small frame and edged away from him, turning my body so that I was now facing him directly. "What happened…?" I asked, paying close attention to his mannerisms with bated breath. *Please, please don't get sick,* I thought to myself.

"I was in love with… a man," he whispered, pointing a shaky finger toward his shrine of sheep. "H-He called me his little lamb. He gave me that lamb doll. I… I was nine."

My eyes widened. My throat got very dry, "Blythe," I addressed him sternly, albeit unable to hide the tremor in my voice. "You *can't* be in love when you're that young. You were just a baby, then."

Blythe's lips quivered. "He… He t-told me… 'The lamb wanders far from greener pastures.' I was out buying bread for the orphanage. He gave me the doll that day, and he even walked me back. A few days later… h-he took me."

I felt as if *I* would be sick now. "Where is he now…?" I asked.

"He was angry with me. He said I got too old. I… My body, it…" Blythe drew in a deep breath, followed by a rocky exhale. "It *bled*. He called it unnatural. *Disgusting.*"

"Bled…?" I repeated. "What do you mean it bled? You mean he—?"

It was as if any light that remained behind Blythe's eyes had been sucked out from him like a snuffed candle to the wind. He locked his deadened gaze with mine. "He touched me," he softly spoke, his voice a detached monotone. "*Used* me. Sometimes it would hurt. He said love does hurt sometimes, and I would bleed out a little when he'd *love* me. But once… once, I bled out and he didn't even touch me."

There was an icy sinking feeling in my gut. "What are you saying…?"

"My body developed as a female would," he said. "H-He only minded the bleeding... when it wasn't him that caused it."

There was a long pause as I searched for the words to say something, anything at all, but there was no condolence nor reassurance I felt right about offering to him. "How long did this go on?" I asked, finally.

"Three years," he said.

I gaped for more words. "So... you're a wom—?"

"No," he interrupted. "I'm a *boy*."

Another pause. I truly felt at a loss for how to respond with this revelation. His body was so skinny, so waiflike with such smooth skin; I did not know how I could have missed it. Regardless, I knew this was not something I could share with anyone else; perhaps not even the personnel at the asylum, least of all my uncle.

"Y-You believe me," Blythe pleaded. "Don't you?"

"Yes," I replied. "But it might be in your best interest not to let anyone else know about this. At least for now."

He scoffed, bitterly. "I *hate* my body."

"I can relate," I said with a weak smile. "There would be days sometimes where I'd scrub my skin so rough that it bled, hoping it might make me lighter. I'd pray to God at night over my bed, begging him to make me just one shade *better*. I still dream about having skin as white and pure as snow, that maybe even my uncle could love me for. Maybe then, my father wouldn't want me hidden away so much anymore."

Blythe wiped his eyes and nose on the back of his hand. "Count Amadeus is all over the papers," he commented. "That's what I hear, at least. Can't read. I figured it was because you're his daughter."

"I'm sure that's part of it," I sighed. "Who knows; maybe I'll actually trick myself into believing I'm fairer-skinned one day and forget all about my struggles. I forgot about praying to God, after all. Sometimes I like to imagine my mother is the one in the sky that all the people pray to. It makes me feel a little less uneasy with how she died... how senseless it was."

"Maybe you'll go *crazy* like me and we'll end up roommates or something," Blythe sardonically chuckled.

I flinched at his off-color sense of humor. "Or maybe you'll see something in me that you don't like, and it repels you from me..." I added, reluctantly.

"What, like, something worse than you being a Negro?" he innocently inquired.

"Please don't say that," I said. I couldn't decide whether it was because I didn't want to think of that as being something bad or because I didn't want to think of myself as *black*.

"For what it's worth," Blythe said, "I don't see you as a Negro."

"Then you need to tell me right now how in this *stupid* world you did that," I frowned defensively; almost resentfully, even. "Because when I wake up every day and catch a glimpse of myself in a mirror, that's *exactly* what I see. I'm black, and no amount of your not seeing that is going to change the *millions* of others who do!" I was almost shouting now. I rose off the mattress and stood before him.

Blythe looked distraught. "Hey, that's not what I—"

I didn't care. "The lawmakers who make all the laws explicitly tailored to incarcerate more people like me than people unlike me, *they* see me! Or my uncle telling me that my mother's presence in this neighborhood was lowering property values; *all* those people see me too! Or they *would* if my father didn't keep me cooped up inside to where I need to *sneak off* like I did when I found you…"

Blythe began to tear up again. "I—… I'm *sorry*, I didn't realize…!"

"Well, you know what *I* didn't realize…?" I asked, my question a part of the rhetoric that now flowed out of me closely followed by tears all my own. "That those *degenerates* who killed my mother weren't all degenerates after all. Most of them were just common, white, everyday working class men—all of whom got away with what they *did* to her. I was only a year older than you were when I watched them kill her. I hid, and all I could do was *watch*."

There was a brusque rapping at the door. I turned, startled, coming face to face with my father who peered in through the square glass window. The knob turned and he stepped inside, glaring from beneath his narrowed bushy brows, his mouth pursed in a small frown that could barely be seen as his mustache overtook it, dominating much the majority of his facial characteristics.

He stared sternly at me for a few seconds, his face flushed red, before turning his attention to Blythe. "Do you know why these doors lock from the outside?"

"To… To keep us in, sir," Blythe stammered meekly.

"For your *protection*," my father corrected him, his voice a booming, bodied resonance that shook me to my core. Still, I could distinguish that he was not yelling. I wondered in that moment how Blythe must have felt about it.

"Yes, sir," was all Blythe could muster.

"Doors are only to be shut at 'lights out,' or the next time I see it closed while you are in here, it *will* be locked; do I make myself clear?" my father warned.

Blythe nodded his head vigorously. "Y-Yes, sir," he sniffled.

My father refocused his attention on me, now. "Rivkah, what are you doing in here? You're supposed to be cleaning your uncle's study, are you not?"

I nodded, silently.

"You're not supposed to be in here. I don't want to catch you bothering another patient again, is that understood?"

Again, I nodded but said nothing.

"Come with me," my father sighed. "I'll walk you back."

He turned and walked from the room and I quietly followed, craning to look at Blythe once more whose head was buried in his knees pulled up to his chest. Part of me couldn't help but feel bad, but I was unable to understand just what he was feeling right then. I joined my father, walking alongside him down the hallway in steady stride. We passed the open doors of other patients, though I cared little to look in on them to see what they were up to.

"I heard yelling," my father said after a while of walking in silence. "That could not have been *you*, now could it...?"

I shrugged, but still said nothing in response.

"No," he concluded. "I suppose it couldn't have been. You haven't spoken a word since you were a little girl. Still; your uncle is in the middle of counseling a new patient. You'll meet him, I'm sure... *Demetrius Slater.* I would remind you to be mindful of them and go about your business quietly so you aren't a disturbance."

I nodded in obedience.

From there my memory faded in a slow awakening, my footsteps alongside my father becoming more the consistency of floating as the floor fell away from me and the walls opened up. I realized as the fog lifted from my mind that he was already long gone. My surroundings became a conscious darkness through heavy eyelids. I became aware that I was laying in a bed. The air around me was cool and still, and I could sense the room I was in had been dimly lit. I opened my eyes, then squeezed them shut a couple of times, as what little light there was enacted just enough an irritant that the cool air stung.

"Bern?" Rafe tenderly addressed me. "You coherent now, darlin'?"

"Why you always... gotta be *callin'* me... *pet* names...?" I groggily replied.

"It's just my way," he chuckled softly. "I know you said you don't like it, but I'll admit, it's a tough habit to break."

"You wouldn't call me 'darlin' if I were a boy," I muttered, coming more to.

"Well," he smirked, "ya ain't no boy; yer a pretty little lady."

"Not so little," I grimaced, opening my eyes all the way, my vision blurry as he came into full view at my bedside to my right. He was wearing his chainmaille.

The dim light came from an overhead ceiling fixture my tired eyes could not quite make out. It was hard to say where I even was, looking around the dark room and seeing only curtains and an expanse of obscured wall.

"How long have I been out?" I asked.

"You been in n' out for 'bout a week," he replied. "You prob'ly don't remember. This the first time you been talkin' coherent enough to ask any sort of questions since you was shot six days ago."

"All Mother," I gasped, incredulously. "Six days. How could I have lost *six* whole days?!"

"Well, you done lost a lot a' blood," he informed me. "Also, there was an infection all through the entry area of the bullet; 'bout an inch more to the left, and it woulda been your heart. You got real lucky this time."

I looked down at myself, at my dark skin and my bandaged chest. I felt strange, as though by some intrinsic sixth sense I was aware that something was unsettlingly different, like a fracture in the reality I had known.

"How were you allowed in here to see me?" I asked. "I thought the hospital staff restricts visitation."

He fished into his surcoat pocket and whipped out a black leather wallet. I noticed small gold line art in the shape of a scorpion decorating one of the corners before he flipped it open and presented me his police badge and ID. "Everybody's real compliant when I got this to back my entitlement complex," he grinned.

I smiled back for a fleeting moment, but my expression soon faded into distant worry that came stampeding into the forefront of my mind as I steadily continued regaining my senses. I decided I should be upright, propping myself up on my arms and shakily coming forward off my back.

"Whoa, whoa," Rafe exclaimed, deftly returning his badge to his pocket before raising his gloved palms to steady me. He clicked something into place which raised the head of the bed, then braced my shoulders to ease me back down. "You been *shot*, remember? Gotta take it easy so's you ain't injurin' yourself worse."

"Rafe," I breathlessly urged. "I… I think I'm stuck between worlds. This doesn't *feel* like a hospital. You have a badge. I *know* you're a detective, but you're wearing armor, remember? The armor we got from the Widowsgrove blacksmith…? Y-Your horse is a car!"

"I know," he softly replied. He sounded sincere.

I could feel my heart lift with his acknowledgment. "You do…?"

"You don't know this, kiddo," he smiled, "but I been in my share of counselin' too. Went to see one of them head doctors and you know what he said? …He said I got a entitlement complex. Some kinda… *syndrome* or somethin'. Can't remember. Y'know what I think, though?"

"I guess you're gonna tell me," I said.

He frowned. "Well, I don't *have* t—"

"Please," I sighed, "tell me what you think."

"...I think in the end it don't matter 'cause if you think about it, we're all a little crazy one way or another. It's only human for us to share in this wild spectrum of emotion, and sometimes what we feel rules out over what's rational. Emotion is the purest form of insanity."

There was a brief silence between us as I absorbed his words. "Y'know," I exhaled weightily, "I always suspected, but I guess I was never willing to confront it as a reality..."

"What, the human condition?" Rafe smirked.

"No," I clarified. "That even my father's insistence that I cleaned my uncle's study, especially whenever my uncle was with outpatient visitors, had all been part of an effort in making it appear as though I was just another *worker* there, and not his daughter..."

Rafe's cheeks tightened to pull back his mouth from a playful smirk to not quite a frown. It was clear that a response was lost on him to make.

"Rafe," I said, meekly continuing my thought, "do... my differences matter to you at *all*...?"

"Well, if you was just a decade older—"

"That, um, isn't what I meant," I interjected, fidgeting uncomfortably.

"I'm just kiddin' around," he assured. "I know what'cha meant, and no, it don't matter. It never did. Orel's been a good friend of mine for a very long time. I saw second-hand the kinda hell he had to go through to get to where he is today, and I know it ain't much easier for your generation neither."

It was my turn now to be lost for words. I downcast my gaze, my eyes resting over my still fidgeting fingers interlacing both my hands in my lap. I wished in that moment that I had the words to express what I was feeling; the awkward inadequacy and unworthiness that followed. He seemed to sense it through my demeanor alone.

His gloved hand closed around both of mine. "Bern... Rivkah... *Viscountess*... your lineage alone demands respect. There ain't nothin' wrong with you. There never was," he encouraged, giving my hands a firm, reassuring squeeze. "Now, your uncle's been put under house arrest for investigation. Got my protective custody over you finally approved by my department; go figure, right?"

"How?" I asked. I felt hollow, even though his words allotted me some capacity of comfort.

"I had to acquire legal guardianship over you from the state," he answered me, softly. "In the times you was in n' out of consciousness, Ovocula spoke to me. She was able to sign for you, giving your consent—as someone who is mentally ill, or disabled."

"Peachy," I grimaced, hopelessly.

"As far as the courts are concerned, you're a poor, dumb, sick black child and they shouldn't care about you, bein' that you're more of an expense and liability to the state than anything else," he continued.

"Rafe," I bristled, looking up at him angrily. "Where's the part where I have *more* reason to be alive right now than not?"

"I'm just bringin' you up to speed right now, sweetheart," he replied, withdrawing his hand. "…Tigerlily's fiancé, Dragonfly, is a lawyer with the *National Association for the Advancement of Colored People.* He's gonna be representin' you in court 'cause we got a battle ahead of us, pressin' charges against your uncle for criminal abuse and neglect and that's just the start of it. We're also gonna *prove* you ain't crazy and that you was wrongfully committed."

"And get Demetrius *recommitted*, I hope," I muttered darkly. "Is he out of recovery and in jail yet, at least? I'm assuming we'll be facing him on trial too for all he's done."

Rafe seemed to shrink in his seat at my bedside, his broad presence diminishing at the very mention of Demetrius. My heart slowly sank with every fragment of a second he waited to reply.

"Rafe…?" I followed up, my nerves wrenched with anticipation. There was a growing sickness rising up from inside of me that only worsened with his words which finally came after a few more beats of silence.

He swallowed hard. "Demetrius escaped the recovery facility he been taken to. It happened just a couple days ago."

—(♥)—

CHAPTER 30
Tall Tale

The weeks that followed were a blur. I was eventually discharged from the hospital and living with Rafe at his hideaway abode amid the desert sand. My wounds had all but recovered, save for the once gaping hole through me which continued to scar over. The antique heirloom key had expelled itself from my person, or was taken out of me; that much is unclear. Its presence outside my body further blurred the lines of the merging worlds I knew, its size relative to my mother's mandolin, large enough to be cradled in both my arms or strapped to my back as I would a quiver. I could not have swallowed the key as it appeared to me now, but my gemstone brooch was no longer able to lock into it so that it could be wielded. I feared that I was losing my ability to harness its powers no matter the words I spoke.

I pleaded with Rafe to let me visit with my uncle while he remained under house arrest, and I remember being unreasonably upset with him that he disallowed me to do so; that it was "complicated," and would hurt our case if I did. There was just so much I needed my uncle to answer for. I was informed I would have to wait until the scheduled court date when my uncle would take the stand in defense against myself as well as the state, for his crimes.

"Rafe," I drudgingly moaned, "how can I possibly fight them without my powers? Why would they have been taken from me *now*...?"

"Well, you remember what Orel told ya," he replied. "And I reckon he's right. Prob'ly a side effect of the worlds havin' merged by whatever's goin' on in that pretty little head a' yers."

I scoffed resentfully at that last statement. "Well golly gee, I best not think too hard on it, lest I damage the pretty little goo grapes *inside* my pretty little head."

Rafe let out an almost startlingly boisterous guffaw. "Darlin', you already *know* I think you're sharp. Ain't nobody gonna convince me you ain't smarter than *me* in a lot of ways! All I'm sayin' is, you can't be frettin' over this. Orel didn't seem too worried about it; he thinks it's gonna work out bein' a good thing."

"I guess I just don't see how," I resignedly sighed.

"Well, 'cause you're more grounded now, for one," he grinned, patting me heavily on the shoulder.

I winced, the force from what was likely only a moderate pat by his standards sending shock waves through my chest and back. "Hey," I gritted, "watch the contact, slobberface."

"Right. I'm sorry," he said with a crooked smile. "I'd never do anythin' to hurt ya—my beautiful butthead."

I smiled, lips parted with my teeth as I stared at him, slack-jawed. "*Beautiful* butthead," I repeated after a brief pause. "If I ever fall my ass in love again, I hope that's how my significant other addresses me. Preferably at our wedding reception." My words dripped with sarcasm.

"If it weren't for them same stupid laws my position forces me to uphold, I'd marry you up right now," Rafe grinned.

"Oh?" I smirked. "You said I was too *young* for you."

"I got a li'l time," he replied. "I got no problem waitin' for you to catch up."

My brows lowered at his words, as I was uncertain whether we had breached the invisible wall between us which separated teasing from intent. "…I thought you were waiting for Tigerlily," I tactfully replied.

He looked surprised. "Tigerlily? Where'd *that* come from…?"

"Nowhere," I said. "Never mind." Immediately I felt embarrassed that I'd even brought it up, the words having fallen from my mouth without reflection. I knew it was too late to take it back now.

"Hey, now, wait just a tick…" he smirked impishly. "You're *jealous* of my friendship with Tigerlily, ain't ya!"

My face flushed red. "I—… *No!* I'm just… I *assumed*, since you were both so close, that—"

"That maybe I was bidin' my time for the right moment to steal 'er away from Dragonfly?" he chimed, relieving me of my fumbling words.

"You two share history together," I was quick to add. "I spoke with Dragonfly and I get the sense he's often felt like a third wheel around you two."

He laughed softly. "Yeah, I reckon so. She'll always be nearest and dearest to my heart… just as my son was, and in some ways, just as Carlyle is in a lesser, kinda *distant* fashion…"

"Dearest, but less dear," I flatly replied, now cocking a brow to his ridiculous sentiment.

"Y'know, *you've* become my nearest and dearest too over the time I spent with ya," he continued, talking over me. He loosed a husky sigh through the parting of his teeth. "Anyhow, Tigerlily's a dear friend n' all, but I long since accepted that ship done sailed. It's nice to play around some, knowin' that ain't no other ship gonna be comin' in for me. Not since my wife."

"You've never talked about having a wife before," I remarked, somewhat curiously. "Would it be rude if I asked where she is now?"

"Not a clue," he shrugged simply. "One day she up n' left me and our son. Never came back. I just came home once, and all her stuff was gone. That was many years ago. Haven't heard from her since."

I thought for a moment about asking what he did to track her down, or if he made any sort of effort at all. I wondered what the nature was of the relationship they shared, being that this had been the first time of my hearing about it. These musings flashed through me in an instant, replaced by the consideration of offering condolence. *I'm sorry*, I thought. Or, *that must have been hard for you.* I didn't know how to make it sound anything but disingenuous. Thankfully I did not have long to search awkwardly for an empty or altogether insensitive response.

"Rafe!" Tigerlily exclaimed as she came bursting down the hall leading into the modest living space where Rafe and I were seated for food.

There was little time for either one of us to react, sitting across from one another at his end table. Before Rafe knew it, Tigerlily had thrown herself at him, and of the only two seats present, he had chosen to perch himself precariously over the stool this time leaving the wooden chair to me. I braced against the chair's backrest as I watched the slender blur that was Tigerlily's form clear the tabletop and into Rafe's arms – crashing to the floor.

"We let ourselves in. Hope you don't mind!" Tigerlily beamed, her arms draped around Rafe's neck as she sprawled out on top of him with his legs still interlocking the stool.

"Dang it, I ain't young n' pretty no more," Rafe wheezed, gently taking her by the waist and rolling her off him before propping himself upright on his elbows. "…Just pretty. So's I can stay that way, you can't be pouncin' me like that."

"Who's 'we'?" I asked.

"I'll apologize on her behalf, Rafe," Dragonfly smirked, indirectly answering my question by entering the room from the hallway with his slow and steady gait. "She ran up ahead of me and I couldn't grab her in time."

Tigerlily climbed to her feet with a scoff that came out in the form of a snort. "*Grab* me?! I'm not Penny; you don't gotta apologize for me like I'm your pet!"

Dragonfly extended a hand to Rafe, but Rafe ignored it as he too slowly picked himself up off the ground.

I shifted in my seat, somewhat agitated. "I didn't know either of you would be coming over," I grumbled, shooting Rafe a sidelong glance. "Really wish people would start telling me things; *especially* considering current events…"

"Oh!" Tigerlily flushed. "I'm sorry, Lady Rivkah, I—"

"It's *Bern*," I snapped.

"*I'm* sorry, Bern," Rafe quickly cut in. "Dragonfly is here to go over details for your court hearin', tomorrow. We got a lot to discuss. I been jugglin' so many details I guess I forgot to tell ya 'bout who was comin' over, when."

I unconsciously lifted my hands from fidgeting in my lap to clutch at the closing of the terrycloth robe I had clothed myself in. As short-fused as I was in the moment, I could not help but feel embarrassed by my reaction more than my form of dress in the presence of company. "It's okay," I reassured, my gaze downcast over bare knees and feet. "I guess I'm just a bit high strung from everything."

"We all are," Dragonfly said. "It's been a long uphill battle. We are fortunate you have your right to a speedy trial; our chances are better while the scandals of the LaCroix asylums are still fresh in everybody's minds. I'm sure you're aware of the media frenzy that's been showing no signs of letting up."

"I really haven't kept up with it," I sighed, distracted. "Does… Tigerlily really need to be here when you go over this…?"

"Don't worry, I'm leaving," she frowned. "I just wanted to say hi to Rafe… and to personally tell you both that I got Kael to agree to testify."

"Whoa, girlie, that's some *real* good news!" Rafe beamed.

I smiled weakly. "I'm sorry; that *is* good news. Please thank him for me. I don't mean to seem rude. It's just that I'm not used to all this attention, and the circumstances that led to it make this even harder for me. I'm sure you've read plenty of paper headlines highlighting what a sheltered shut-in I am."

"That ain't your fault, darlin'," Rafe softly interjected, cupping my shoulder with a gloved hand.

"Okay," Dragonfly clapped together his palms, assertively, "here's how this is going to go…"

"Bye," Tigerlily whispered, allotting Rafe a cheesy wink before slipping out of the room and back down the hall. I watched her leave, smiling and staring at her portrait as she passed it, which had since been rehung.

"...We all know your uncle is guilty of some pretty heinous crimes," Dragonfly continued. "The hard part will be getting the jury to know it, too. You're at a disadvantage here, even in lieu of a laundry list of charges we've got to stick him with."

"How many charges?" I asked.

"Well over a dozen—and we'd be lucky if even one of those stuck," he grumbled.

"Why," I demanded.

Dragonfly sighed weightily, raising his fingers to pinch at the bridge of his nose. "Your uncle is innocent until proven guilty which means we must provide substantial evidence that cannot be dismissed in court as circumstantial, or otherwise that he is guilty of those charges he is presented with. In addition, many witnesses may not be considered *reliable* if they have a history of mental health issues or have a bias—which definitely includes residents at the asylums. Lastly, if the defendant chooses to have a trial by jury it will need to be a jury of his peers. Mostly white men."

"Crotchety *old* white men," Rafe playfully added. "Older than even *me*."

I rolled my eyes, humorlessly. "Older? I don't see how you're not fossilized."

"Let's stay tasked, please," Dragonfly interjected, drawing our attention back to him. "We have lots to go over, and I got little time to do it. I wanted to add that I'm sure Doctor LaCroix will want to go the 'trial by jury' route... so we'll need to be prepared for that."

Rafe cocked a brow. "How you figure that? Unless..." he trailed, thoughtfully.

"The reason why he would choose to have a trial by jury is to have the benefit of his peer group. He's committed obvious felonies but a trial by jury would be much more lenient. If he goes with the judge, then the judge is obligated to rule by what's legally mandated—and ethical. Going with the jury increases the possibility of a popular decision being made. Pretty much it allows for an emotional appeal as well as preferential treatment."

Dragonfly's words inundated me like ice cold water. The chair slid back as I stood from the table, my heart sinking in my chest with each slow, steady beat. "I need to get some fresh air," I spoke quietly, my eyes downcast toward my feet once again.

"Well, okay," Dragonfly responded hesitantly. "But try to make it quick."

"Stay close to home," Rafe warned. "Dragonfly'll fill me in on finer details on the meantime."

My perceptions of reality were still a surreal haziness as I took off down the hall leading outside Rafe's hideout. Suddenly my surroundings were no longer the expanse of rolling desert dunes they once were, but the outskirts of a cityscape set against an expanse of gold and crimson sky. I stood a distance from the dirt cliffside which plunged downward to the dead canyon thicket, where beyond that the city of Widowsgrove shone the beginnings of light as slowly the sun moved to set. I spotted a child toward the cliff's edge, seated against the bark trunk of an overlooking acacia with dirt on his crestfallen face and messy tufts of hair peaking out from under his worn bowler cap. His clothes were patchy and torn, his filthy bare feet poking through the fallings of his baggy pant legs. He reminded me of Blythe.

I approached him. As I neared, I noticed his flushed cheeks shone the sheen of bitter tears. I wondered whether he had come from Widowsgrove, despite the distance on foot or the city's disallowing of residents to leave. I wondered if he was even real. "Boy, why do you cry?" I gently inquired.

He shyly gazed up at me beneath lowered lashes. There was a moment's pause before he pulled his shaky hands from his lap with a wince, turning out his knuckles for me to see. They were badly bruised; enough that I wondered whether they might have been broken, the skin raw and lacerated on a couple of his fingers.

I stood, aghast. "What happened to you? Did you get into a fight...?"

"N-No," he replied, sniffling. "Well—sort of. This other kid was pickin' on my friend in the schoolyard, kickin' sand at her an' pullin' her hair. I got him to stop. He ratted on me to the teacher, and she whacked my hands with a ruler." Fresh tears welled up in his eyes to trickle down his cheeks.

I felt a flame stirring in my belly with his words. "Did your teacher discipline the other boy?" I asked.

He solemnly shook his head. "She's his mother."

I knelt down in front of him so that I was level with his eyes, bringing my hand up to cup around his chin for but a moment until his sorrowful gaze met with my own. "Now you listen to me," I said. "This world is unjust, and by no fault of your own is it that way. Do you know *who* makes the world unjust?"

"Yeah," he sniffled. "The stupid bullies."

"The *adults*," I corrected him. "The ones who have all the power. And sometimes, adults can be bullies too. You're taught to mind your elders because they're your elders, and to be respectful of them, but that's wrong. Do you know what they *don't* tell you?"

He silently shook his head.

I narrowed my brows at him. "We're all still kids; every one of us. We just grow taller."

CHAPTER 31
Phoenix Rising

"I love it when you get that crazy sexy look in your eyes," Kael said, marching alongside me.

"Crazy sexy look?" I repeated, incredulously.

He grinned wryly. "Yeah, that psychopath murderer look. It's hot."

I had been scowling without realizing it. He had broken the long held silence; Carlyle, Seth, Dragonfly, and Rafe each marching in pace and not saying a word. It was the day of court, and we were each outfitted in our finest armors: Carlyle in his usual maille garb complete with surcoat, shield and sword, Seth toting his packs of supplies, equipped with his shield as well, Rafe outfitted in a full suit much the same as Carlyle, and Dragonfly clutching his mighty crossbow in a single hand, his long daggers crossed on his back. He wore his long ebony hair in the tight bun of a warrior, his face striped in warpaint of bright yellows and reds.

"I'm planning on *dominating* this sordid system run by these old men in their monkey suits, Kael," I spoke matter-of-factly, my tone steadied to match my conviction. "You'll forgive me if I forget to smile."

"You know what I don't get?" he said, still grinning that stupid grin. "How's it possible that a woman be dominant over a man? Women get fucked."

"*Kael...*" Dragonfly warned.

"That's perspective," I replied, not bothering to look over at him.

Kael chuckled. "How do you mean?"

"Let me put it to you this way..." I started, just as we had come upon the tall double doors outside the courtroom. "A man does not penetrate me. I engulf him."

The words fell from my mouth before I realized what I was saying, but I was too focused in my quiet fury to spare feelings of inhibited regret. If nothing else, it was the first time I had seen Kael at a loss for a wisecrack or a rebuttal of any kind. I had effectively turned his joking demeanor around on him, and caused each of my other companions noticeable discomfort in doing so. Standing in place before the double doors, both Seth and Rafe eyed one another apprehensively while Carlyle flushed red, but remained still. Kael stared up at me, jaw gaping in silence.

Dragonfly cleared his throat, shifting his weight from one foot to the other. "Is… everyone ready…?" he asked.

We burst through the double doors together, entering the courtroom. There were rows of seating and aisles where nondescript people were each settling in. There was a center podium for the judge, toweringly tall, with half a dozen security guards—imposing suits of metal armor—lined against the wall on either side behind it. The judge took on a woman's form, and as I drew nearer, my heart pounding with anticipation, her visage that of Hi-Yoon's, black veil over her eyes as she brandished a sword in her right hand and the *Scales of Justice* in her left. She wore a black robe and sash.

"Lady Justice," Carlyle marveled, under his breath.

There were a few familiar faces among those who would see my uncle under trial, albeit not to testify: an uncharacteristically tidy Blythe locking eyes with mine only briefly before quickly averting his gaze, a court-kempt Tigerlily nodding to each of us a few aisles away, Arnie from the coal mines, Bill from the Rogue Musket entrance, a 'Clyde' from the bar, a number of past pit fighters—and then my eyes drifted to where my uncle was standing. His glowering, contemptuous gaze pierced me like needles through the pincushion of my heart, bidding it to beat sharply in my chest. He was wearing his fine eggplant dinner suit, his graying greasy hair slicked back into its usual ponytail. His beaklike nose was noticeably more crooked and not fully recovered.

Standing next to him was a man I recognized only vaguely as once having boarded my father's ship, the Wild Rose. He attended the twentieth birthday of the Viscountess in me, among the twelve guests gilded with dead beasts and salad hats, none of whom were any friend of mine nor would they prove to be my father's. He was just another high society schmoozer, and presumably smooth-talking enough as a lawyer for my uncle to have chosen him to champion his defense. He too wore a suit, his square shoulders evening his confident posture, glasses adorning his angry beady eyes that rested behind his

jumbo ears. The each of their attires wildly contrasted mine and my comrades',
as I too had been dressed accordingly for battle. Still very much caught between
opposite extremes with my perception of reality, my leather-clad ensemble was
accompanied now with shining steel pauldrons and gauntlets with which I
clutched the heirloom key in my fist like a sword of valor.

"I recognize that man," I said quietly, gritting my teeth.

"His name is Kent Cunningham," Dragonfly informed. "He's one of
the best lawyers in the state."

My muscles tensed with burning rage. "He was at my birthday party—
the night they burned my father's ship to the ground. He told my father I took
after him, over dinner. I hadn't met him before then."

"Wait," Kael interjected. "*Cunningham?* Like, Francis Cunningham's
brother, who went to law school?!"

"Who…?" Rafe asked, just before I could do so myself.

Kael smirked wittingly. "Francis was one of the pit fighters. He was
the guy who busted up my eye pretty bad that one time. He's here, right now;
the heavyset beast in the aisle behind us now. Can't miss 'im."

We each looked back, and there he was, unmistakable. I often paid
little mind to the other fighters, but he was vaguely recognizable to me now.
He stared us down, unabashedly.

"Bern," Orel greeted me solemnly, stepping up beside me and tearing
away my gaze. He spoke to my good ear, his voice abnormally steady. "I was
wondering when you all would get here—"

I looked him over with still the surreal haze which clouded my mind.
It was difficult to get used to the idea that I had selectively recategorized foes
and allies alike, banishing from my mind the reality of who and what they
were—who *he* was—as I could not accept it let alone within myself. My eyes
danced around his face, his hands; his dark complexion as he pushed his
glasses up the bridge of his nose. As I watched him, I could feel the courtroom
expanding all around me, the podium growing taller and the already vast
walls, further apart. I felt the sound of the judge's cudgel booming against the
podium deep within my chest, but in the form of Lady Justice beating the hilt
of her sword over the raised railing of her trial arena.

"All rise for the honorable judge," the suits of armor spread around the
arena floor spoke in unison.

Everything was changing before my eyes. I looked around me now,
and those in court attendance suddenly made up an audience in great numbers
spread throughout the coliseum, each overlooking us everywhere I turned. I
found my back to Seth and Carlyle, both their shields raised, with Rafe and

Dragonfly each drawing their ranged weapons; rifle and crossbow, together, simultaneously. Kael stepped out of the formation to join Orel, who stood still but the distance between us seemed to grow as the battlegrounds continued to expand. Its expansion did not cease until both Kael and Orel had been removed from our party, disappearing among our spectators to later testify.

"The criminal case of Rivkah Abernathy LaCroix versus Acanthus LaCroix is now in session this Tuesday, October 23rd, 1956," Lady Justice spoke, her voice a familiar resonance except never so cold and distance. "Doctor LaCroix, you are currently on trial for the charges presented to you prior to the date of court; malpractice on the grounds of negligent behavior, malpractice on the grounds of illegal activity and treatment, felony false imprisonment for lengthy terms of unlawful imprisonment, a federal offense of owning and orchestrating an illegal gambling business, tax evasion, involuntary manslaughter due to criminal negligence, patient abuse in the form of withholding treatment, patient abuse in the form of intimidation, patient abuse in the form of harassment and ridicule, patient abuse in the form of permitted physical harm, assisted assault criminal harassment, assisted destruction of private property, misuse of public funds, and fraud. You have chosen to plead innocent to these charges presented. We will begin with opening statements."

"I would like to begin, with your permission, Lady Justice," said my uncle's attorney. My eyes followed his voice to where he stood since the transformation of the courtroom; atop a pillar raised off the battleground alongside my uncle.

Lady Justice returned him with a nod. "State your name for the court."

"My name is Kent Cunningham and I will be representing the defendant, Doctor Acanthus LaCroix. I would like to start by stating that my client is an honorable man of the community. It's true that he may not have always managed his affairs well but my client always acted in the best interest of the community and his family. He voluntarily committed his life to the study of those people whom society has deemed mentally unfit and devoted himself to treatment of these individuals working in the public sector. He worked hard to better our proud community providing *excellent* quality health care. The charges against this man have been made assuming his fault and intention. Perhaps my client is guilty of poor management, but he must be found guilty without doubt of knowledge and direct action permitting these things of which he must be willful to do for us to bring him to the status of criminal."

While he spoke from his elevated position above us, my eyes drifted to the beginnings of a flame swirling the air several feet from where we stood.

The air rippled with heat as the flame took shape, the fiery whirlpool soon like the flapping of wings as a bird of pure fire materialized into existence.

"In addition," he added, "I hope it is considered that the institution that had given him his position is our very own government and a conviction of this family man, this man of the people, would be a statement of disapproval of the very people who gave him his position's decision, and *not* a conviction on definite evidence for criminal activity, as is my client's direct actions. I challenge the prosecutor to bring definitive evidence of criminal activity against this hardworking man."

The flaming construct arched its back in a flourish as its fiery wings doubled in size, a wingspan that nearly brushed either side of the coliseum walls. Its white hot eyes honed in on us, and it let out a screeching battle cry which swept us through in a mist of steam.

"All Mother! It's a phoenix," Dragonfly warned under his breath. "The defense is strong. We will need to fight it with everything we've got."

Before I realized what was happening, the steamy mist transformed the air into a foggy haze which obscured our surroundings except for the manifest phoenix and the suits of armor lining the walls. Six of them came alive; one for each of us—or what *would* be if Kael were still near—dropping into a battle-ready stance with weapons drawn. They started in on us, shuffling between their every heaviest footsteps with the rattling clash of metal armor and unsteady joints.

"Please," I breathed. "Tell me you're all seeing this and it isn't all in me. Please tell me I've got a grip on reality."

"Are you familiar with the Greek philosopher, Plato?" Dragonfly asked.

"No," I admitted, my heart racing.

"He created the idea of *Two Worlds*," he replied, talking fast. "Kind of like how I mentioned before about Tigerlily being two-spirit, except instead of being, you are experiencing. One world, the world of *Becoming* is the world we know to be true around us, the physical world we inhabit. This world continually changes, evolves, and disappears…"

There was no sight nor sound of anyone else in the courtroom coliseum as the fog had quickly risen to rooftop heights and thickened so that only the phoenix and the would-be knights were seen. I felt a sharp chill rise up within me, prickling every vertebrae up my spine.

"This 'Becoming' reality we take in through our senses," Dragonfly fervently continued, "and it is impossible to develop any genuine knowledge of it since we can only describe its changing nature as it appears to us. Do you follow me?"

"If you're asking whether she understands, damn it, *I* sure don't!" Carlyle interjected, tensed with an impatient snarl.

"I-I'm not sure!" I said anxiously, darting my eyes between each approaching armored foe, alarmed by my own inability to distinguish man from sorcerous construct.

"What I've just described to you is our world of appearance," Dragonfly replied, maintaining his fast-paced diction. "It is not the same as *reality*. Reality is much different; it is the second of Two Worlds. Reality is the world of *Being*, a realm that is unchanging, eternal, and knowable through what we reason."

"Better hurry up n' make a point," Rafe warned, taking aim at the armored figure nearest him.

"Plato did not mean that the everyday world of Becoming is an illusion, he meant that the physical, changing world is *not as real* as the eternal world of Being! You exist right now between both worlds, and right now you must choose to Be!"

The armored figures continued to advance, drawing so near I could see my reflection in the shining armor of the construct a few paces directly before me. I barely recognized myself, my visage split between the metal seam down the center of the breastplate, my left side the familiar fair-skinned Bern with hazel eyes and long braids of fiery red playing stark contrast to my right side, the deep complexion of Rivkah with honey brown eyes and hair a lustrous ebony. In either side, my own armor took on a consistent appearance—shining, silvery plate pauldrons adorning my shoulders, a knight's breastplate to match the metal gauntlets clutching at the key I drew into both my hands.

I brandished the key like a blade, raising it over a shoulder and swinging wide to connect with my foe the moment it was within my range to do so. There was a pulse of white light as I made contact, washing away the fog and everything else. A moment later I was seated in a chair of rigid wood along the left side of a suited up Dragonfly, across from the judge. It was not Hi-Yoon, the Lady Justice.

"Counselor," the elderly man of pale complexion and snowy hair scowled, not of general disposition but of face at natural rest. "You may approach the bench and question your first witness."

Dragonfly allotted me a reassuring nod before standing, the chair he had been seated in dragging over marble flooring, pushed out from his backside. He walked around our table toward the circle floor, stepping from the aisle which separated us from the table my uncle and *his* mouthpiece sat at. The members of the jury appeared to be looking intently at him with contemptuous glares which surely were not in my head just as everything else seemed. He was headed for Kael, as the smaller man sat fidgeting in a lower seat adjacent to the ghoulish judge.

"Mister Iron Cloud," Dragonfly formally addressed him, as Kael looked back, seemingly startled by the use of his surname. "Tell me where you were on the evening of December 28th, shy of two years ago."

Kael swallowed hard. As I looked to the back of Dragonfly's head, his hair coiled up off his neckline, he seemed to be giving him a nod of reassurance. I carefully surveyed Kael's expression as his anxiety appeared to subdue. "It was raining," he said after a moment's pause. "I heard it outside… between Alasdair's screaming. He was louder than the thunder, but, I heard that too. Demetrius was torturing him strapped to a chair next to me. We were in the basement where they keep the medicines. Galvinsglade."

"And do you believe Doctor LaCroix was aware of the events which transpired that day?" Dragonfly sharply continued.

Kael's brows furrowed, presumably with the recollection of his terror to accompany the righteous indignation with which he spat. "*He* was the one who issued the command."

My mind cast me back without warning into the fog. I stood over my felled foe, the suit of armor a pile of rusted metal before my knightly boots wrapped in chain. I glanced to my right where Dragonfly was deftly reloading another bolt into his crossbow having already downed two more, each metal carapace rusting over and collapsing into a heap on the ground to be overtaken by fog. Carlyle and Seth each thrust their tall, weighty shields against the plated chests and gilded swords of these enchanted beings, holding off the other two while Rafe took aim with his rifle, a lone baby blue eye wide open and focused on his target, the silvery soldier marching nearest him.

I wondered whether there would be more back and forth, snapping between the two existences which made up my whole universe. I gritted my teeth, honing in on the mighty phoenix as it flapped its powerful wings of flame and hurled steamy gusts of hot air into us. I braced against it and raised my key, slowly building up into an angry charge. I did not even bother to look back at the sound of Rafe's gun going off, or the sounds of blunt force echoing off the far walls unseen from the brother's onslaught. With every point made against my uncle, a husk of a knight would be vanquished. Even if I did not understand the proceedings of a court, I understood the fight for justice. I decided in that moment that I would stay *here*, mind willing.

As I ran toward the phoenix, my perception of time seemed to bend.

I could hear voices jumbled all around me, voices whose words I could only catch in broken fragments. I identified Orel echoing through my head and reverberating in my chest.

"H-He never carried out his own d-dirty d-d-deeds," I heard him say. "He had me l-locked away with B-… R-Rivkah. He let Demetrius—"

"Oh, yeah, she'd babble nonsensically at times," Carlyle's voice echoed loud and clear all throughout me. My heart skipped as I glanced back for only a moment to see where he was, but the fog had closed in, leaving me to the flaming bird all alone.

Is he talking about me? I thought.

"The only way to reach her would be to babble right back at her in that strange tongue of hers; pretend it meant something…"

Pretend.

"Sage hajish kalehkt," I snarled. I felt vibrations in my sternum as a blue circular light rendered my flesh and even the armor I was wearing all but completely translucent. The energy pulsated through my pauldrons, my shoulders, and down my arms until it reached the base of my key. I held on tightly with both hands, my gauntlets exploding from my knuckles and fingers into pieces, the light expanding around me to make up an aura as it shot through the key and careened into the wild firebird with enormous force.

The recoil sent me sprawled across the coliseum floor. The power behind my blast also sent back the fog, and as it did, the voices inside my head became a medley of foreign resonance like a unified piercing hum.

"If she isn't insane, then she's guilty of *murder* on multiple counts!"

"She was as much a conspirer in her father's slaying as is accused of her illegitimate uncle."

"How *patient* he is, the burden of a mulatto bastard thrust upon him in wake of great family tragedy…"

And so set the tone for the proceedings of this *trial*.

CHAPTER 32
Three Wise Men

    I stood at water's edge under a starry night's sky, gazing down at my reflection which took the form of Rivkah, her tired eyes and the solemn natural frown of her lips at rest. It appeared as if the stars among the heavens were also reflecting off the surface of the water, but I knew better from Orel—it was in fact the bioluminescence of marine microbes... phytoplankton. Hundreds, perhaps thousands, all gathered here to light up the expanse of sea and all around my legs with the gentle tide. If not for the great weight looming over my restless mind, it would seem so peaceful, a part of the natural world so rich with beauty and wonder. Even without the sound of steady footfalls in the sand behind me, I would have felt not quite so alone.

    "You should be pleased, my lady," Dragonfly spoke gently. "At least we were able to pin your uncle with one charge of tax evasion."

    "Please do not tell me how I should feel," I said, my voice a quiet monotone. I was drained. Empty. I did not have to look back at him to feel his silent understanding rolling through me in waves to match the steady waters.

    "Are you familiar with Leviathan?" Dragonfly asked after several beats of silence between us. "It is a book. Thomas Hobbes."

    "No," I replied simply. "Between my father's old texts and my mother's romance novels, my reading has been limited. Before I... had become *one* with myself, I'd forgotten I could read at all."

    "It's not my place to lecture you," he continued, "but you should know that a citizen does not have a duty to his government, but an individual has a duty to other individuals within society. We all operate under a social contract, written or expressed in other means. Since I spent the better part of my life growing up on a reservation I had to be learned in this."

I turned to face him. His deep eyes were calm, if searching. His square jawline framed over the collar of his business suit and tie, kempt and still much the opposite from how I'd first made his acquaintance. I said nothing, curious to know where he could be going with this.

"Individuals create a social contract with other individuals forfeiting rights in the hopes of producing more goods within a system of the 'commonwealth.' The goods within this grouping of people, the commonwealth, is the common good. If a government oppresses, or limits the goods of its people, it must be understood that it is the people which make up the body of the Leviathan, and it is the Leviathan which is the entity that rights are forfeited to for the production of goods."

"What sort of *goods*...?" I frowned.

Dragonfly smiled wryly. "Anything that helps our fellow man in some way. You have to understand... the government, social contracts; they are all *intangibles* that exist only by the trust and consent of the people who establish them. While coercion may exist, you have to also understand that there is a communal response to any action and that these coercive forces may only be empowered by the few. The majority will always rule, but the minority should be identified as part of the community. *We* are that minority."

"We are," I agreed. "And we should be identified as such, yes. So, why does it not feel that way?"

"Once a government has begun to oppress its people... limiting not only their rights but also doing them wrong and limiting their goods... it is the assumed duty of the people that are governed to correct injustices as part of the body and actively fight for that which they believe will produce more goods."

There was a spark in Dragonfly's eyes as he spoke. His posture was relaxed, hands joined behind his back with his legs in an open stance. I realized only then that he had waded into the water with me, the bottoms of his pant legs soaking up the elements.

"However, it is the governing bodies who must understand that which is good for the people—and it is *their* responsibility to not only perpetuate these goods, but enable the layfolk to produce more goods for society as a whole. If the governing bodies do not operate under this understanding *then the citizens must **fight***. If the structures which govern our society are tainted, then we must change it with our rebellion."

I felt a rush with the last of his words. "You must be one of the advisers Zebadiah had prophesied," I marveled, with great sense of clarity. "But, he said there would only be three…"

"He's a Dutchman," Carlyle joined, his voice recognizable before his form as he too now approached. He was like Orel. He and Orel were like me. "Zebadiah, that is. He speaks of the Castle in the Sky sometimes as, *luchtkasteel.*"

"Luchtkasteel," I repeated. "What's that?"

A wry smirk tugged at the corners of his mouth. "He told my brother and me that it's a dream you hope to see fulfilled… a goal you set for yourself that can never be achieved for how vast, and immense it is."

The rush I had felt before was all but diminished with Carlyle's humored callousness. "But I believe restoring the earth *can* be achieved," I urged. "I believe we *can* have peace, and justice for all under the framework of society Dragonfly speaks of."

"Don't ever change, darlin'," Rafe too now approached. He was the only one of us whose complexion remained so light by comparison. "You took on that phoenix of a case head on. *You* were the one who won your freedom. You got'cherself acknowledgment, an' you never gotta go back to that place again. All we did was back you up."

I smiled weakly. "So what am I gonna do now? I've never had to live on the outside before…" My tone darkened. "And Demetrius. He's still out there."

Rafe's baby blue eyes transformed by the light of the stars and aquatic organisms encircling us. Where once his softness lent comforting reassurance, his visage had darkened considerably. "My bullet pierced straight through 'im. You n' me both know it ain't Demetrius walkin' around in them britches he got on."

My heart sank. "If Roland is dead," I exhaled, "if Demetrius is dead… then all that's left of him is the Governor."

"This may seem like I'm changin' the subject," Rafe went on, "but just humor me for a minute. Did you know there's a direct correlation between how *adorable* an animal is, and how delicious it tastes?"

It took me a moment to collect myself from my dwelling thoughts enough to answer him. Each of the other men glanced at him out from the corners of their eyes with bated uncertainty. "Would you eat Penny?" I replied, finally.

Rafe grinned toothily. "Nah. I don't care much for dessert."

"Rafe, I've always known you to be pretty levelheaded," Carlyle commented. "But—"

"My point is," he talked over him, "we don't know *jack* about nothin' unless we try things out. And all I know is, lamb chops taste better n' a full grown sheep."

I felt a slow shiver run through my spine, numb to his attempt at lightening the mood. "I have a friend who would agree with you."

"Maybe you should answer your own question, for yourself," Dragonfly interjected, his eyes piercing mine as he drew my attention. "What *are* you going to do now?"

I began reflecting in my head, but felt urged by the quiet demeanors of each man before me. I opted to talk myself through it. "I once thought that living internally, navigating the world around me, was a means to cope. Perhaps also *escape*. It never occurred to me that the way I think, and feel, and see things, was also a tool for facing elements outside my control on my own terms. I never realized it to be a means of creating power all my own. I want to see what that power is capable of. As you said, Dragonfly—I am a citizen, and I must fight. The world outside myself is as much my own to be a part of as the others who share it with me, and we all have a right to inhabit it."

"Even people like the Governor…?" Rafe spoke.

The surface of my skin flushed hot with resolve. I waded further into the reflective waters.

I let myself slip under.

About the Author

If you know anything about Taversia, you would know she doesn't like to write about herself, and yet here she is again writing in third-person narrative. This is another set of randomly assorted facts about her, and this book!

♕ Taversia just completed her first semester at Ivy Tech Community College with 12 credit hours and a 4.0 GPA!

♕ She resides in Indiana with two ex-stray cats she decided to invite into her home—all the way from Texas.

♕ She also decided their names are Jiji & Nutella.

♕ Currently, Taversia is lobbying to get Indiana Code § 35-45-4-1 to decriminalize women going topless in public spaces, same as men.

♕ From 2011 – 2014 (earlier this year), Taversia was an active part of the RLSH (Real-Life Superhero) movement known as the Crimson Catalyst. She formed a team and passed out food/supplies to the homeless on the streets of Chicago. This marks her coming out of the phone booth, as well as her "superhero" retirement.

♕ Taversia has been an active supporter of Love146, an organization working towards the end of child trafficking & exploitation. She participated in Comic Creators for Freedom, drawing comics to help raise money for donations, and more of her work is published in 146 : a collection of love stories.

♕ Some of the dialogue in this book were actual words spoken to Taversia which helped her through some rough times.

♕ The back cover of this book features Penny, an actual cat who lives with Taversia's brother.

♕ Taversia no longer cries late at night about her life.

CPSIA information can be obtained
at www.ICGtesting.com
Printed in the USA
FFOW04n1828090516
23874FF

9 780991 528233